PRAISE FOR KAREN KELLEY'S
HOT PARANORMAL ROMANCE

"[Kelley's] books are funny and romantic with the perfect blend of spice!"

—Gena Showalter, *New York Times* and *USA Today* bestselling author of *The Darkest Surrender*

"Karen Kelley is romance's rising funny girl."

—Sharon Sala, *New York Times* and *USA Today* bestselling author of *Blood Ties*

Bad Boys Guide to the Galaxy

"Delightful… a charming novel that will tickle your funny bone and melt your heart. Karen Kelley proves yet again why she is the queen of sensual comedy."

—*Romance Junkies*, 4 1/2 ribbons

Dating Outside Your DNA

"The sex is steamy and the pacing gallops along in this readable romp."

—*Publishers Weekly*

"Karen Kelley has offered up yet another fun and fabulous read brimming with her trademark humor and sensuality. Quirky, sexy characters and non-stop action."

—*Romance Junkies*, 4 ribbons

where there's Smoke

KAREN KELLEY

sourcebooks
casablanca

Published by Sourcebooks Casablanca, an imprint of Sourcebooks, Inc.
P.O. Box 4410, Naperville, Illinois 60567-4410
(630) 961-3900
Fax: (630) 961-2168
www.sourcebooks.com

Library of Congress Cataloging-in-Publication Data
Kelley, Karen.
  Where there's smoke / Karen Kelley.
  1. Paranormal romance stories. I. Title.
  PS3611.E443W48 2012
  813'.6—dc23
                          2011050773

Printed and bound in the United States of America.
VP 10 9 8 7 6 5 4 3 2 1

To Karl, the love of my life

Chapter 1

DESTINY CARTER WAS SIX years old when she had the first inkling that her life wouldn't be a fairy tale. That was the day her mother left her in a grocery store and never came back. Destiny was right, her life went downhill from there. Bad foster homes, bad boyfriends, and really, really bad choices.

Then she died and went to Hell.

Until she was kicked out.

Destiny landed on the sidewalk with a hard *thump*.

"Son of a bitch!" She grimaced as she came to her feet, rubbing her hands over her tender backside. She was probably the first person ever to get kicked out of Hell. Temporarily, that is.

Hysterical laughter bubbled inside her, but she quickly tamped it down. She was not going to lose what little bit of sanity she had left. She would get through this like she did everything else, by gritting her teeth and doing what she had to do.

All is not lost. Just take a deep breath.

She inhaled.

Ugh! Her nose twitched as a god-awful stench filled her space. She glanced down the deserted street. Faded army-green painted letters on a shabby storefront window proclaimed it as Ft. Worth's finest resale shop.

Uh hell, she'd landed close to the stockyards in Ft. Worth, Texas, but this wasn't Billy Bob's. No, skid-row bars and vacant buildings lined both sides of the street.

Could her day get any worse?

Not that she had anything against Texas, except it was hot as hell. The dry heat was not helping her mood.

"I couldn't manage to steal one more soul?" she grumbled.

Okay, so she wasn't the best salesperson in the underworld. Why didn't that lawyer just sign on the dotted line? He insisted on reading the fine print and before she knew it, poof, he was gone. One more soul and she would've been a full-fledged demon with all the rights and privileges of that position—like drinking, gambling, and lots of sex.

"Sex," she breathed on a sigh as she slowly combed her fingers through her long, black hair. Naked, straining bodies. Hands touching, caressing. She bit her bottom lip and forced the vision to go far, far away before she grabbed the grungy-looking bum leaning against the vacant store front and had her way with him.

She grimaced. Maybe she wasn't *that* hard up. But Destiny did really miss sex. Everything about her life might have been lousy, but never the sex. And right now she was so horny she figured she'd start sprouting a pair any time, except people at the trainee level couldn't grow a set of horns to save their lives.

Now she was one step farther from her goal. The ones in charge were really pissed, but at least they had given her another chance, and new orders: corrupt someone and drag the unwitting person back to Hell. She had one week to do it or else. Why the fuck had they tacked on "or else"? What were they going to do? Send her to Hell?

Okay, shake it off. Getting kicked out was only a minor glitch. She could take a soul in less than a week. A moment of panic sent a shiver down her spine and her bravado drained away. Who was she kidding? Only dying souls caught between Heaven and Hell were sent to the sorting station. Her job was to convince them Hell was their best choice. She didn't have to search them out. Nothing ever went right for her in life. Why did she think being dead would change things?

No, she could do this. She *would* survive.

A flashing neon sign suddenly caught her attention when one of the bulbs popped and blew out. THE STOMPIN' GROUND. A bar. Her mouth watered. Demons-in-training weren't allowed to drink, or do much of anything on the job, and they were always on the job. One drink wouldn't hurt, and a bar would be a good place to start looking for a corruptible soul. In fact, it was her duty to go inside and check the place out.

A slow smile curved her lips as she slid her hands slowly over her body and the plain, butt-ugly, black wool uniform shift became a tight-fitting, low-cut, fuck-me red dress that shimmered with each slow, seductive step she took. Yeah, she was bad. Life made her that way. That's why she went straight to Hell. You never saw a good girl in Hell.

The bum's mouth dropped open. He looked at his wrinkled brown paper sack that obviously held a bottle of booze, then back at her. She grinned and winked. He tipped the bottle to his mouth, guzzling down more alcohol.

"See you in Hell," she muttered.

Destiny made her way to the bar, then pushed on the door, stepping inside the cool, dimly lit interior. As soon as her eyes adjusted, she glanced around. A haze of cigarette smoke formed a gray cloud above the patrons.

Slim pickings. Only a handful of people sat at tables.

Two worn out hookers were strategically positioned close to the door. Too easy. They already had Hell stamped on their foreheads. Destiny wanted to impress the powers that be. Used-up hookers would not make an impact on them.

A couple of men sat at another table deep in conversation about a stupid football game. Not bad looking. Wedding rings glinted on their fingers. Married. Too much trouble.

Hmm… But the demons might be impressed.

Before she could take a step toward them the bathroom door opened, spilling a patch of light into the bar. Two laughing women joined the men at their table. Scratch that idea. Two was company, four was a crowd.

There was a lively group of barely legal college boys chugging pitchers of beer. Hmm, certainly corruptible. From the way they were dressed, they were definitely slumming. One guy glanced her way, eyes practically bugging out.

Oh hell, was that drool? No thanks!

Someone put money in the jukebox and a slow country song began to play. For a moment, she let the deep voice of the singer wash over her. She didn't even mind that he was crooning about his cheating wife and losing himself in a bottle of whiskey. Damn, she missed being alive.

Her gaze languidly drifted around the rest of the room, past dark walls with posters of country singers plastered all over them. The bartender wiped a damp cloth across one end of the bar. Destiny's eyes narrowed as she sized him up. The potential was there.

He raised his head, saw her, then smiled. The kind of smile that made her feel good all over. He wasn't bad looking, in a good-old-boy sort of way.

Destiny drew in a deep breath as she readied herself for a full assault, but at the last minute a movement at the other end of the bar caught her eye.

A lone cowboy sat on one of the stools nursing a beer, his back to her. He wore a black T-shirt that deliciously hugged his broad shoulders. Her gaze dropped. The jeans weren't bad, either. Nope, not bad at all. The guy had a great ass from this angle. *Sweet!* Cowboy had just enough muscles that he created a fantasy, but not enough that she would be in competition with his ego.

He turned and looked her way, his gaze sliding sensuously over her body. Tingles of excitement tickled her spine. She had such a fondness for cowboys. They knew how to ride 'em long and hard, and she was all for long and hard.

She devoured him with one long lazy look. His black Stetson was pulled down low on his forehead as though he didn't give a damn about anyone or anything. It didn't help that, for some insane reason, black cowboy hats turned her on.

Oh baby, she was about to make his wet dreams come true. Yee-haw, ride 'em cowboy.

The bartender was forgotten as she locked on target. Destiny slid her hands over her hips nice and slow before sauntering toward him, putting just a little bit of swing in her hips.

This time she would be the one calling the shots. The one in charge. No one would ever control her again like they had when she was alive. She would take what *she* wanted and to hell with the rest! Literally.

The cowboy watched her every step of the way. She was already wrapping him around her little finger and the poor guy didn't have a clue. She stopped beside him.

"Buy a lady a beer?" she asked. Her words held enough invitation that only an idiot wouldn't guess she wanted more than a beer, and this guy didn't look like an idiot. She slid onto the stool next to his, propping her elbow on the scarred wooden surface of the bar.

Over the haze of smoke, over the smell of alcohol, Destiny caught another scent that weaved its way around her, making her lean in a little closer. It was spicy and held a promise of nights filled with down-and-dirty sex. She could feel the waves of heat radiating off him, curling around her body and wrapping her in a sensual cloud of sexual awareness.

"A beer for the lady," he drawled, breaking into her fantasy and nodding toward the bartender.

His voice sent tingles down her spine. It was just a little raspy—low and sexy.

Cowboy swiveled his stool around to face her and tipped the

brim of his hat with one finger so she got a better look at his face: the strong jaw, the slight stubble, and the most intense blue eyes she'd ever encountered.

Destiny had her first mini orgasm, and it felt so fucking great! This guy looked good enough to eat. She was going to enjoy corrupting him.

"What's a cowboy like you doing in a bar all alone?" Okay, that sounded pretty cheesy, but she was a little out of practice; she'd died in 1959.

"Waiting for a woman like you," he replied and again his words caressed her as his blue-eyed gaze drifted lazily down her body before returning to her face. Her nipples tightened.

The bartender set a beer in front of her. Cowboy dropped a few bills on the counter and the bartender left.

She grinned as she took the bottle, her tongue sliding nice and slow around the rim before she brought it the rest of the way to her lips. She tilted the bottle a little and ice-cold liquid slid down her throat. Nice. She'd missed the taste of alcohol.

"So, what's your handle, cowboy?" she asked after she lowered the bottle.

"Chance. Chance Bellew."

"Well, you've just met your destiny." She grinned. "Destiny Carter." She thought she might have crossed the line of cheesy, but his eyes began to sparkle and his slow, sexy grin made her tremble.

"And maybe you're taking a chance by sitting so close to me."

She leaned nearer. "Maybe I like taking chances." And she'd certainly like to take this Chance!

"You may not know what you're letting yourself in for," he told her.

"Oh, I think I might."

"Are you a bad girl, Destiny?"

His slow Texas drawl washed over her like liquid fire. It was all she could do to even breathe. She took another drink of her beer, then set the bottle back on the counter before turning and looking him right in the eyes. "You've never seen bad like me."

He casually placed his hands on her knees. She drew in a sharp breath.

"You think so? I've been with some really bad women."

His fingers left trails of fire as he began to draw slow circles on the insides of her knees. She sucked in a deep breath as delicious sensations rushed through her.

"You don't mind my touching you, do you?"

Destiny met his gaze head on and shook her head. "I don't mind at all, but don't you want to find someplace quieter?" Someplace where she could tear off his clothes and make wild, passionate love all night long. Her body was starting to freakin' burn she was so hot. After that, she would take him to Hell.

Chance shook his head. "It's dark enough. No one is watching."

Destiny scanned the bar. The college boys were just leaving. The married men were still talking football. The women with them were starting to look bored. The bartender had walked over and joined in the conversation. The hookers still looked bored. Chance was right. No one paid attention to what they were doing.

He propped his foot on the outside rail of her barstool to block anyone's view, and then his gaze dragged its way down her body. Her nipples hardened to tight little nubs. They ached for him to tease with more than his eyes.

Some small amount of sanity returned. "You want to fuck in the bar?" How much could they experience here? She wanted him totally naked and lusting for her body.

Still, the idea did hold some merit. She was always the one who loved living on the edge. The one who took a dare at the drop of a hat, no matter the risk. She never had anything to lose.

"It's your choice," he told her. "I can stop. I can walk out of your life forever."

His fingers inched higher.

She bit back her moan. Walk away? Leave her aching for more and not even look back? She slowly shook her head. "No way, Cowboy. Like I said, you've never met a bad girl like me."

He met her gaze, and for just a second Destiny thought she saw something—something telling her that she might be in over her head with this guy; but when his hands moved a few inches higher, she dismissed the warning bells.

Chance continued moving his thumbs in slow, seductive circles on the insides of her thighs. She sucked in a mouthful of air, her bottom squirming on the seat as she gripped the edge of the bar with one hand and his thigh with the other. He was so close... so close... to that secret spot that would send her over the edge.

"You know what I want to do?" His voice washed her in sensual fantasies.

She shook her head.

"I want to rip off your dress. I want to see your breasts, hold them in my hands right before I suck on them, teasing each nipple with my tongue."

She automatically thrust her chest forward.

"Can you feel my tongue scraping across your sensitive nipples?"

She whimpered, nodding her head.

"Then I would slide my hands down your body, over your hips. You're fucking hot. I love looking at your nakedness. I'd spread your legs wide and, for as long as I wanted, I'd stare down at you, seeing all of you."

Her legs automatically opened for him. Yes, hell yes. She wanted him to look, to see, to take pleasure in her body.

"I'd lower my head, inhaling your musky scent. Nice."

His fingers continued to draw circles on the insides of her thighs—closer and closer.

"Then I would taste you." His words were spoken low, but it

was as though they ricocheted inside her head, bouncing off the images he created.

She trembled. Even when she was alive, no one ever did that. The thought of him licking and sucking caused an ache to settle in her lower region. Maybe she only misunderstood.

"Tasting all of me?" she croaked.

His hands inched higher still until he brushed lightly through her curls. "Especially here."

Her thighs quivered and her imagination kicked into overdrive. She was damn glad the dress and her stiletto heels were all she wore.

"Do you like that?" he asked as he continued to move his fingers through her curls.

"Oh yes." She bit her bottom lip, scooted to the edge of the stool, spreading her legs a little wider.

He fanned open her labia, running his fingers up and down before working the pad of his thumb against her clit. She whimpered.

"Lean in against me," he told her.

She blindly obeyed as little earthquakes began to erupt inside her.

"I want to suck on your pussy," he whispered close to her ear as his hands continued to massage and stroke. He slipped his tongue inside her ear and swirled it around. "I want to suck on your pussy until you cry my name."

It was all she could do to take a breath, and every breath she drew in burned her throat.

He slipped two fingers inside her, sliding them in and out, in and out. "You're wet. I want you to come for me—right now."

His hot breath stroked her neck. She nodded, grabbing his shoulders. She couldn't form one cohesive thought. Every fiber of her being was centered on what he was making her feel—and it felt so good!

He slipped his fingers out, running them up and down her pussy, then slipped back inside. In and out. In and out. The heat inside her began to build hotter and hotter. Flames licked over her as spasms gripped her body.

The room grew darker, everything blurred.

It was only the two of them.

No one else mattered.

Destiny met his gaze and saw the fire burning in his eyes. His fingers continued their assault on her body, pressing against her, massaging, working her as if he knew exactly what to do, what she so desperately needed.

"What do you want?" he whispered.

"More. I want more."

He slipped two fingers inside her.

In and out. In and out.

She was so close, so—

"Don't stop. Please don't stop."

She moaned, her body trembling with release. Her breathing came in short gasps as she tried to draw in enough air to fill her lungs. He held her close, pressing his fingers against her until her body stopped quivering, and the bar came back into focus, then he slowly slid them out of her, scraping against her, making her body quiver one… last… time.

"You've been a very bad girl, Destiny. I think next time I'm going to have to show you what I do to bad girls."

Flames licked up her body at the thought of Chance showing her anything.

He suddenly straightened. He was tall. At least six feet four inches. She grabbed the edge of the bar so she didn't lose her precarious position on the stool and slide off onto the floor. Destiny doubted she would have the strength to get back up.

"Another beer for the… lady," he told the bartender before dropping some more bills on the counter.

When had the bartender returned? Did it matter? No, not really. Destiny felt far too satisfied to let anything bother her right now.

Chance leaned down and brushed his lips across hers, then stood and walked away.

For a moment, Destiny thought Chance might be going to the men's room, but he walked past the sign directing him to the restroom and out the front door.

What the hell? He was leaving?

Nothing ever changed. They got what they wanted, then left. Just like when she'd been alive. Tears welled in her eyes.

The bartender placed a beer in front of her.

She gripped the cold bottle, blinking back the moisture in her eyes. What did it matter? She'd used him, too. Chance had given her exactly what she'd needed, and he'd done it very well. And maybe she wanted more—so what?

"Who is he?" she asked before the bartender turned away.

He looked at her and shrugged. "Some cowboy. He's been coming in here for about a week now. I asked him once if he was from around here. He only said he was waiting for a lady." The bartender's gaze swept over her. "I thought you might be her."

A cold chill ran down her spine.

He was waiting for her? Why? Who was he? Did he know she was in search of a soul?

Idiot!

Of course Chance wasn't waiting for her specifically. He was just a cowboy looking for some female company. Any willing lady would have satisfied his needs.

She glanced toward the door, felt his lingering presence. Chance was good, real good. He had her wanting more. Why shouldn't she test the waters again? She would wait for him tomorrow night. He'd told her "next time." She smiled. Yes, he'd be back.

Chance Bellew won the point for tonight, but tomorrow—he'd soon be all hers. She planned to take him higher than he'd ever been before. By the time she was through with him, Chance would beg her to take him to Hell. He might have been waiting for a lady, but he found a demon instead. Well, a demon-in-training. Close enough.

Her lips curved upward. Tomorrow night couldn't get here soon enough.

Chapter 2

It took all Chance's willpower to leave Destiny. His dick hurt so bad that if anyone bumped it, the damn thing might break off. Walking away was the most difficult part in any assignment.

Once outside the bar, he took a deep breath, then slowly exhaled. Destiny was some kind of hot. Chance was tempted to turn around and go back inside. Just say screw it to the way he'd always done things. There were other ways he could handle the situation.

Chance shook his head, quickly dismissing that idea. Why fix what wasn't broken? His way always worked well for him. He had to make Destiny want him so much that she would do anything to have him, including giving up her soul. He had a week—and one day—to do it.

Oh yeah, he knew exactly what she was—a demon wannabe, and he knew her timeline. Idiot, that's what she was. The demons always failed to mention the fine print that told the trainees they would burn in Hell until there wasn't one speck of anything human left inside them—once they made it out of the sales department.

Most people who gave up their souls only saw and heard what they wanted. Who the hell would think to read the fine print anyway?

Then the trainees had to get their own contracts for souls while promising other poor saps a better life. The demons were running their own pyramid scam, with Satan at the top raking in souls.

Yeah right, a better life his ass. Like that would ever happen. Chance made it his job to set the trainees straight.

He walked behind the bar. After looking around to make sure no one watched, he closed his eyes, and thought about where he wanted to go. Air swirled around him and the ground was no longer beneath his feet. The sensation of traveling through space was an odd feeling, but he'd gotten used to it over the centuries.

When Chance was on a firm surface again, he opened his eyes. He stood in the middle of the rec room. He supposed people nowadays would call the spacious room a man cave. A bar stretched across one end. An assortment of cattle brands were burned into the surface. The branding irons now hung on the wall. Cowhide-covered stools were lined up in front, ready to invite a tired cowboy to sit and have a drink.

A scarred, red felt-covered poker table was in one corner, a seating area with overstuffed, black leather furniture in another. Dillon liked beating them at pool, so he made sure the room had a table. Sliding glass doors led to a covered patio. From there, a path wound its way to the stables.

The ranch had almost five hundred acres, more cattle than he knew what to do with, and some of the finest saddle horses around. The ranch house itself had twelve thousand square feet of living space. More than enough for one, but just right for the four immortals who lived there. It was home. The only real one any of them had ever had.

Chance glanced around the rec room. Ryder was shooting pool with Dillon, and Hunter was watching TV—the guy was seriously into television, especially *Survivor*.

Ryder glanced up, casually asking, "How'd it go?" Ryder was the Romeo of their rag-tag group. He wasn't as tall as the rest of them, only six feet one inch, but his dark hair and smooth good looks made up for his height. He'd romanced more souls on their way to Hell than Chance could count.

"I finger-fucked her in the bar," Chance told him.

Ryder grimaced. "That had to be hard."

Chance was sure his expression was equally pained. "It still is. She's freakin' hot. All curvy and soft—and tight." He drew in a ragged breath. "She's got a body that would make a dead man come." And long, thick, black hair that begged him to run his fingers through the silky strands.

Ahh, but that wasn't even the half of it. No, there was something in the way she looked at him with those deep green eyes—kind of misty. Bedroom eyes. Yeah, that's what they were. Chance was afraid he might have met his match with Destiny, but he loved a challenge.

Dillon, the blond Adonis, sank the eight ball with a loud clunk, drawing Chance back to the present. Dillon returned his cue stick to the rack. He was six feet three inches of raw male power. The guy had six-pack abs that were as hard as concrete, and even though he seemed to take everything in stride, he didn't mind busting some demon heads together. Or anyone else who got in his way. But right now, Dillon looked concerned.

"Are you going to be able to save her soul?" Dillon's forehead wrinkled.

Truthfully? Chance wasn't sure. "I don't know," he told them. "Destiny likes being bad."

He sensed her presence before she even opened the door. The mirror behind the bar confirmed his suspicions when she stepped inside, looking hot in her body-hugging red dress and those four-inch stiletto heels.

What the hell was it about stilettos that turned him on so much? That and long legs, and hers were long and then some. They were the kind of legs that wrapped around a man's waist and sucked him in deeper. Now that was an image. His body ached with need.

"Yo, Chance, you still with us?" Ryder asked.

Chance looked around the room, startled for a moment. The vision of Destiny had been so clear that he felt as if he was there with her. God, what was it about this woman that had him living in a fantasy world? He shook his head and looked at Ryder.

"She's hot, all right," Chance told them. "And she wants my soul."

Hunter turned away from the TV long enough to snort. "Just make sure she doesn't tempt you too much, buddy."

"I'm not a fool." She might be sexy, and different from other women he ran across, but no, she wouldn't get the best of him. Besides, he'd been saving souls way too long to get caught in a demon's trap, especially one still in training. He would do whatever it took to save Destiny. Yeah, sure, he skirted the very edges of what was legal—for an angel—but he would do whatever it took.

Not actually an angel when he thought about it. A nephilim, to be exact. All their fathers were angels. Centuries before, they mated with mortal women. When the women bore children, a new race was created. Immortals with powers—demigods.

The children didn't live by the same rules as mortals, nor that of the typical robe-wearing, bright-light-surrounding-them angels. Hell, most of the time the nephilim were breaking the rules and making up new ones as they went. As long as they didn't cross over to the dark side, everyone pretty much stayed out of their way.

After decades passed, the nephilim decided they needed something to do. Saving souls and maybe answering a few prayers on a slow day was as good a job as any. If they had to walk a fine line to do it, so be it.

He sighed. And sometimes a demon-in-training who looked like Destiny came along. Chance had a feeling helping her see the error in her judgment might take a while. At least he hoped so.

Ryder bumped him on the shoulder. "Hey, you look like you could use some distraction. Why don't we see what's happening in town?"

"Yeah, come on, go with us," Dillon chimed in.

Hunter even stood, turning off the TV. "Yeah, I'm bored."

"You're watching *Survivor*," Chance reminded him.

Hunter shrugged his wide shoulders. "It's a rerun." Hunter was six feet three inches of pure muscle and power. Nobody got in his way. In fact, most times they just ran the other way. He looked mean, but he was a big teddy bear. He'd once answered a prayer that involved a kitten stuck in a drain pipe. No prayer was too small. And they still hadn't let him forget that one.

Chance looked at them, each waited for him to say something. They knew how tough it could be, trying to turn someone. They were there for him. He only had to say the word. God knew he could use a break. "Yeah, okay."

"Where to?" Ryder asked.

"My turn to choose," Hunter told them as they stood in a circle facing each other.

Chance groaned. The last time Hunter chose, they all ended up in a barroom brawl. Hunter had a touchy temper, although that time wasn't really his fault. A couple were arguing at one of the tables for most of the night. The dude was being a pain in the ass and his date just looked as though she wanted to crawl into the nearest hole. The nephilim normally didn't get involved in shit like that.

Until the dude slapped his date.

Hunter lost it and took the dude out with one solid punch, but he didn't count on the creep having friends. Nor did the dude's friends count on Hunter's cohorts.

Chance grinned. Damn, that was a fun night when he thought about it.

His smile slipped into a frown. They'd almost blown their cover, though. Mixing with mortals was risky at best. Sure, they answered prayers now and then. Playing demigods and granting wishes could be pretty cool. Revealing their true identity was the one gray area where they could get called on the carpet.

Not that any of them had ever seen their fathers, or any angels for that matter. No, they had other ways of communicating their displeasure. The angels upstairs merely blocked the nephilim's powers.

Before he could remind Hunter about that, they were off. When the four of them traveled, it always took at least a minute to get to where they were going. Chance closed his eyes and hoped for the best.

Cold air whooshed around him before turning into a warm breeze. He inhaled the scent of earth and cedar, right before the hiss of a pissed-off bobcat filled the air.

Not a bar then.

They began to drift downward until Chance's feet landed on solid ground. His stomach dropped, then settled.

"Where the hell are we?" Ryder asked.

Chance opened his eyes. Dillon's eyebrows were veed, Ryder scratched his head, and Hunter beamed. Chance felt pretty much the same as Dillon and Ryder—confused as hell.

"Yeah, where are we?" Chance asked. The area looked familiar. Rolling hills were dotted with oak and cedar trees. Much like the ranch. To the north, the trees were thicker. Something told Chance that he'd been there before, and there was a reason he didn't return sooner.

"We haven't been here in at least a hundred and fifty years, but I didn't think any of you would ever forget the place we created. We wanted a challenge." Hunter's grin covered his whole face. "This was the reason we bought the land for the ranch."

The bobcat that hissed earlier padded out of the woods. The feline raised her head, then screamed loud enough to make the birds squawk. Hunter squatted and the bobcat ran to him, barreling into Hunter. A normal man would have been bowled over, but then Hunter wasn't a normal man. He only laughed and scratched the beast behind its ears.

The guy attracted animals everywhere he went. He was Tarzan of the nephilim.

Dillon scanned the hills. "Didn't we have Indians and—"

The pounding of hooves shook the earth beneath their feet, followed by the sound of war cries.

Ryder snickered. "I forgot about the holograms. Scared the hell out of me the first time."

Indians suddenly swarmed over a distant hill like ants at a picnic, and they were coming their way, bows drawn. Chance took a step back, then remembered they weren't real. Okay, he'd admit the holograms startled him the first time, too. Hunter told them they were a challenge to see who was the best at escaping danger. Except they all managed to elude the marauding band of Indians, so there was never a clear winner.

"I thought we'd outgrown Cowboys and Indians," Dillon drawled.

An arrow flew through the air in a wide arc before landing between Ryder's feet. "That looks real." He reached down and pulled the arrow out of the ground. "It is real."

They turned to look at Hunter.

"I tweaked the holograms. Makes the game a little more interesting."

"Yeah, and you watch too much *Survivor!*" Chance whirled around and took off at a run toward the trees. They were immortals and healed fast, but they still felt pain, and right now there were arrows flying all around them.

They had some protection in the woods. Chance was glad to see four saddled horses waiting for them. Without pausing, he jumped, planting his palms on the horse's rump and leveraging himself into the saddle. Before he drew another breath, he kicked the horse's sides and they were off, dodging trees and low-hanging limbs. The Indians weren't slowing down.

Chance would kill Hunter. As soon as they were back at the ranch, he would kill him.

He cast a quick glance at the others. Maybe it had been too long since their skills were put to the test, but Chance would still kill him.

"Split up!" Hunter yelled. "We'll meet at the lake."

Ryder went to the right when they cleared the woods, Dillon to the left. Hunter and Chance topped the next hill, then both veered in opposite directions. Chance glanced over his shoulder. There were five Indians on his heels. An arrow suddenly whizzed past his ear.

"Crap!"

He could be enjoying a beer in the rec room. But no, Hunter had them playing Cowboys and Indians.

Chance quickly looped the reins over the saddle horn. In one smooth motion he swung his leg over the saddle, turning at the same time, until he faced backward. He tightened his legs against the leather to keep his balance and jerked the rifle from its scabbard. In quick succession he cocked, then fired the gun, getting off three shots, dropping three of them, and pissing off the other two.

"Not too smart, are you?" he yelled. He cocked the gun and fired again.

Click.

Well hell, it was just like Hunter to keep the odds even. He flipped around in the saddle, kicked the horse into a dead run. He had a fifteen second lead when he topped the next hill. As soon as he was on the other side of it, he laid back on the reins. The horse's back hooves dug furrows into the earth, but slowed enough for Chance to jump off and run back up the hill. Just as he topped the rise, the two Indians were reaching it, too.

Chance swung his rifle, butt first. The wood splintered when it connected with the surprised warrior. Blood spurted from his nose as his head reared back and he flew off the back of the horse.

"One down," he muttered as he turned.

The other warrior jumped off his horse, feet landing with a dull thud on the ground. He bared his teeth, pulling a knife from the sheath at his side. Chance crouched low when the Indian ran toward him with a fierce war cry that should've had Chance shaking in his boots.

It didn't.

The Indian slashed downward. Chance feinted to the right, then grabbed the Indian's arm. Their gazes locked. Chance saw the same excitement that he was feeling mirrored in the Indian's eyes.

And the Indian's arm felt just a little too real. Up close like this, he also looked a little too real.

Chance only had a moment to wonder just how much Hunter had tweaked the holograms. The Indian pushed hard against his chest. Chance lost his balance and fell to the ground, landing with a hard jolt that knocked the breath out of him.

He recovered quickly and planted a booted foot against the Indian's chest, using the momentum to push the Indian over his head. The Indian landed on his shoulder, the knife flying from his hand. Chance jumped to his feet and ran toward him. Just before he reached the Indian, he drew back his fist and landed a solid punch that connected with his jaw. There was a loud crack. The Indian spun around. Chance drew back his fist again and connected with his gut. When the Indian doubled over, Chance brought his knee up. As if in slow motion, the Indian fell back, crumpling to the ground.

Chance drew in a deep breath and looked around.

All clear.

A slow grin curved his lips. Damn, he missed all of this. Herding cattle and fixing fences just wasn't the same thing as tangling with someone who was trying to kill him. He almost hoped one of the Indians would get to his feet, but just as quickly as the thought came to him, the warriors disappeared, leaving only a sprinkling of glitter dust in their wake.

A shame. He was just getting started.

His horse was at the bottom of the hill, munching on grass. He waited, but the horse didn't vanish. Chance only hoped Hunter brought the real thing for them to ride. He'd hate to be galloping along and have the horse disappear from under him.

Excitement still flowed through his veins when he caught up with the others about a mile north. Chance nudged his horse, joining them.

"Next time you might want to mention just how much you *tweaked* the holograms."

"Had fun, didn't you?" Hunter asked.

Chance leaned forward in the saddle, resting his arm against the saddle horn. "That's beside the point."

Hunter laughed. "I knew everyone would enjoy the challenge."

"We could've been at a bar," Ryder grumbled.

"You just want to get laid tonight," Dillon said.

"And that would be a problem, why?"

"You know, you can go blind from overuse." Chance laughed.

Ryder and Dillon joined in. Hunter was the only one who wore a serious expression.

"What?" Chance finally asked.

"We still have one more place to go," Hunter told them.

They looked at each other. All joking stopped. The others knew what Hunter was talking about.

"We have to?" Dillon bumped his gray Stetson up a little higher on his forehead.

"Yes, we do."

"Then let's get it over with." Chance nudged his horse forward, dreading what was to come, but Hunter was right. They couldn't forget who they were. If they grew careless, it could cost them their lives.

They rode side by side. Before they were even around the lake, Chance heard the flames crackling and spitting. He hesitated, his horse prancing beneath him. He calmed her fears with a few whispered words and a soothing caress down her neck before he climbed down. The others followed suit. Without speaking, they walked farther down the mountain, leaving their horses behind.

As they drew closer, the heat was like an electric blanket turned on high in the middle of a blazing hot Texas summer. When they rounded the corner, each man came face to face with his worst nightmare. No one spoke as they stared at what was before them. A blazing inferno, at least a mile high, rose into the sky, reaching toward the clouds, red and yellow flames whipping about like snakes caught in a tornado. There was only one way to get across.

Is everyone ready?" Hunter asked.

"Who came up with this insane idea, anyway?" Dillon grumbled.

"You did," the other three replied in unison.

"It's a reminder of what the fires of Hell will feel like if we should ever lose our souls," Chance said.

Every time they faced an assignment even remotely involving demons, they knew the risks were higher.

"Maybe it's a good thing you brought us here." Chance drew in a deep breath as he mentally prepared himself for what was to come.

"Are we ready?" Hunter asked.

"Let's go for it," Dillon said.

"If we must, but I would never be in danger of losing my soul. Nope, no way in… hell." Ryder snickered.

Ryder wasn't as brave as he pretended. Chance heard the edge in his friend's voice.

"We can do this," Hunter said.

They locked hands and stepped into the flames at the same time. Together, they were four times stronger, four times more able to stand against evil.

The heat immediately spread over Chance—licking, burning. The pain was intense, almost too much to bear.

Chance continued forward, gritting his teeth and clamping his lips together. He could stand the pain because it would soon be over, unlike a demon who would feel the fire for decades. Only when any trace of kindness and compassion was burned away, when all that was left was the anger and torment, only then would the fury be released into demon form.

By then, demons were so consumed by pain and anguish they only wanted to wreak havoc on the innocent. As Chance forced his way through the fire, he kept seeing Destiny's face before him. She didn't deserve that kind of torture.

Flames licked at his arms and legs, branding him with pain. The stench of burning flesh filled his nostrils. Taking one step at a time, making it through the heat was all he focused on.

He could do this. He *would* do this for Destiny!

Beside Chance, Ryder stumbled. Chance tightened his grip. They would make it together or not at all! Ryder squeezed his hand, letting him know he was okay, and they continued forward, four nephilim as one.

Chance stepped out of the blaze, Dillon, Hunter, and Ryder with him. Fire fell from his body. He raised his arms to the heavens above. His roar of anger caused the cloud above him to grow black, and then it showered rain down upon them, cooling their burning skin. The pouring rain soon became a light drizzle. Once again, their bodies healed.

Damn it, Chance had to save her. If he could keep her here a week and a day, she would be safe from those fires. He would do all that was in his power to make that happen.

"I will set Destiny free!" Chance vowed to the heavens above. "Satan will not have her soul!"

Chapter 3

THE ROAR OF THUNDER shook the bar. Destiny flinched, looking around, but no one else seemed to notice anything out of the ordinary. Maybe the crash was meant for her ears alone. A demon could be sending her a warning. A cold chill ran down her spine.

When did she get so jittery? She wasn't sure, but the odd feeling stayed with her. Chance wasn't at the bar. Maybe that was it. Destiny felt as if she'd been stood up. Her life was littered with people who'd dumped her—starting with her mother. Destiny hadn't thought about her in a long time.

Her hand trembled when she reached for her beer, bumping it instead. The bottle tilted; she grabbed it before it could fall. Destiny's heart pounded inside her chest. She drew in a deep breath, forcing herself to relax. How could she let Rose hurt her after all these years? Her mother was nothing to her.

And she could tell herself that all day and it would still be a lie. For a while, Rose made a decent mother. Destiny remembered hugs, a second-hand doll from a dirty thrift store, food on the table. Rose worked two jobs. Her eyes had been a pretty blue, but they were always tired. Then a man came into Rose's life and promised to make everything better. He hadn't. Wasn't that the way it always happened? Men could really screw things up.

She brought the bottle to her lips, taking a long drink of the cold liquid and letting it wash away her past.

Chance hadn't agreed to return that or any other night. No big deal. She wouldn't even let it bother her except the night before was so unbelievably good that she hoped for more of the same. Why not take what she could get for a change?

Her gaze moved around the dimly lit room. Everyone else seemed to be at the bar, though. The place was crowded. A typical Friday night. People were off work and ready to party.

Except for Chance.

Was he out on the range rounding up cattle? She wasn't sure what hours cowboys worked. Her mouth turned down. Or if he was even a cowboy in the true sense. Just because he wore a cowboy hat and boots didn't make him a cowboy. She tapped her ruby-red nails on the bar. Hell, she knew nothing about the man. Well, except that he could give a girl one hell of an orgasm.

Her eyes strayed to the beer mug clock hanging on the wall behind the bar. Almost eight thirty. Damn, she was so pathetic, but all she was able to think about was the way his magical fingers awakened her body. Her motor was purring. Downing three beers certainly didn't help slow it down. Now she was even more revved, and she was starting to get irritated.

Why did she even wait for him? She'd already been hit on by no fewer than four eager men looking for hot sex, and every damn one of them wore a blasted black Stetson. She could've taken any one of them up on their offer of a good time. Before the night was over, she'd have more than one soul under her belt, and be on her way back to Hell.

Just as quickly as the thought entered her head, she dismissed it. No, she knew it wouldn't be the same with someone else. That was why she didn't take one of the offers. She wanted Chance, and only Chance would do.

The door opened, letting a sliver of light into the otherwise dim interior. She held her breath, then exhaled in a whoosh. The hookers again. They must be regulars. Business was booming. They should be able to make a little extra money. It was a sad day when they would get laid before her. Life could be a cruel bitch when she wanted to.

Destiny brought the bottle of beer up to her mouth and closed her eyes as she took a long draw, draining it. The beer was still ice-cold and it had been a long time since she'd had alcohol. She lowered the bottle, already feeling a little tipsy.

Ah, hell, where was he anyway?

"Can I buy a lady a beer?" Chance asked in his slow, sexy drawl.

She stiffened, then relaxed. Her world felt right. She almost hated him for that.

The cowboy definitely had some moves. She hadn't even seen the door open. Not that anything mattered right now. Chance was here. Destiny didn't care about anything else.

"You're late," she told him as she swiveled her stool to face him. Her thighs tingled. He looked all cowboy in a deep blue, button-down western shirt and snug-fitting jeans. And yum, he wore his black Stetson low on his forehead.

With one finger, he raised the brim and sat on the stool next to hers. His gaze roamed down her body, touching, caressing, before slowly moving back up and meeting her eyes once more.

"I didn't know we had a date." His words were low and husky, sending goose bumps spreading over her arms.

She drew in a deep breath, looking away. Chance had a way of making her want to strip out of her clothes and let him fuck her brains out. That thought had merit, except being discreet was a must, so stripping probably wasn't wise. Demons were touchy about people knowing they really did exist. Which was odd because they offered so much: No more pain, no sadness, a life of luxury even Donald Trump would envy. She frowned. Except she had yet to see any of it.

She shook away her doubts. As soon as she brought in one more soul, she would have everything she dreamed about. No one would ever be able to hurt her again. Besides, she had other things she wanted to think about—like the sexy man in front of her.

She slowly slid her fingers up and down the condensation on the empty bottle. "After last night, you and I both know we aren't finished." She studied him for a moment. "Why did you leave? Surely you didn't have a wife to get home to." Perish the thought!

"No wife. I had to be someplace."

Relief swept over her. Not that it mattered to her one way or the other if he was married. She was there for one thing and one thing only: to steal his soul. A wife didn't play into her scheme of things. She rationalized that a wife would only have made her job more difficult, but secretly Destiny liked the idea that another woman hadn't sunk her claws into him.

Chance looked around, then came to his feet.

Was he about to disappear again? Her heart pounded. Oh damn, she really needed him. The night before was just a teaser. She wanted the real thing—every delicious inch!

But Chance didn't leave. He held out his hand. As if on cue, someone put money in the jukebox and a country ballad began to play.

"Dance with me." His eyes bore into hers—hungry, as if he couldn't stand not touching her one more second.

The air around them almost crackled from the passion building between them. She slid off the stool. He took her hand and led her to the dance floor. There were other couples moving to the rhythm of the music, not really dancing, just holding each other. It made the dance floor crowded. She didn't care. She wanted to hold him close, feel his warmth.

Chance pulled her into his arms, her breasts pressed against his chest. Her nipples immediately tightened. It didn't take much friction for her body to come alive because her short black dress hugged every curve, and the material was so thin it bordered on naughty. But then, she liked being naughty.

"You look sexy tonight," he whispered close to her ear before his teeth captured the lobe. He tugged lightly before letting go.

She moaned. Her head was already spinning with visions of them having wild, mind-blowing sex.

"I can feel your body heat. Damn, you're so hot," he said. He brought his hand up, cupped her breast, then lightly teased her nipple. "You're not wearing anything under your dress. You are bad, aren't you?"

Bad? He had no idea how bad she could be. She was ready to show him, though. "Let's get out of here," she said, biting her bottom lip.

"Not yet. Just a little more."

A little more what? He was right when he said her body was burning up.

He moved his head until his lips brushed across hers. She sighed. His tongue scraped over her bottom lip, then delved inside as they swayed to the throbbing music from the jukebox.

They explored each other's mouths, his tongue thrusting then softly teasing. She captured his tongue and caressed, then released. He drew in a quick breath. She smiled to herself. Oh yes, she was going to be the one in control.

She lightly massaged the back of his neck with the pads of her fingers. His body grew taut, but just as suddenly relaxed, surrendering to her touch. He was hers for the taking.

"Make love to me," she whispered when the kiss ended. "I'll take you higher than you've ever been."

"Soon, sweet lady. Soon." He ran his hands down her back, cupping her ass, pulling her in closer. "I'll give you everything you want." He moved his hand between their bodies, then stroked his fingers up her thigh, not getting in any hurry.

Destiny trembled, holding her breath as he teased the inside of her leg. Suddenly she didn't feel in as much control as she had a moment ago.

His body swayed, keeping up with the tempo of the slow sultry beat on the jukebox. She followed his lead, letting each new sensation sweep over her.

Did he know the fire he created inside her? Did he realize how much passion was building between them?

She nudged her hips forward to let him know she was more than ready and willing, but all she got from him was a deep rumble of laughter.

Anger fused through her. He laughed at her? She pulled away, but his fingers stroked a little higher and, just as quickly, her anger dissolved. He was so close to the sweet spot. She couldn't stop her whimper as he teased her flesh.

She had to get control of the situation. She was the demon. The one in charge.

He scraped his fingers through her curls, then tugged on the fleshy part of her sex. Spasms trembled through her body. Oh yes, that was the spot!

All thoughts about being in charge flew out the window. One touch from him and she had a mini orgasm. Who the hell was this guy? Could she keep him when she returned to Hell?

"You like that?" he asked.

She nodded, but when she reached for him, he shifted away until she straddled one of his legs. There were more people on the dance floor so they could barely move, but it didn't take much movement from his thigh for her to feel the pressure riding against her.

"When I get you alone, I'm going to slowly undress you. I want you naked, your legs spread open. I want to see every inch of you. I'm going to slide inside that hot little body."

"Yes," she moaned. The people around her faded, replaced by shadows as she focused on his words, as she listened to him telling her exactly what he would do to her, and the whole time she rubbed against his leg.

"I'm going to slowly enter," he told her. "Inch by inch. It will be all I can do to keep from ramming myself inside you. But I don't want to start hard and fast. I want to savor each second of slipping inside you, feeling the way your hot body closes around my dick. I'll go deeper and deeper."

The heat inside her rose higher and higher until she couldn't stand any more. She gripped his shoulders. "Please," she whispered, her voice breaking.

"Feel me going deeper, then sliding out. In and out. In and out," he said. He rubbed her nipple between his finger and thumb, pulling and squeezing.

She tried to swallow and couldn't. Her mouth was too dry. Each ragged breath she drew into her lungs reminded her how badly she needed release.

He moved his jean-clad thigh just enough so that he could slip two fingers inside her.

In and out. In and out. Touching, pressing, massaging.

"I can't," she whimpered.

"Shh," he whispered close to her ear. "I'll take you to the place you want to go." The pad of his thumb pressed against her clit and began to massage.

Her body ached.

She clasped his arm, squeezing.

"Let yourself go," he murmured close to her ear.

She bit her bottom lip.

"Feel me fucking you."

"Yes," she moaned.

"I'm going harder, deeper."

"Yes. Don't stop."

He massaged, then slipped his fingers inside her body faster and faster.

The room swirled around her, lights danced in front of her eyes.

Heat swept over her in waves as she climaxed. She bit her bottom lip and pressed herself tighter against him as her body throbbed.

Chance held her tight, his tongue delving inside her ear.

Her thighs clenched and unclenched, pressing against his muscled thigh.

A tear slipped from the corner of her eye as weakness settled over her. She clung to him, unable to move, barely able to breathe.

Destiny vaguely knew when Chance led her back to one of the booths rather than the barstool. She slumped down, resting her elbows on the scarred surface, her head in her hands. Moving wasn't an option. If someone claimed this booth, they could roll her onto the floor and everyone could step over her. She closed her eyes and concentrated on breathing in, then breathing out, and letting the world around her catch up.

The next thing she knew, a waitress was setting a beer in front of her. She so needed a cold beer right now. Destiny dragged her eyelids open and looked up.

"The cute cowboy said you might be wantin' a beer." She smacked her gum and rolled her eyes. "Lucky you, he's some kind of hot."

Destiny looked around, her heart sinking to her feet. "Where'd he go?"

"Said he had to be somewhere." The waitress danced off when someone called to her.

"Well, hell." He did it to her again. Left her feeling like a limp dishcloth.

But a very satisfied dishcloth.

Chance would be back. Destiny smiled right before she tilted the bottle and swallowed down a third of the beer. Her body felt like mush—but in a really good, relaxed way.

Next time, she wasn't about to let Chance get away. He had no idea what it would be like fucking a she-devil. His lust would drive him insane with desire. He'd burn for her before she was finished. Oh yeah, his soul was already hers for the taking.

Then why did she feel just a little niggle of alarm? A little voice whispering in her ear saying she wasn't even close to stealing Chance's soul. He played her all the way.

Who the hell was this guy?

She took another long drink, then came to her feet. Her purse was lying on the counter at the end of the bar. Amazing. What was this world coming to when no one bothered to steal someone's belongings? She slipped the strap over her shoulder and left the bar.

It was still hot outside. Figured. Hell was cooler than Texas. The sooner she left the better. Next time Chance showed up, Destiny would be prepared. She was positive there'd be a next time, too.

A smile tugged at her lips. Her passion might be spent, but Chance left her with a warm glow that made her feel more alive since way before she died. It was almost as if Chance had a few special powers of his own.

"Hey, lady, spare some change for a vet? I haven't eaten in over a week."

The voice was male, deep and gravely. She spotted him just inside the dark alley. Big and burly, the bum wore filthy army fatigues and hadn't shaven in weeks. She didn't even want to know what kind of bugs were making their home in his beard.

The slight breeze changed direction. Her nose wrinkled and her eyes burned. She took a step back.

Oh crap! Which was an apt enough description of the smell. What dumpster had he crawled out of? The guy had a distinct odor that drifted over to her like a black, rotting cloud.

"Please, lady. Spare a war veteran a few dollars for a hot meal?"

Oh, what the hell. She was feeling generous. She dug some money out of her purse and handed the bills toward him.

One of her foster dads was a vet. Charlie was an okay kind of guy. He drank a little too much, and couldn't hold down a job for more than a few months, but he never slapped her around like some of the others.

The guy reached out to take her money, but instead grabbed her arm and pulled her into the alley. "Thanks, lady." He grinned and raised a gun. "Now we'll have us a good time. You ain't never been fucked the way I'm gonna fuck you."

That's what she got for trying to do a good deed. It was the story of her life. Someone always wanted to screw her over.

She sighed. This wasn't going to be pretty.

Chapter 4

"YOU REALLY DON'T WANT to mess with me." Destiny didn't even try to struggle or break the mugger's hold.

"Yeah, and why's that?" He grinned as he shoved her against the side of the brick building, his forearm against her throat. His face was only inches from hers. If he didn't move, she was going to puke. His fetid breath became a putrid fog surrounding her.

She pushed against his arm enough so that she could talk. This guy was starting to piss her off. "Because I can get real ugly."

"Not a babe as hot as you." He sucked in air on a whistle as his slimy gaze slid down her body then returned to her face. "Sweetheart, I'm gonna make you scream."

"How about if I make you scream?"

He was momentarily startled, then he smiled, showing yellowed teeth. "I like that even better. I bet you make men scream all the time."

"You tell me." She drew in a deep breath and transformed into his worst nightmare.

He screamed, immediately loosening his hold. His feet moved backward at a speed not known to mortal man—well, until he ran into the side of the other building. His body began to shake as bad as an unlevel washer on the spin cycle, then he took off running in the opposite direction with a disjointed gait.

"I guess I was right. I did make him scream." She straightened. "Veteran my ass," she muttered, changing back into her human form. She smoothed her hands down the sides of her dress and turned to leave.

Destiny stopped short. The same bum from the first day she arrived was staring at her. His slack jaw and wide-as-saucers eyes told her that he'd witnessed her transformation into a monster, followed by the panic-stricken vet bolting down the alleyway. His hands shook as he raised his bottle to his mouth and guzzled the liquid as if he could somehow block out the hallucinations that were plaguing him of late.

Rather than drown his problems in alcohol, the bum should try changing his ways. No one ever did. People never learned. Not that she'd been any different.

She shook her head and aimed toward her apartment. The night was still young, but she was in no mood to hunt for some poor bastard she could drag back to Hell with her.

Nope, she wanted Chance and she was more determined than ever to have him. It was a matter of pride now. And she would have him. She only needed a better plan. Leaving her seduction in fate's hands certainly didn't work. No, as soon as she returned to the apartment, she would map out a foolproof strategy.

She liked the sound of that—her apartment. She never really had a home. Well, not one all to herself, and this one was only temporary.

Her mood began to lift. She rather liked the place where she was staying. A nice couple *loaned* her their apartment for the week—after she did a little trickery. They won an all-expense paid trip to Hawaii—lucky them.

Destiny was apartment sitting. So far, rummaging through their stuff only produced a lot of unpaid bills. It was a good thing she came along or it looked as though it would have been years before they could afford to take a vacation.

She could have drained their brains and left them wandering under one of the bridges. Kind of like zombies. They would've been homeless of course, until she was ready to return to Hell. That is, if she put everything back the way it had been.

They seemed nice though, and she had to admit, she was feeling sentimental at the time. Not a good thing when she was so close to getting demon status. And when she did, her life would finally be everything she wanted it to be, at least, as close to perfect as it would ever get.

Before she went up to the apartment, she stopped in the convenience store across the street and grabbed some magazines, a bottle of wine, and a tub of ice cream—double chocolate brownie. Damn, she was born in the wrong time period! Brownie and chocolate ice cream, a win-win combination.

She looped the plastic bag over her arm, which was so much better than lugging a paper bag all the way back, and thumbed through one of the magazines as she strolled down the street. Hmm, it didn't look as though much had changed since the fifties. The kitchens just got bigger. She dropped it into the bag and pulled out another magazine and slowly fanned the pages.

Starving models draped their bodies in designer clothes and expensive jewelry. Nice stuff. The sequins were a little too sparkly for her taste, but she could see herself wearing some of the outfits.

"Hi, aren't you staying in Max and Jennifer's apartment?" The voice was soft and feminine.

Destiny glanced up from the magazine as she strolled down the sidewalk. The girl was cute, not as young as she sounded. Maybe twenty-six, the age Destiny was when she died.

"I'm sorry, what did you ask?"

The girl smiled, showing pretty, white teeth. "I asked if you were staying in Max and Jennifer's apartment. The Dunlops. I thought I saw you leaving earlier, but just missed saying hi."

Max and Jennifer? Dunlops? Of course, the young couple. "Yes, apartment sitting while they're in Hawaii."

The girl's expression turned dreamy. "I'd love to go to Hawaii. I'm happy for them. They've really had a hard time of it lately." She blushed. "I'm LeAnn West."

"Destiny." Starting conversations with mortals wasn't good. They always wanted more than she was prepared to give. It was the same thing when the recently dead came through the sorting station. They always wanted to get to know her better. Knowing people only made things worse. When she was alive, she'd start to like someone and the next thing she knew, they would start taking and taking.

Destiny mentally shook her head to clear it. The life she once had was over and done, and she was glad of it. No one would ever hurt her again, she wouldn't let them. She focused instead on what LeAnn was telling her.

"I'm going to be a singer." She wryly grinned. "If I can save enough money to go to Nashville, that is. I kind of made it this far, then had to get a job."

"Well, good luck." Destiny stepped inside the elevator.

The young woman laughed. "Going up?" She stepped into the elevator. "I usually take the stairs but I'm feeling lucky tonight." Her chuckle echoed inside the enclosed space after the doors scraped closed.

Great. Destiny punched the number three button and attempted to bury herself in the magazine. Hopefully, LeAnn would take the hint that they would never be friends.

"Oh, clothes. I love clothes!" The woman leaned over and looked as Destiny turned the page. She sighed. "Someday I'm going to wear an outfit just like that on stage."

So much for escaping LeAnn. But Destiny couldn't help glancing at the model wearing a pair of black jeans and a fitted black jacket. On the lapels were sparkly, black gems. The shirt beneath looked like any ordinary black knit. But the necklace caught her eye. The beads were a muted pink surrounded by clear pink crystals.

Dangling from the end was a prism in the shape of a pink heart that captured the light and sent out brilliant shades of pink and gold.

It sparkled. A lot.

"A suit like this could make someone feel like a star. Sweet bling-bling, too."

"Bling-bling?" The woman was talking in a foreign language.

"Yeah, the necklace. Bling-bling."

Bling-bling. Okay, Destiny would admit the necklace was nice. She'd never had bling-bling.

The elevator suddenly jerked.

They both grabbed the dubious metal railing. One thing Destiny totally agreed with LeAnn about was the state of the elevator. It banged and clanked its way to the third floor before coming to a jarring stop. If she wasn't already dead, Destiny would have been afraid for her life. LeAnn was either courageous or really stupid for even stepping into the death box.

As soon as the elevator door opened on Destiny's floor, she hurried off. "Good luck with the singing," she tossed over her shoulder.

Once Destiny was safely inside the apartment, she breathed a sigh of relief. LeAnn wasn't that bad, but Destiny never had a girl-friend and she didn't want one now. Man, she would be in trouble with the demons if she did!

She dropped her magazines on the coffee table and carried the bag into the kitchen. After taking the wine and ice cream out of the bag, she eyed her purchases.

Decisions, decisions, decisions.

She put the wine in the cabinet and grabbed a spoon out of the drawer. The wine would come later.

When she was comfortably ensconced on the sofa, she began flipping through another magazine. Her third choice looked a lot more interesting than the other two. Not that she was against all the recipes in the first one. She loved to eat. But she was not a cook, and never planned to be a cook. Sandwiches were good enough, or sweet talking some guy into buying her a meal worked just as well, although someone coming through the sorting station mentioned women's lib and fast food. She was all for equal pay and not having to cook. It was about time women wised up.

Not that women having power helped her situation. Chance took control of each encounter. She was doing something wrong. Women with opinions had probably changed things in the bedroom, too. Not having sex since before she died put Destiny at a disadvantage. She could be doing everything totally wrong. A dark thought hovered over her. Maybe Chance had only felt sorry for her. She certainly didn't want to become a pity fuck.

No! She would not let her thoughts move in that direction. No fucking way was she a pity fuck. She'd checked herself out in the mirror and she was pretty damn hot. The world hadn't changed *that* much! Any man would give up his soul to have sex with her.

Her forehead puckered.

Except Chance. So maybe she *was* doing something wrong, but she planned to change all that. Her next moves would be the right ones.

She flipped to the next page.

Destiny choked on the ice cream she'd scooped into her mouth as she stared at the page and tried to get her breath back. When she was capable of breathing without snorting ice cream through her nose, she set the carton on the coffee table and brought the magazine closer.

Sex toys?

Sex toys!

Damn, they actually advertised sex toys in a women's magazine. She was definitely born in the wrong time period. She quickly scanned through what they had listed. Vibrators, breast massagers, bondage kits and—oh, wow—a glow-in-the-dark dick. She could wake up in the middle of the night and there would be her dick, glowing like a beacon of light.

She stared off into space, picturing the fluorescent green dick glowing on her bedside table, gently vibrating like a pet waiting to be loved.

There was a sudden thud against her door. Destiny jumped, pulled out of her fantasy. What the hell was that?

She uncurled from the sofa and went to the door. When she looked through the peep hole, she had her answer. Not what, but who. Great, Little Bo Peep. Or as she'd called herself, LeAnn.

Destiny could pretend she wasn't home. Maybe LeAnn would go away. She held her breath.

The doorbell rang this time. Three short jabs.

This lady was quickly becoming a pain in the ass. She would find out what she wanted, then get rid of her.

"Did you need something?" Destiny asked after opening the door.

LeAnn raised a casserole dish that she held securely with two potholders. "I had Lasagna heating, but I hate eating alone. I thought we could share." She wiggled around Destiny and hurried toward the kitchen. "I've been here before so I know where Jennifer keeps everything." She glanced over her shoulder. "I kicked my foot against your door, but I guess you didn't hear me until I rang the bell."

"What the fuck," Destiny muttered. But as she followed, her nose caught the aroma of the food and she realized she was hungry for more than ice cream. But she wouldn't be making a habit of having the girl over.

"Sorry to shove my way inside, but the potholders were getting a little too warm." She smiled her perky little smile. "You haven't eaten, have you?"

"No."

"Great." She peeled back the foil. On top of the lasagna were slices of garlic bread. She went to the cabinet and grabbed two plates, then scooted right down to one of the drawers and got utensils. When she had everything arranged, she looked at Destiny. "I guess we'll have to drink water."

"I bought a bottle of wine." She pointed toward the cabinet. Not that she really wanted to share. She'd planned on getting drunk later—all by herself.

"Perfect!" LeAnn proceeded to get the bottle and unscrew the cap. The woman was moving in.

"Oh, did I see an ice cream carton in the living room? We better put that in the freezer before it melts." Zip, she was out of the room. She was like a freaking bee that overdosed on speed.

"Sit down," LeAnn said as she came back into the kitchen.

Destiny still wasn't sure, but she took a seat. LeAnn joined her. The next thing Destiny knew, there was food on her plate. She took a tentative bite. It was good, she conceded, then looked across the table. "Not bad."

"Thanks." LeAnn beamed as if Destiny had told her she won a Country Music Award. "I'm just glad we met. It gets kind of lonely in the city."

Well, they weren't about to become best buds! Not in this lifetime. Her forehead wrinkled. Not that she was alive. Besides, LeAnn was too sweet. Not her type.

They ate for a few minutes in silence. The lasagna was pretty good. LeAnn was a regular little homemaker.

"Why Ft. Worth?" Destiny finally asked when the silence started to get to her, but as soon as the words left her mouth she wanted to call them back. She was breaking her cardinal rule not to make friends, but then they weren't actually friends. They were only sharing a meal. As soon as it was over, bye-bye.

"Ft. Worth was a town along the way to my dream." Her eyes suddenly grew wide. "That would make a good song. I'll have to remember that." LeAnn blushed. "I write a little, too."

LeAnn continued her inane chatter during the rest of the meal. Her conversation didn't mean a thing, of course. Just words to fill the void. Destiny nodded in all the appropriate places. But after the meal, LeAnn was apparently not through bonding. The bad thing was that Destiny was starting to like her. This wasn't good.

"Let's take our wine to the living room," LeAnn suggested.

Before Destiny could disagree, LeAnn was heading toward the other room. She plopped down on the sofa, then grabbed the magazine Destiny had been looking at.

Destiny was careful not to let LeAnn see her smile. Little Miss Puritan would be out the door in a flash when she saw the page of sex toys.

"Oh, that's sex gadgets," LeAnn said, her expression puzzled.

"I thought I would buy a few things." Destiny moved to the chair across from LeAnn. "Do you have any recommendations?" Destiny innocently quirked an eyebrow. Okay, that should do it. LeAnn would run from the apartment any second now.

"Well, actually, I've never ordered from a magazine, but I do know this great little shop not far from here. I mean, that's where I get mine. The store owner, Maggie Jean, she's great about helping her customers."

Destiny's mouth dropped open. She snapped it closed, then asked, "You use sex toys?"

LeAnn shrugged. "Well, yeah, I thought everyone did. Sometimes I don't have time to get dressed up and go out on a date, and I'm not seeing anyone steady now so that makes it even more difficult. I won't just take any guy to bed, but a girl has to get release somehow or she could blow an ovary."

LeAnn had to be joking. Any second she would burst out laughing and say of course she didn't use sex toys.

Except she didn't.

"You're going to tell me you've actually walked into a store that has sex toys, and you've bought them."

LeAnn nodded. "Maggie Jean is very discreet, and I don't think a guy would be caught dead in her store. It's very frou-frou. Kind of like a lingerie store with pretty stuff in the windows. Pfftt, I don't think guys even know what kind of store it is. The toys are at the very back."

Wow, Destiny really was born way too soon.

"If you want, we can drop by the store." She glanced at her watch, then grimaced. "She's probably closed." She brightened. "Sometimes Maggie Jean locks up but stays late to do inventory. Let me make a quick call. She won't mind at all if we drop by."

"Sure." Why not? Nothing would surprise Destiny about this woman now.

LeAnn's grin stretched across her face. Destiny tried to wrap her brain around the fact that LeAnn, who looked like the perky cheerleader next door, was actually a nymphomaniac with sex toys. Nope, she just couldn't see it. So maybe she would go to this so-called sex toy store and see if LeAnn was ribbing her or telling the truth.

Mixing with mortals was a big no-no, but she couldn't resist. Really, what harm could there be in going to a sex store? It might even help her cause. Not much information about changing times came to her at the sorting station. Didn't she have a duty to know about the ways of the world and all the changes that had taken place since she'd died? Not to mention it might give her the edge she needed to seduce Chance—and she so wanted to turn the game they played back to her favor.

Chapter 5

SOMETHING DIDN'T FEEL RIGHT to Chance. He had a great sixth sense that usually told him when something was out of kilter. His intuition warned him to watch his step.

No one saw him materialize. He was pretty sure about that. Still, he slowly scanned the area behind the bar. An overflowing dumpster braced a partially crumbling brick wall. Other than a few boxes that looked as though they were tossed out the back door, nothing seemed that unusual.

It was the safest place for him to land and not be detected. He learned long ago not to pop in just anywhere. Especially during the Spanish Inquisition and the witch trials. That had been a little uncomfortable, especially when that crazy puritan started yelling, "Burn the witch!"

There were no puritans behind the building. He'd stake his immortality on that. Even so, he had a bad premonition.

Chance sniffed the air. The only bad odor he detected were the fumes from empty alcohol bottles. There were definitely no demons around; they had a distinct odor, like garlic and rotting flesh.

His bad premonition could only be something he sensed, rather than something actually there. Destiny might have gotten pissed because he'd yet to make love to her. She might have decided not to show. She could already be seducing someone else's soul away from them.

He cringed at the thought. Chance didn't like thinking she

was out in the world trying to get her stupid quota. He'd promised himself he would save her from the path she seemed determined to travel. He'd do his damnedest to make her salvation happen.

There was only one way to find out what was going on. He started around the corner, heading toward the bar, but he only went a few feet when he came to an abrupt stop.

"Hello, Chance," a familiar, sultry voice said. Destiny stepped from the edge of the shadows.

Crap, that was his premonition. Destiny turned the tables on him. He caught her scent on the light breeze. She smelled sweet, musky. Like a woman ready for sex. Nope, she definitely wasn't a full-fledged demon because her delicious scent wrapped around him and was tugging him closer.

Ah, man, and what the hell was she wearing? The dress was light blue, the material illegally thin. So thin he knew she wasn't wearing a bra because he could see the dark outline of her tight nipples.

God help him!

Those were the same breasts he dreamed about taking in his mouth—teasing and sucking on each one.

He swallowed past the lump in his throat, his gaze moving slowly downward, drinking in every sexy inch. Not a difficult thing to do when the material of her dress hugged every single curve.

Did she know what she was doing to him?

He met her eyes. Oh yeah, she knew exactly what she was doing. She stepped farther away from the bar. The streetlight bathed her in a soft glow. Then she did the unthinkable. She parted her legs and the light shot between them, leaving nothing to his imagination. Especially the fact that she wasn't wearing panties.

His dick immediately grew hard, throbbing and aching. He forced his gaze away from the dark thatch of curls and dragged his eyes back to her face.

He knew that look. She had him by the balls. Chance was afraid it would take all of his charm to get her into the bar where he'd be safe from temptation.

"Little warm out here," he told her, walking closer and taking her elbow. Chance hoped like hell he could lead her inside.

"You're right, it's really hot." She moved so that she held his hand rather than him holding hers. "And the bar is stuffy."

So much for his charm. He had a feeling there was no way he would get her back inside. "I could use an ice-cold beer, though."

Destiny tugged on his hand. "My apartment is nearby. I have beer and wine."

She had an apartment? Of course she had an apartment. Destiny probably had enough magic to get almost anything she wanted. Could he hope for a roommate, though? Probably not. Her eyes told him she had it all planned out.

Sweat beaded on his forehead. He didn't think air conditioning would help—or an ice-cold beer. The tension began to build inside him. It was going to be a long, hard night.

"We could go dancing," he suggested, not quite ready to give up.

"Maybe later." She smiled up at him.

"Or a movie."

"I bought some DVDs."

He breathed a sigh of relief. If he could get her interested in a show, then he might be able to make it through the night.

Yeah right, as if he really thought that would work. Chance had a feeling he was in deep shit and it was going to get a whole lot deeper.

If the others could see him now, they'd be laughing their asses off. They thought his technique was way too complicated. Ryder told Chance that his arguments for staying celibate during the process of saving a soul or answering a prayer were ludicrous.

Ryder was just too scared to find out if he could last a whole week without getting laid. Hell, not a week went by that he wasn't trying to seduce some female—whether he planned on saving her soul or not!

No, the other three had their way of doing things and Chance had his. He liked to seduce women in a way that made them hungry to turn their lives around, then gently aim them down the right path. It always worked in the past, well, most of the time.

"We're here," she said.

They came to a stop in front of a dirty gray apartment building. His head jerked around. Damn, he'd been lost in thought. He'd missed the opportunity to talk about how good life could be in general while slowly introducing the idea that demons lie about everything, without letting on he was an immortal. Tricky, but he could have done it. If he'd paid attention!

They stepped inside the apartment complex and made their way to the elevator. Two silk ivy plants in need of dusting were strategically positioned near the front doors. If the owner of the building meant to welcome someone, then he'd missed the mark. The place was showing signs of wear and tear. Definitely not upscale like his apartment downtown.

Stained carpet led the unsuspecting on a winding trail to a questionable elevator with smudged metal doors. He grimaced as they entered the suffocatingly small space. When Destiny pressed the button for the third floor, the doors didn't quite close all the way. A sliver of dreary light attempted to make an escape through the opening, but gave up when the elevator began its ascent.

If he wasn't immortal, Chance would have taken the damn stairs.

But he was.

The rickety elevator trudged upwards like an overweight old woman carrying too many groceries up a steep hill. Chance breathed a sigh of relief when the ancient contraption groaned to a stop.

Maybe he would take Destiny to his penthouse apartment sometime. The nephilim each had an apartment in the same building, not that they were there very often. They preferred the ranch. There was nothing better than waking up in the country.

"This is where I'm staying," Destiny told him, opening the door.

He took a deep breath and stepped across the threshold. His gaze quickly swept the room. It was worse than he imagined. Candles burned low, not enough so that the room was too warm, just a few for ambience. The fragrance tickled his nose.

"It smells nice," he told her, and it did. He felt very relaxed. That wasn't a good thing when he needed to stay on guard.

"It's called ember."

Figured.

"I'll be right back."

She strolled out of the room. He couldn't take his eyes off the seductive sway of her hips, and when there was nothing else to watch, her essence lingered. If he was that susceptible to her charms, what was it going to be like when he had her naked? His dick jerked at the image *that* created.

Deep breath.

He breathed in, then out, then in—

You're hyperventilating, idiot! He slowed his breathing down and the lights stopped dancing in front of his eyes.

Better.

He could do this. He only needed to remember what was at stake. Chance wasn't about to let a damned demon torture Destiny for all eternity.

He scanned the room, taking stock of everything. Overstuffed pillows were plumped on the sofa, romantic music played in the background. Red silky material was draped over the two lamps, creating a cozy glow. She didn't leave out one detail in her attempt to seduce him. Oh yeah, she was good—for a beginner.

"I hope you like wine," she said as she sashayed back into the room.

She probably thought she could get him drunk, then have her way with him. After that, she would tell him how great it was to be a demon-in-training. A mortal would probably believe Destiny and happily follow her back to Hell like a little puppy.

Except he wasn't a mortal or a puppy. It was time to turn the tables.

"I love wine." Chance smiled as he took the glass she offered. He swirled the dark purple liquid around, then took a drink.

His lips puckered. He was afraid the insides of his mouth might permanently cave in. How could anyone get away with selling wine this bitter? And where the hell did she buy it? The market on the corner?

One thing Chance hated was cheap wine. He'd become a connoisseur over the centuries. The Romans could make great wine. Napa Valley was the next best thing. They even beat the Italians at their own game, but it was a close call. Competition was good sometimes. Kept people on their toes.

Chance guessed it had been a while since Destiny crossed over. Six dollars and ninety-eight cents had probably been a small fortune when she was alive, which was what he estimated she'd spent on the wine. Now, it just meant cheap wine. But he smiled. "A good year."

Destiny preened. No, he didn't think it would take much to convince her the demons had lied.

"I have movies, too." She hurried over to the DVD player.

Just for a second, Destiny was like any young woman, proud she had thought of everything. He wondered what she could possibly have bought. Probably something totally innocent, then she would be disappointed, but it would be for her own good.

"LeAnn showed me how to work the player," she admitted, not realizing she dated herself to some extent.

Then it hit him. "LeAnn?" Were there more demon wannabes in other apartments in the building? It was going to be difficult enough squaring off with Destiny. A threesome might be hard to resist, especially if LeAnn looked as sexy as Destiny.

"You have a friend here?" He glanced warily around.

Destiny looked up. "She wants to be a country and western singer. LeAnn is trying to make her way to Nashville."

Probably a mortal then. He wondered if Destiny knew how much trouble she could get in by even talking to someone when she wasn't trying to steal their soul. The demons didn't like mixing with the humans any more than angels did.

Destiny put the DVD in the slot, then stepped back. "Make yourself comfortable."

He took a seat on the sofa. She hurried over and sat beside him, then snuggled in nice and close. Her breasts mashed against his arm and his dick saluted them, which seemed to be its normal position since he laid eyes on Destiny. She pushed play on the remote, but had already started to make her move.

Please let it be *Bambi*, he thought to himself.

The title whipped up on the screen, *Bad Girls in Lust*. It wasn't *Bambi*.

He was in so much trouble.

His eyes were transfixed on the screen as three girls stood in front of a small pond. The scenery was cheap and made to look as if they were in the woods. The pond was obviously someone's backyard pool, complete with a fake-rock waterfall.

That wasn't what grabbed his attention. Nope, it was when one of the women began to do a slow striptease. The other two danced over and began to help her remove her clothes. Oh God, girl-on-girl action. He was definitely in trouble.

Destiny moved to her knees on the sofa cushions and leaned in nice and close before whispering in his ear, "Do you like the movie?" Her tongue darted inside his ear, swirling around.

His dick began to throb. He had to get hold of himself. His gut clenched at the image that brought to mind. Any release at all would feel damn good. "Yeah, I like the movie," he croaked.

"I thought you might." Her hand snaked downward.

Chance had to take charge of the situation or all would be lost. He grabbed her hand. "You've been very naughty, Destiny."

Her eyes grew wide, her nostrils flared.

"You went shopping, didn't you?"

She slowly nodded.

"You went to a sex store."

Again she nodded.

"What else did you buy?"

She visibly swallowed. "A vibrator, and some other... other things—toys."

He shook his head. "That was very naughty. I think I'm going to have to spank you."

Her forehead furrowed. "I don't—"

He patted his thighs. "Bend over."

She scooted back and crossed her arms in front of her. "No man has spanked me since I turned fifteen."

So much defiance. It would be fun taming her. "Then maybe it's time someone did." He reached out, slipping his hand beneath her dress, fondling between her legs. She gasped, closing her eyes. He fingered her labia, stroking up her flesh, then slowly moving his fingers down. Her pussy was already getting hot and moist and it was a hell of a turn-on.

It took extreme effort on his part to move his hand from beneath her dress. "Or I can leave."

Her eyes flew open, her expression shocked and disappointed. "You would leave? Right now?"

He shrugged. "It's up to you." She didn't move. He started to get up.

"Okay, okay."

He grinned. Her eyes narrowed. He patted his thighs.

Her lips pursed right before she lay across his knees.

For a moment, he couldn't move as her weight rested across his dick. He'd never wanted to fuck a woman as much as he wanted to fuck this one. But not yet. He had to save her soul first.

Chance inched her dress up until her ass cheeks were exposed. Fuck, she had sweet cheeks. He pushed her dress higher, exposing the curve of her back. Very sweet. She wiggled her ass. He gritted his teeth. Her movement against him was heaven and hell at the same time.

If he didn't do something fast, he was going to be in more trouble than he might be able to get out of. He brought his hand down lightly across her ass. The sound echoed in the silent room. She gasped. He knew he didn't hit her hard enough to cause any real pain, not the kind that hurt.

"You've been a bad girl, Destiny."

"Yes," she moaned.

He brought his hand down again. Her ass shot up. Pale cheeks taunted him. He tried to swallow but his mouth was too blasted dry. He needed to think about something, anything except what he wanted to do to her.

His gaze strayed to the television screen. The woman who'd stripped was on her back. One girl sucked on her breast while the other had her face buried between the girl's legs.

Oh hell.

He tried to swallow past the lump in his throat, but couldn't.

Chance wanted to do the same thing to Destiny. Suck on her pussy until she screamed his name. Maybe he would before the night was over.

He reached for his wineglass and took a long drink. The wine did nothing to cool him down, but the bitterness brought him back to reality. He started to set it back on the end table, but changed his mind at the last second.

He lightly slapped Destiny's ass again, then drizzled the wine over her bottom. She gasped when it ran between her cheeks. He knew the instant the liquid touched her pussy because her gasp turned into a moan. He emptied his glass, then leaned forward and began to lick it off.

"All better?" he asked.

"You didn't really hurt—"

He nudged her onto her back. Her dress twisted around her waist. Yes, this was exactly how he wanted her. "I think I might have hurt you right here." He ran his finger up her slit right before he lowered his head. He'd wanted to kiss her in that very spot the minute he first laid eyes on her.

She grabbed his head, crying out, "Oh damn, that feels so fucking good."

It tasted good, too. Just like he imagined she would taste. Ahh, but he needed so much more. He came to his feet, scooping her into his arms.

Chance carried her into the bedroom and laid her on the bed. In one swift motion, he had her dress off. He stood at the end of the bed, then grabbed her ankles and spread her legs wide. Nothing was left from his view.

"Where's the vibrator, Destiny?"

"The dresser," she croaked.

He could tell by the way her voice cracked that she was near the breaking point. He went to the dresser and opened the top drawer. Inside was every imaginable sex toy known to women. He grinned. They didn't let demons-in-training have sex, and Destiny was a very sensual woman. It wouldn't take much to show her that being good wouldn't be so very bad.

He brought out a vibrator shaped like a penis, and a bottle of cinnamon-flavored syrup. He was glad to see the vibrator wasn't nearly as big as he was.

Okay, Chance would admit that sometimes his human side crept up and reared its egotistical head. He grinned. He never had any complaints in the sex department, though.

Chance turned back around. Destiny's legs were closed. He moved back to the bed and stood at the end.

"This isn't how I left you."

Her body trembled.

"Open your legs so I can see all of you."

She drew in a sharp breath, but spread her legs wide.

"That's better." He moved between her legs. For a moment he just sat there on his knees, staring at her. Damn, she was so freakin' hot.

"Chance," she moaned, raising her hips.

And more than ready. He opened the bottle of cinnamon syrup and, holding it high above her, let it pour on her breasts, her nipples, her stomach, then her mound, drizzling between her legs.

"Cold," she said, reaching down.

He'd already anticipated what she would do and grabbed her hands. "I'll warm you up." He lowered his head and began to suck. She tasted musky, and like cinnamon.

She cried out. Her hips rose higher.

When he stopped, she began to whimper. "Please," she begged.

"Please what? I want to hear you say it."

"More. Don't stop."

He began to lightly spread the syrup over her breasts, tweaking her nipples. "Is this what you want?"

She shook her head, biting her bottom lip.

He leaned forward, taking one nipple in his mouth, scraping his tongue across the tight little nub before he released it. "Better?"

She shook her head.

"Tell me exactly what you want me to do."

A sigh escaped her lips. "Suck my pussy."

"My pleasure," he told her, but before he lowered his head, Chance lubricated the rubber penis, then turned it on low. He ran it down her slit before inserting it inside her vagina.

"Oh yes," she cried. "Right there. Yes! Don't stop!"

But she didn't have to worry, he wasn't about to stop his assault on her luscious body. He lowered his mouth again and began to suck and nibble the fleshy part of her sex. She squirmed beneath him. Her hips raised and lowered.

"Oh fuck, oh fuck," she began to mutter. Her head moved from side to side, her fingers curling in the bedspread.

He straightened, watching as the throes of passion swept over her. She was getting close to the edge. "Do you want more? Or should I stop and let you rest?"

"No! Don't stop!"

"Spread your legs so I can see more of you."

Her legs opened wider. This was pure torture for him. He couldn't take his eyes off her as he inserted the vibrating dick in and out of her hot body. He had to end this now or it wouldn't be a fake dick he plunged inside her. He nudged the vibrator on high speed, then lowered his mouth and began to suck again.

Her hips raised and lowered. She panted now, her breath coming in short gasps.

She suddenly stiffened, crying out. He moved his mouth, but replaced it with his hand, applying firm pressure. He wanted to watch her come. She didn't disappoint him. Her body trembled with the force of her orgasm.

A tear slipped from the corner of her eye. When her body stopped quivering, he removed the vibrator. She curled on her side, legs pressed together, whimpering.

Chance pulled the spread over her naked body. "Sleep, beautiful lady. Sleep." She drew in a deep breath and closed her eyes as he eased out of bed, stealing one of the pillowcases as he went.

Every part of him ached so bad he could barely hobble to the dresser. He slid the top drawer open and removed all the toys, slipping everything into the pillowcase.

As he walked into the other room, his eyes moved to the movie still playing. There were six people on the screen. Three men and three women and everyone was fucking.

His dick jerked.

Maybe he should change his technique and go ahead and fuck Destiny. He certainly needed some relief. Just as quickly as the thought entered his head, he pushed it away. Why fix something that wasn't broken? Although right now, his dick would argue the point. God, he had to get out of the apartment.

Instead of going back to the ranch, he went to his penthouse apartment. He didn't want to face the others. He closed his eyes and thought of where he wanted to be. Seconds passed. He felt a cool breeze on his face. When he opened his eyes, he was standing in his living room, facing a wall of windows.

Darkness had crept across the city. Lights from the nearby office buildings made it look almost like Christmas. Chance dropped the pillowcase on the carpeted floor and made his way into the kitchen.

He needed something to cool him down, and the beer in his refrigerator was ice-cold. He got one out and twisted off the cap, tossing it toward the sink. The cap skittered off the counter and pinged when it landed on the tiled floor. He didn't really care. He just wanted to clear his mind of the vision of Destiny, legs wide open, her pussy inviting him to do more than tease and taste.

He strolled back to the living room and opened the sliding glass door, stepping to the balcony. The sweltering heat of the day had cooled somewhat and there was a light breeze. He glanced up. A few stars were scattered across the night sky. He stared at them, as though he could see past. For a moment, he forgot about Destiny. Just the same, a new tension began to build inside him.

Their fathers were up there in the heavens somewhere. They'd never met them. Sometimes Chance wondered if they thought about their offspring. They were supposed to be angels, for God's sake. You would think they would care just a little.

Ah, fuck, why the hell did it even matter? How could he miss something he never had?

Destiny was different. He could have her, even if it was just for a little while.

He raised the bottle to his lips as she filled his mind with erotic images. The beer was cold going down, but it really wasn't helping his dick feel any better.

He missed her with an ache that ran from his head to his toes. The beer hadn't made him want to fuck her any less. It was time to resort to other measures to get rid of his killer hard-on. He made his way to the bathroom and turned on the shower. No hot water, only cold. He needed relief.

He quickly stripped out of his clothes, gasping when he stepped under the spray. For a moment, he let the water sluice over him. Ahh, better.

Until he closed his eyes. A vision formed of Destiny with her ass exposed to his view, him spanking her, then her naked on the bed, her legs spread wide, her tits pointing toward him. She tasted so great. Musky and ready to be fucked, and fucked hard.

He pushed the button on the soap dispenser and a glob of gel landed on his palm. Destiny created an ache in him that wouldn't go away. No other woman had ever affected him like she did. He slid his hand over his chest, then down farther, until his hand encircled his dick.

His thighs clenched and he sucked in a mouthful of air. He'd wanted to plunge inside her body, feel her heat wrap around him.

His hips shot forward as his hand began to move up and down. Slowly at first, then faster. He could barely take a deep breath. He leaned his other hand against the smooth tiles and pictured Destiny raising her hips to meet each thrust. Her legs opening for him. Sliding the vibrator inside her.

He could almost feel her hot, moist body closing around his

dick. Chance's vision clouded. He gasped, then threw his head back and yelled as release came.

Water poured over him as his breathing slowed.

If he didn't fuck her soon, he might just go blind.

Chapter 6

DESTINY COULDN'T BELIEVE IT happened again! How did he manage to seduce her every single time? Destiny planned every last detail of her seduction. She strummed her fingers on the table and glanced through her notes. The mood lighting, the alcohol, the sexy dress, the naughty DVD—Destiny did everything she'd read about in the magazine. The plan was foolproof. Then what went wrong?

Nothing!

It was stupid trying to figure out what went wrong. She shoved her notes to the floor. She'd executed her plan perfectly, then awakened in a sticky, syrupy cinnamon mess. First thing, she took a shower and stripped the bed. Served her right for giving up control of the situation when she should've been the one dictating what happened.

What did she forget?

When she shifted in the chair, spasms of pain erupted down low. Damn, she was so freakin' sore! She eased her body into a more comfortable position, which wasn't easy after last night.

Last night… She found it difficult to swallow as visions of the night before swarmed across her mind. The way Chance had looked at her, as though she was the most desirable woman in the universe. His burning gaze had caressed her body, his hands had…

A light bulb went off inside her brain.

Damn, she knew exactly what she forgot. She didn't take into account how susceptible she was to *Chance's* seduction. The man had his moves down pat.

Warm tingles spread over her as her eyes drifted closed and she once again lost herself in the memory of the previous night. Man, Chance had some fantastic moves, too. His touch… ah hell, the way he spanked her. His mouth covering her most intimate spot… the way he took her to the edge, and then…

She drew in a ragged breath and exhaled on a whoosh. The wild uncontrollable orgasm—

Her pussy clenched.

"Ow, ow, ow!"

She quickly pressed her hands against the tender spot in the hopes she could ease the pain. She cleared her mind of all the delicious thoughts going through her head. No more thinking about last night. It hurt too much. Besides, she absolutely refused to waste the time she had left on earth drowning in sexual fantasies when she could have the real thing. She grimaced. Except she might be too sore to fuck anything. But when her soreness eased, look out, because she was going to take Chance on the ride of his life!

He was good, even though he hadn't actually fucked her yet, but she was better. After all, she was almost a demon, and he was a mere mortal. Determination stole over her. She would win this game he played.

She jumped to her feet, but had to grab the edge of the table when the burning ache between her legs became almost unbearable.

"Ohttpw." Her bottom lip puckered. Okay, she'd stop thinking about sex—at least until she wasn't quite as sore!

Destiny hobbled toward the bedroom, mentally making notes of what she needed to do when Chance came around again. And he would. She had no doubt about that. She would be more than ready next time.

The shower she took earlier had gotten rid of the sticky syrup, but once she soaked in a tub filled with hot water, look out! She'd be able to tackle anything.

As she made her way through the bedroom, her eyes strayed to the dresser. The top drawer was open just a crack. After buying all the fun sex toys she could carry, she neatly arranged them in the dresser drawer. Vibrators to the far right, the nipple clamps in the middle, lotions and tasty syrups on the left.

She distinctly remembered telling Chance where her vibrator was located. She smiled. He definitely used it well. Her smile curved downward. He better not have left them in a mess. She cautiously moved to the dresser and peered inside.

Empty.

Great! Just fucking great!

Dammit, Chance took all her sex toys. Her lotions, her clamps, every last vibrator—she'd gotten a little carried away buying vibrators. The damn things cost a fortune, too!

Well, not that she actually had to fork over the cash. When she needed money, she made it magically appear inside her purse—which was pretty cool when she thought about it.

But hellfire, Chance stole her glow-in-the-dark, vibrating dick! Her shoulders slumped. She was really going to miss it. Except the thought of actually using the darn thing made her hurt even more.

Not having sex since 1959 really cramped her style.

Her frown deepened. And why hadn't he fucked her yet? Even if he got his jollies from watching her have an orgasm, wouldn't he want satisfaction, too? Hmm, something was going on and she intended to find out exactly what it was, even if it killed her.

Okay, technically, she was already dead, but she still wanted to know what was up. Well, she hoped he could get it up.

She drummed her fingers on the dresser. She had to come up with a new plan or she'd never steal Chance's soul. Just the thought of returning empty-handed left a sour taste in her mouth, not to mention a twinge of fear.

Demons were not creatures she wanted to mess with. They had

unfathomable power and could crush her in an instant. She didn't even want to imagine what they would do to her if she didn't bring back a soul. The thought of going before the demon tribunal made her knees knock. She had a feeling it would be far worse than just going to Hell.

The ringing doorbell made her jump, bringing her out of her dark thoughts. A demon? Shivers of dread rushed through her. How would she explain her failure?

She frowned, shaking her head. A demon wouldn't ring a doorbell. Sheesh, now she was getting paranoid.

Chance then? Her nipples tightened. Her thighs clenched.

"Ow," she whispered as she grabbed the edge of the dresser. She wasn't sure she was up to an all day sex orgy.

She really wanted to soak in a hot tub filled with bubbles. That would have to go on the back burner. At least until she got rid of whoever kept jabbing the doorbell.

Destiny made her way to the other room, still as naked as the day she was born. Clothes were such a bother. She reached out and pulled a white terrycloth robe out of thin air. After slipping her arms inside the sleeves, she belted it at the waist.

Whoever was on the other side of the door jabbed the bell a couple more times.

"I'm coming, I'm coming," she muttered, then groaned at the image *that* created. Hell, she hadn't been this sore the day after she rode a horse for the very first time.

She looked through the peephole then groaned again. LeAnn was quickly becoming as annoying as a fly on a hot summer day. Destiny opened the door.

"I brought breakfast. Do you have coffee on yet?" She pushed past Destiny and headed toward the kitchen, the scent of doughnuts trailing after her.

If Destiny's mouth wasn't already watering, she would have

thrown LeAnn out on her ass, but not only was the aroma tantalizing enough to tickle her taste buds, her stomach started to rumble like a coal train chugging up a steep mountain. That's when she realized she didn't eat last night.

"By the way, you look like hammered shit," LeAnn said over her shoulder.

Destiny opened her mouth, then snapped it closed. What the hell did she mean by that? Of all the nerve! She dragged her fingers through her tangled hair, glancing into a mirror hanging on the wall as she ambled past.

She came to a screeching halt and stared at her reflection.

A tuft of hair poked out on each side almost looking like a pair of horns. They so didn't do anything for her. She quickly raked her fingers through her tangles, taming her hair.

Were those dark circles under her eyes? She stepped closer to the mirror and intently studied her reflection. And bags! She was too young for bags! She mentally figured her age. No, she wasn't going there. Besides, she was twenty-six at the time of her death and she hadn't aged since.

But maybe she did look like hammered shit.

When she stepped inside the kitchen, LeAnn was rummaging through the cabinet but turned as Destiny walked into the room. "Rough night, sweetie? You really have to be careful using the sex toys. Kind of like a kid in a candy store. You can get too much of a good thing."

"I'm sore." Destiny eased down onto one of the chairs at the table.

LeAnn grabbed a hand towel out of one of the drawers, then went to the refrigerator and opened the freezer door. "I've got the perfect cure." She scooped some ice out of the bin, then folded it in the towel. "Here, try this." LeAnn shoved it toward Destiny.

Destiny raised one eyebrow as she took the homemade ice pack. "Put it between your legs. It will help with the swelling." Her laughter tinkled through the room. "We've all gotten a little carried away at one time or another." She turned back around and continued making the coffee, then got down cups when it began to drip into the glass carafe.

What the hell, Destiny would try anything. She placed the cold towel between her legs. At first it felt a little awkward and uncomfortable, but then the pain began to ease. The cold compress actually began to feel pretty good.

"Better?" LeAnn asked.

She shrugged. LeAnn just sat there, watching Destiny as if she expected her to ramble on about LeAnn's fantastic nursing skills. It was too damn early for Destiny to deal with her. "Yes, I do feel better." There, that should satisfy her.

LeAnn's smile spread across her face, making her look like Pollyanna. *Give me a break!*

Something just didn't fit, though. "How do you know so much? You look too—"

LeAnn rolled her eyes. "Please don't say innocent. Like Britney sings, 'I'm Not That Innocent.'" She belted out part of a song.

Catchy tune. LeAnn had a great voice, too. Strong for someone so petite. She could have a hit with that one, except apparently this Britney chick had beat her to it.

"You do look innocent," Destiny told her.

LeAnn went back to the coffeepot, but not before Destiny saw a flash of pain.

"I've been on my own since I was seventeen," LeAnn finally admitted as she poured the coffee and then carried it to the table. She went back for the sugar and powdered cream.

"That's kind of young to be facing the world," Destiny casually pointed out.

"And maybe not so young." LeAnn wouldn't meet Destiny's eyes as she pulled out a chair and took a seat.

"I bounced around from foster home to foster home myself," Destiny told her, feeling a kindred spirit in the other woman. "I know what it's like to hit the streets at an early age."

"I'm sorry," LeAnn told her, pity filling her eyes.

When would Destiny learn to keep her mouth shut? This was not a bonding moment, but before Destiny could think of something to say that would end the conversation, LeAnn began to speak again.

"I didn't have it quite so bad. I mean, with foster parents and all." LeAnn's expression softened. "I had the best parents and an older brother I adored." Her laughter was light, musical. "I used to tag after him wherever he went. Sometimes he acted mad, but I knew he wasn't. I think he enjoyed my hero worship." She sniffed.

Something squeezed Destiny's heart, and before she could stop herself she asked, "What happened?"

"Car wreck." LeAnn added cream to her coffee so that it turned almost white when she stirred. "A drunk turned in front of my dad. Everyone said I was lucky to survive when everyone else… didn't." She brought the cup to her lips, blew, then took a drink.

"But you didn't feel lucky," Destiny guessed.

LeAnn lowered the cup to the table and shook her head. "Not even a little bit. What twelve-year-old would? Not after everything I loved was destroyed."

"What happened after that?"

"They sent me to live with my aunt and uncle. I'd never even met them. My parents hadn't spoken to them in years. Then I was dumped on their doorstep. They resented my intrusion into their perfect lives. They didn't have kids and they didn't want kids. I had a dog, too, but they made me give her away. Just a mutt, but I really loved that dog." Her bottom lip trembled. "I called her Rebel. She was always doing stuff she shouldn't."

Destiny never had a pet. It was always better not to get close to anyone or anything. If only she'd kept her vow, her life might have turned out differently.

LeAnn opened the lid on the box of doughnuts. "I really need chocolate." Her hand shook just a little as she brought out a chocolate-iced doughnut and took a big bite, chewed, then swallowed. "On my seventeenth birthday I'd had enough and went my own way." She paused, then continued. "I thought I could do better."

"Have you?"

LeAnn smiled wryly. "Not at first. I was pretty gullible. I'm doing better now." She took another drink of coffee, then set her cup back on the table. "So what's your story with the foster parents?"

"Not much. My mother left me in a grocery store when I was six. I guess she thought she could do better on her own, too. I never saw her again. The courts placed me, but I acted up a lot, got knocked around a bit." Her words tumbled out before she could call them back.

She drew in a deep breath, forcing the bad memories to the far recesses of her mind, then smiled, hoping it didn't come off as feeble as it felt. "All water under the bridge. You can't live your life in the past."

LeAnn was quiet.

Destiny looked up, surprised she'd told so much about herself. LeAnn reached across the table and took her hand, squeezing lightly. A ripple of warmth washed over her.

"I'm sorry your childhood was so bad," LeAnn said. "Maybe it was fate that brought us together. We could be sisters. You know, pretend ones?"

Fate? That was laughable! If LeAnn knew what Destiny really was, she would run from the room screaming her head off.

What was she thinking to tell this mortal her life story? This sister relationship was definitely not going to work. She had a soul to steal, and getting chummy was not on her list of things to do.

"You're right about living in the past," LeAnn agreed, then abruptly changed the subject. "Is the ice working?"

"Is the ice—"

Destiny started laughing, she couldn't help herself. It was all so ironic. Even being dead, she was fucking everything up. She was bonding with a mortal woman and had yet to get laid by a mortal man. And now LeAnn wanted to know if the ice was working.

"Is it better?" LeAnn wore a puzzled expression. "The soreness," she clarified.

Did LeAnn think Destiny's brain was fried or something? Maybe.

But surprisingly, Destiny did feel better. "Yes, it worked. I feel great." She was sitting in a puddle of cold water, but she wasn't sore.

LeAnn looked at her watch. "Crap, I have to get to work. I waitress over at the Cow Patty." She downed her coffee, then jumped to her feet. "See you later!" She was gone almost as quickly as she'd appeared.

Destiny shook her head and stood. The soppy hand towel slid off the chair, making a plop when it landed on the floor. Water dripped down her legs. "Yuck."

She made her way to the bathroom and turned on the water in the tub. She missed taking baths. She thought they would have steam baths or something in Hell. Nope, nothing. She supposed any kind of luxury was reserved for those with demon status. What was the harm enjoying some of the finer things while she was on earth?

She untied the belt, then let the robe slide to the floor right before she stepped into the tub filled with warm water. She sighed as she sank down, the water lapping her naked skin. Nice. As soon as she was comfortable, with the water just kissing her shoulders, she closed her eyes and let all her worries float away. Baths were one of the few things she let herself indulge in when she was growing up.

Crystal, one of her foster mothers, used to get so freakin' pissed when Destiny would lock herself in the bathroom and soak in a tub filled with Crystal's scented bubbles. That was probably when she actually started taking long hot baths. A smile curved her lips. She enjoyed pissing Crystal off. It only made up for a fraction of the pain the bitch had heaped on her.

When the water started to cool, Destiny reluctantly climbed out and dried off, tossing the damp towel over the side of the tub to dry. She was going to miss all this, but she was certain it wouldn't be long until she reached demon status, then she would have everything she dreamed about.

She padded naked into the living room and opened one of the magazines, flipping through the pages until she came to a woman wearing a low-cut, deep red T-shirt and a pair of jeans. Destiny grew up in a backwater Texas town and hoped never to return. Dying hadn't exactly been her idea of an escape route. She turned the magazine page and sighed. She'd only missed one thing, her jeans. And boots. She really liked the looks of the red ones the model wore.

"Nice." Destiny might not have many powers, but she planned on using the ones she did have.

She laid the magazine on the coffee table and skimmed her hands over her sides. When she glanced down, she was wearing the sexy little number. She pulled her hair back with a red clip on each side, tagged a little black shoulder purse, and out the door she went.

The world waited for her beyond the apartment and she planned to see everything she could before she had to leave. This was her time to play.

"What are you doing?" a gravelly voice behind Destiny asked as she closed the door.

Startled, Destiny jumped. The demons changed their minds and they were going to drag her back to Hell. It was too soon. She still needed a soul!

Would she ever see Chance again? Have sex again? Was this the end?

Quick, she had to think of something! Whatever she had to do, she would do it, even if it meant resorting to begging and pleading. She wasn't ready to go!

She swallowed past the lump that had lodged in her throat and turned.

Eww, this was one ugly fucking demon.

Chapter 7

DESTINY WAS PRETTY SURE the demon was female, but it was hard to tell. It had salt-and-pepper hair, wore a baggy blue shift bunched and belted at the waist. The creature's skin was wrinkled and dry. The... thing... had a thin line of whiskers on its upper lip and one small mole on its chin that sprouted a long, black hair. The hair curled on the end and bounced around whenever the creature exhaled.

The demon raised a wooden cane with a brass handle and shook the stick threateningly toward Destiny. "I asked, who the hell are you? What are you doing coming out of the Dunlops' apartment?"

Destiny watched in fascination as the long hair coming out of the mole bounced around on the creature's chin.

"They're gone on a trip," it continued in a scratchy voice. "Although how they could afford to take the prize of a trip to Hawaii beats the hell out of me. They should've cashed in their winnings and used the money to pay off their blasted bills."

Okay, maybe not a demon—not one from Hell, anyway.

"Well, you just gonna stand there lookin' like a dead frog on a tree stump or are you gonna answer me?" The sexless creature bounced the rubber end of the cane on the floor a few times to show its impatience.

"Who are *you*?" Destiny asked. The creature had boobs. She was nosy, too. Clearly female. The old hag didn't know who she was talking to. If she didn't watch out, Destiny would vaporize her. Actually, she couldn't. It was the thought that counted, though.

"I'm Beulah, the next door neighbor. I heard you and that man in there last night. You was hollerin' like a banshee." Her eyes narrowed. "Having sex, I suspect."

What a rude old biddy. "Yes, we fucked most of the night." There, take that, you jealous old crone.

The old lady opened her mouth, then snapped it closed, pursing her fat lips. "Shame on you…" Her words drifted away as the door on the other side opened.

The woman's demeanor instantly changed when a thin, older man stepped from the next apartment. He was bow-legged and wore a gray handlebar mustache and a worn cowboy hat that looked almost as old as him.

Beulah didn't seem quite as aggressive as a moment ago. Destiny had a feeling the man intimidated her.

The old cowboy looked up and caught them staring. When his gaze landed on Destiny, he sucked in his slight paunch.

"Well, bust my chops," he said as he walked nearer. "I didn't know we had a new tenant." He yanked his hat off before smiling broadly and bowing in front of Destiny.

At least he had more manners than the hag.

"I'm Charles Dickens. Not the writer, of course. Although I have been known to spin a few yarns in my time, me and Mr. Dickens only share the same name." He was thoughtful for a moment. "But, I did work in a newspaper office back in my younger days. Not writing, mind you. Only sweeping, but I picked up a lot of what goes on." Confusion showed in his eyes as if Charles forgot the original thread of conversation.

More mortals! They were coming out of the woodwork! She didn't need anyone in life and she certainly didn't need anyone now.

Charles suddenly smiled, his eyes twinkling with humor. "It's hell getting old, but having a beautiful woman around makes living a little more bearable."

Destiny's defenses began to crumble. She gritted her teeth, willing herself not to fall for the old man's charm. It didn't work. The twinkle in his eye was too much. She returned his smile.

Then the dark cloud, aka the mortal demon, cast its ugly shadow over the land. "Old coot," the crone muttered.

Destiny started to tell her to butt out, but at the last minute she stopped. The woman wasn't worth the trouble.

"I caught her coming out of the Dunlops' apartment," the old biddy informed him.

"I happen to be apartment sitting," Destiny told them both.

"Of course you are," he said, then turned toward the old woman. "Now, Beulah, how could you accuse someone so lovely of breaking the law?" He raised his eyebrows and looked down at Beulah.

Beulah glared at Charles. If she hoped for an ally, it wasn't going to be him.

Why the hell was Destiny even hanging around? She didn't have the time or inclination to become involved with mortals. Besides, it was a huge no-no unless she planned on dragging them back to Hell.

Hmmm?

Nope, it wouldn't work. Beulah would scare the hell out of the demons, and the demons certainly wouldn't be happy if she stole old souls. Most of them had already used up their energy and were practically worthless.

These two were sucking her energy, not to mention her time. "If you'll excuse me," she hurriedly told them before rushing down the hall and escaping. She jumped on the elevator and jabbed the down button just as Charles rounded the corner.

"Oh, sorry, I can't find the open door button," she called out, pretending to look for the button to hold the door open.

"No problem, little lady," he yelled back.

Destiny snickered. She was so bad. The elevator shifted and she had to grab the rail to keep from losing her balance, but exhilaration swept over her when the elevator clanked to a stop and the door scraped open.

Free!

Her exhilaration vanished when she nearly ran into the mortal on the other side of the elevator doors.

The perky little redhead looked up and smiled as she stepped inside the deathtrap. "Oh, hi. Are you new? I'm Pam."

"Gotta run," Destiny called over her shoulder.

"Maybe we can meet up later," the girl called out.

"And maybe not," Destiny said under her breath.

As she stepped out of the building, she breathed a sigh of relief. Freedom!

Her forehead creased in thought. Now what?

Destiny wasn't sure what direction she wanted to go. The street was flat so there was no question about going uphill or downhill. The buildings looked as though they were all leased as apartments.

She wanted to do something daring, something fun! Nothing boring for her. No, she wanted to live. Even though technically she was dead. Surely, she could find some excitement somewhere.

South, maybe?

Before Destiny even took one step, a motorcycle rounded the corner and roared up to the curb where she stood. A motorcycle like none she'd ever seen. The bike was sleek black with chrome so shiny she could see her reflection, and it was sexy as hell. Chance straddled it like he was born there.

"Want to go for a ride?" he drawled. One side of his mouth curved up in a slow grin.

She definitely wanted to ride him, but when he patted the seat, Destiny knew they weren't thinking along the same line.

She eyed the motorcycle with more than a smidgeon of trepidation, but Chance's words had a way of caressing her body and causing tingles of excitement to run up and down her spine. He was definitely stirring something forbidden inside her. Chance made her want to rip off her clothes and let him take whatever he wanted.

He turned the throttle, gassing the motorcycle. The machine roared to life like a lion ready for its next meal. "Come with me," he urged.

Still, she hesitated. Motorcycles made her nervous. A few tough guys had tried to get her on the seat behind them, but she'd always refused.

"Don't be scared," he said.

Scared? She cocked an eyebrow. "Scared?" She shook her head. "I don't think so."

Still, she paused for a fraction of a second. Oh hell, what was the worst that could happen? She'd get killed? Pfftt, she was already dead.

She flicked her hair over her shoulder and stepped off the curb. "I'd love for you to take me for a ride." She smiled as she climbed on. Her words had never rung more true, and his groan told her he knew she wasn't talking about his motorcycle.

"Hang on nice and tight," he told her after he cleared his throat.

She quickly wrapped her arms around his middle as some of her earlier reservations returned. But when she inhaled she breathed in his scent: the earth, the wind, and all the heat his body promised. She felt each breath he took.

The city was soon behind them. She lost track of time as the morning drifted past. Chance traded the Interstate for a less traveled paved road. The wind blew through her hair. She tightened her grip around Chance's waist and rested her cheek against his back. This was as close to flying as she would ever get. She'd never felt so free! She could ride with him forever.

Would the demons come looking for their wayward trainee? Or was she insignificant enough they would forget she even existed? No, luck was never on her side. They would find her, no matter where she hid.

It felt as if a knife had suddenly been plunged inside her heart. What was she thinking? Being a demon was the life she wanted. She was almost dead when Vetis whispered his offer in her ear. The demon had made the pain stop. Vetis became her protector. He freed her.

Tears suddenly filled her eyes. Problem was, she never felt less free. They had her working at the sorting station. Telling the poor saps that came through they would love their new life—they only had to sign on the dotted line.

Yeah, right, as if she knew anything about what that life was like. Nope, she was just a salesperson, nothing more. A working stiff—in the true sense.

Some signed, some didn't. It wasn't always easy convincing people to give up their souls. There were newbies who thought the price was too high. But who wouldn't want immortality and a life they only dreamed about? It would be like winning a lottery. They were idiots if they didn't sign.

Or were they?

Maybe she misjudged everything, and maybe Hell wasn't the answer. She certainly wasn't living the life Vetis had promised.

She drew in a deep breath. The alternative was unacceptable. The pain was unbearable. For her, there was no other choice.

A chill swept over her. She still needed one more soul. Without it, she was doomed. Determination filled her. She would have it! Things would be different then. Chance was her ticket to freedom, to the life she always dreamed about.

Chance leaned to the right as he went around a sharp corner. Destiny closed her eyes and tightened her hold a little more.

If he didn't die first.

She frowned. No, she wouldn't let that happen. And she had plenty of time to convince Chance that Hell was the place to be, so as the wind whipped past, Destiny decided she would enjoy the moment.

It was too late to change her mind about being a demon, so why worry? She had a job to do. Being in hell wouldn't be nearly so bad with Chance at her side. Damn, they would have an eternity of fun—and lots of sex.

She frowned. They would both have sex, not just one of them.

A sudden thought made the blood run cold through her veins. Oh no, what if there was something physically wrong with him? He could be horribly deformed. What if he had a teeny-tiny penis?

But he was so tall! And he had big feet—or was that only a myth started by guys with really large feet and small dicks?

She swallowed past the lump in her throat. It might be even worse than she could imagine. What if he didn't have a penis at all?

Her heart pounded inside her chest.

No, fate couldn't be that cruel!

Chance gave great head, and she'd swear his fingers were magic, but she wanted him buried deep inside her, really deep. She wanted him to fill her up. Everything had been almost perfect. It couldn't turn sour now.

There was one way to find out. She inched her hands downward. Before she could get lower than the top button on his jeans, he made another sharp turn, then revved the engine. The bike shot forward.

Oh shit, they were going to die! Okay, maybe not her, but definitely him!

Destiny tightened her grip on his waist and closed her eyes tight as fear shot through her. She might already be dead but she could still feel pain, and she really didn't want to crash and feel a whole lot of hurt all at once.

When he slowed, she breathed a sigh of relief. But then he turned down a dirt road with so many deep potholes she was afraid he would drive into one and make a quicker trip to Hell than she planned. As it was, her teeth felt as though they were being jarred loose.

The potholes got bigger, and she no longer worried about driving to Hell on a motorcycle. Not the way Chance swerved around the obstacle course of potholes. She worried more about staying on the back of the bike as heavy dust swirled around her. She clung to his middle and tried not to cough up her lungs.

They didn't drive to Hell, and Chance finally pulled into an unpaved parking space beside a deep green pickup. She breathed a sigh of relief when he turned the key, killing the engine. Except there was still a loud humming inside her ears and a god-awful smell assaulting her senses.

He swung his leg over the bike. "We're here. Did you enjoy the ride?"

His words sounded as if they were coming from a long way off. Rather than answer, she climbed off, but her world tilted. She grabbed his shirt to keep from toppling over. He wrapped his arms around her in a warm embrace.

Destiny looked him straight in the eye.

He smiled down at her as if he just gave her a five carat diamond.

She punched him on the arm and stepped away. "You scared the hell out of me! My hearing is permanently damaged! And I've swallowed half of that blasted dirt road. What the fuck do you think?"

He looked startled for a brief moment, then his gaze slowly moved over her. She planted her hands on her hips and glared at him, but he didn't get in any hurry as he inspected her for possible damage.

"You don't look too bad to me. Not bad at all, in fact." His words were soft, husky, and filled with passion.

And Destiny thought it was hard to breathe going down the dusty road! He made her forget everything around her except him. She couldn't even remember the road being that bad.

"It wasn't horrible, I guess, but the dirt road was full of potholes and—"

Chance moved closer and leaned down, his lips brushing across hers, his tongue darting out, lightly caressing her bottom lip. He pulled her against him as he deepened the kiss. She closed her eyes and melted into him.

The blood running through her veins began to heat, but before they could explore each other further he stepped back, holding her arm so she didn't lose her balance.

"Am I forgiven?" he asked.

Her senses slowly returned. Damn it! How did he make her forget everything? She studied him but had no answer except that the guy could kiss. And he was sexy hot.

"Maybe I'll forgive you, I'm not sure yet," she said as she glanced around. "Where the hell are we?"

Before he could answer, a white double-cab pickup with dark tinted windows pulled on the other side of Chance's motorcycle. ANGEL RANCH was stenciled on the door along with a pair of angel wings. The driver killed the engine. When the door opened, the most beautiful woman Destiny ever laid eyes on stepped out.

The woman wore a white cowboy hat and a sky blue shirt tucked into form-fitting jeans, and she had enough curves to strike out a baseball team. She shut the door on the pickup, her long, blond hair catching the breeze. She casually flipped it back over her shoulder, then looked straight at Chance.

"Hey Chance, you riding today?" Her voice was soft and sweet.

"Maybe." He smiled.

Destiny looked at Chance, then at the woman. Destiny hated her. She hated that she had delicate features packed into a hot body. She hated that Chance knew her.

Then the bitch turned her attention toward Destiny. "Hi, I'm Nevaeh. Chance's… cousin."

All the tension building inside her evaporated. Cousin, huh? "I'm Destiny."

"Glad to meet you, Destiny. Keep this cowboy in line. He can be quite a handful." She winked as she went past them.

As soon as the other woman was out of hearing range, Destiny looked at Chance. "Cousin?"

"On our fathers' sides. Were you jealous?"

She raised her chin. "Not at all."

He laughed, then grabbed her hand and began tugging her in the direction Nevaeh walked.

"Where are we?" she asked.

"Rodeo," he said.

"Rodeo," she repeated as her gaze scanned the sea of pickups and trailers. Her nose wrinkled as an all-too-familiar scent of cattle and horses hit her. At least she knew where the smell came from. As long as she had lived in Texas, she'd managed to stay away from rodeos. The only things she liked to ride were cowboys. As for the rest of it, no thanks. Bulls scared the hell out of her.

"I thought you might enjoy it. Ever been to one?"

She shook her head. Once she rode a horse, and it wasn't so bad, but she'd never been to anything like this. Her life was filled with fun times, nothing as innocent as a rodeo. She was the party girl, the wild child. The bar owners didn't look too closely at her ID back then.

Oh yeah, no one partied harder than her. It didn't matter there was only one reason the guys looked at her like they did. It didn't matter at all. She used them as much as they used her. At least, that was what she always told herself.

But Chance made her feel different. As though she was someone special, someone different than who she'd been. Someone who was worth something.

But a rodeo? This was a first and she wasn't so sure about it.

"Come on," Chance urged.

What she would like was to have sex with him—real sex.

His face was devoid of expression as he held out his hand, but he didn't look as though he would change his mind.

Okay, fine. Since sex wasn't going to happen she might as well go with him. It shouldn't take that much time. They could have sex before the day was over.

If he had a dick.

Chance grabbed her hand and pulled her forward. "We won't stay very long, will we?" she asked. The warmth of his hand holding hers was already sending tingles of excitement over her.

"Not long."

He grinned and butterflies were released inside her belly. They fluttered around like crazy. What kind of spell did he cast over her that she wanted him so much? The man really had charm.

Destiny barely noticed the cowboys they passed. She was too busy eyeballing Chance. The man was built. He had some serious muscles going on. *What'd he do, wrestle bulls all day long?*

His clothes fit different, too. The low-riding black jeans hugged his ass, and every woman they passed turned and looked one more time. He'd rolled up the sleeves of a white button-up shirt and tucked the hem into his pants with a *this feels comfortable* confidence that few men achieved. The clothes could've been the first ones he grabbed out of the closet, but it didn't matter because he wore them with a devil-may-care confidence women couldn't resist, herself included.

She sighed.

No, Chance had to have a dick. Life was cruel. It wouldn't be fair if death was cheating her, too.

"What do you think?" he asked as they made their way up the metal stands and took a seat, one that she thought might be a little too close to the arena.

On the opposite side of them were pens holding snorting, pissed off bulls. Right under the announcer's booth were the chutes where bulls and bucking bronco would be released. A shiver ran down her spine. Why anyone would want to climb on top of a big, burly bull was beyond her. It took a special kind of lunatic to ride a bull.

The gates opened at the far end, and horses carrying riders from various ranches loped into the arena single file on each side. Some of the riders carried flags so the crowd knew who they represented. Nevaeh carried a blue flag that popped in the breeze. Destiny could almost reach out and touch the white fringe as she rode by.

The lead horses on both sides met at the other end, then passed as they circled back so there were two lines passing each other. When all the riders lined the edge of the arena, they stopped, leaving the center open.

The stands were filled with people all decked out in their best western shirts and jeans. Their boots were polished to a high sheen. They all came to their feet, hats off, including her and Chance, when two riders galloped their horses into the center of the arena. One rider held the Texas flag, the other the flag of the United States. The crowd whooped and hollered as the riders came to a stop in front of the stands. Then all went silent as a strong voice began to sing the National Anthem, followed by the state song, "Texas, Our Texas."

Destiny stood beside Chance, barely able to take a breath as her throat clogged. What the hell was she doing? She was never sentimental.

Chance squeezed her hand. She raised her chin. She got a little dirt in her eye, that was all. No wonder, with all the clods the horses stirred up.

The songs ended, the crowd cheered, and the horses, with their riders, galloped out of the arena.

"So?" Chance asked.

"It's okay." When he didn't say anything, she looked at him. The man was exasperating! "Yes, I'm having a good time."

He smiled. "I knew you would."

A few hours at a stupid rodeo wouldn't make that much difference. How many years had she been cooped up at the sorting station?

It was a beautiful day. Clouds shielded them from the overpowering heat of the August sun. There was even a light breeze. Had Chance asked the gods for cooler temperatures and, because he was favored, they had granted his wish? What was she thinking? Chance was a mortal, but he did seem like a lot more at times.

Destiny rubbed a hand across her eyes. She'd like nothing more than to forget she desperately needed his soul to make her quota. It would be just the two of them and a life she always dreamed about having. She wouldn't remember all the bad stuff.

Her heart skipped a beat.

No, she wouldn't let her past intrude.

Not today.

Chapter 8

DESTINY LAUGHED AS A clown danced in front of a bull. The bull was actually a costume with one person wearing the head and another the tail, except they kept coming apart in the middle. When the clown waved at the crowd and then dropped his handkerchief, the fake bull butted him. The clown came to his feet rubbing his backside before he dug his oversized shoe into the dirt as if he was about to charge the bull.

Destiny held Chance's arm and laughed. The bull and clown bowed before leaving the arena. She was still smiling when she met Chance's gaze. A current passed between them. Something she never felt before. She could almost believe they were destined to spend their lives together.

He jumped to his feet before she could dwell on *what ifs*, and pulled her along with him. "Where are we going?" she laughed.

"I'm hungry, and I want to buy you something."

They started down the steps as his words sank into her brain. Chance wanted to buy her something? She thought back and couldn't remember a time when someone spent money on her. Presents were a luxury, her mother had told her, and Destiny figured she was probably right.

"What?" Chance asked when he turned to look at her.

She smiled and shook her head. "Nothing."

"Then come on," he urged. He smiled, and she knew he could ask her for just about anything and she would probably give in.

There were vendors on the other side of the stands. Chance pulled her along until she thought her arm would be yanked out of its socket. He finally stopped in front of a covered booth that displayed every color hat imaginable.

"Here, try this one on," he said as he picked up a deep red hat. "It matches your boots."

Destiny hesitated. She really liked the hat, but she never wore a cowboy hat. When she saw the price tag of $122, she balked. How much could a cowboy make? The hat would be way too expensive.

"Don't worry about the cost," he said, as though he'd read her mind. "I can afford it. Besides, you're worth every penny."

"Okay," she said with a frown as she let him place the hat on her head. It felt odd. Maybe he only wanted to make fun of her. If he laughed, she'd cut his balls off.

She frowned.

If he had balls.

"I like it," he told her.

"You don't think I look silly?" She glanced in the mirror that had been propped on one shelf. The hat didn't look too out of place on her head. She glanced at Chance to make sure.

Fire shone in his eyes and she knew exactly what he was thinking. She was pretty sure it wasn't the hat perched on her head. Breathing took on a whole new meaning as sexy images filled her head.

"I think you look pretty tempting," he drawled as he stepped closer.

She leaned forward, ready for anything he wanted to give and imagining what she would do in return, but she was stopped short when a group of laughing children ran past.

Reality swiftly returned. Who did she think she was? This was all make-believe. "But the hat's not for me," Destiny said. Chance created a fantasy and, for a moment, she bought into it.

"Why not you?" Chance asked.

She shrugged. "Maybe I'm not the cowgirl type." She reached up to remove the hat.

"Today you can be anything you want. This is a day for magic." He skimmed his fingers down the side of her face.

His touch left a trail of heat in its wake, along with a hell of a lot of promise.

One touch and Chance made her forget what she needed to do. First, he brought her to a rodeo. Next, he wanted her to pretend to be someone she wasn't. He seemed to be asking a lot from her lately. But his words were so tempting. How she'd longed for days when she could imagine she was someone else. Days when nothing evil would intrude into her world.

After her mother left her in the store, Destiny had dreamed about being like other little girls. Girls with parents who loved them. She'd wanted it so badly. As if that would ever happen! Her foster parents cared about the check that came in every month, nothing else.

"You can do this," Chance told her and squeezed her arm.

Startled, she flinched, then realized where she was. There were no more foster homes, no more being envious of someone else. And maybe playing make-believe was coming a little too late, but Chance was right, she deserved this day to be perfect. She deserved it all. No one would ever take away her dreams again!

She squared her chin. "Okay, I'll do it. I'll wear the hat because I want to wear it."

"Good," he said, then smiled as he glanced at the saleslady who was beaming.

Of course she beamed. The woman knew she had a sale. Destiny didn't care. With a determined stride, she marched to the small partitioned changing room in one corner. A dark blue sheet on a string closed it off from the rest of the shop. A hundred and twenty-two dollars for a hat!

She turned once more and let her gaze fall on the mirror. For just a moment, she felt as young and carefree as the young woman staring back at her. *The girl next door.*

Where had the seductress gone? The demon-in-training? The girl who stared back at her looked innocent and pure. As if she finally got to play dress up. As if she'd had loving parents. As if nothing bad had ever happened to her.

But none of this is real, her mind screamed. She wasn't the girl next door. Was she ever innocent? She was a troublemaker in school because that was the only attention she ever got. She was the girl who would do anything on a dare. She didn't care about anyone but herself. Why should she? This person staring back at her wasn't who she was. Her hand trembled as she reached to remove the hat.

Chance grabbed her hand. "I like the way the hat looks on you. What would it hurt to just enjoy the day? One day. That's all I'm asking."

She looked away from the mirror, closing her eyes tight. "I don't think I can." She didn't know how to be the girl in the mirror.

"I'll help you. I'll be with you every step of the way. I'll never leave your side. Just one day, that's all I'm asking, Destiny."

She sighed, the fight leaving her when she opened her eyes. Her glance fell once more on her reflection. She'd wanted to be that girl so badly. Maybe Chance was right. No harm would come if she took one day to just have fun. She raised her chin, defying anyone to tell her differently.

"Thank you for the gift," she finally told him.

She stilled. Nothing happened. The world didn't come crashing down on her. No one stepped forward to say she couldn't do exactly as she wanted. She breathed a sigh of relief.

"You're welcome," he said. His gaze slid over her body.

The warmth from that one look made her body start to tingle. She could almost feel him entering her. Slowly moving in and out… caressing her with his dick…

She grew damp as her fantasy played out in her mind.

Her legs would wrap around his waist and pull him in deeper and…

"Are you hungry?" he asked.

"What?" She quickly cleared her mind.

"I need food," he told her, then laughed.

She was hungry too, but not for food. His stomach rumbled. She would let him satisfy his emptiness. Later he could satisfy hers.

After lunch, they watched as most of the children in the stands scampered to the arena. Whoever captured the ribbon from one of two calves turned loose would win a ten dollar bill. They cheered the winners and applauded the ones who didn't win but seemed just as happy anyway.

They drank beer from paper cups until her head was spinning. They watched the barrel racing, rooting for Nevaeh when she raced out of the gate, then stood and clapped when she was awarded a silver belt buckle for second place.

"I'll be right back," Chance told her as he stood and made his way down the metal stairs.

Destiny leaned against the step behind her and smiled. The day was perfect: exactly what it would have been like if she could have led a normal life.

If she'd had the opportunity.

But she hadn't had that choice, and she hadn't been one of the good girls.

Chance made her feel as if everything would have been different if she'd met him first. There was something special about him. She couldn't quite put her finger on what it was, but it was there, and she'd loved spending the day with him. She wasn't ready for it to end.

But did it have to? Every day could be this wonderful. She sighed when she thought how it could be for the rest of eternity. She only had to convince Chance they could have this much fun all the time if he agreed to give up his soul.

She would talk to him soon. He liked her. She was certain of that, and she didn't think it was just about the sex. Convincing him to leave with her wouldn't be that difficult.

Then why did she feel so sad? Why did she delay talking to him about Hell?

As her thoughts tumbled around inside her head, she barely paid attention to the announcer when he told the crowd the main event of the day was next—the bull riding competition. But when he called Chance's name as the first rider, the blood in Destiny's veins chilled.

"No, don't do it," she whispered as she sat forward. Her gaze searched until she spotted Chance. He was just climbing on the back of a bull. Three other cowboys leaned over the chute, helping him get settled on the stomping, snorting beast.

He was going to get himself killed! The bull would throw him to the ground and pummel his broken body!

The announcer began to speak again. "Chance Bellew is one of our top bull riders. He's taken home more first place awards than any cowboy here."

"I don't give a fuck," Destiny said, but the cheering crowd drowned out her words. Were they all crazy? Now she remembered why she never went to rodeos when she was alive!

"This has got to be fate," LeAnn said as she plopped down beside Destiny. "I went by the apartment to ask if you wanted to go to the rodeo, but you weren't at home." Her smile was as big as Texas. "And here you are."

Fate? She didn't think so. "I thought you had to work."

"Water leak. The owner of the Cow Patty closed for the day. I went by your apartment, but I'd missed you."

"Chance has made a special request," the announcer continued. "He's dedicating his ride to Destiny Carter. Just goes to show everyone this must be one special little lady."

"Oh great, he's making me the reason he's about to die."

LeAnn's eyes grew round. "That's you!"

"He's going to get himself killed," she moaned.

"Wow, you're really worried."

Destiny took her eyes off Chance long enough to meet LeAnn's gaze. "Wouldn't you be worried?" And why was she encouraging LeAnn? Oh hell, maybe she did need her right now. Destiny had never been to a freaking rodeo before today. The only thing she knew about bulls was the fact they were big and ugly.

"You're absolutely correct, I probably would be worried too, but if that announcer is right and he's a champion bull rider, I'm sure he'll be okay. I mean, he didn't get a rep for being a top rider not knowing what he's doing."

"She's right, you know." Charles Dickens sat on the other side of Destiny. He planted the heel of his boot on the next seat down. "I love rodeos. Never had them in New York." His normally pale cheeks turned ruddy. "That's where I'm from, but I got to Texas as fast as I could. I figure livin' here since I was ten is almost as good as being born here."

Oh hell, she was surrounded by mortals. They weren't helping her, either. Their words didn't ease her worries at all. "He's about to ride a bull that doesn't look happy about the whole thing. I can't believe he'll be fine." Why was she even having this conversation?

"I'll stay right here with you," LeAnn vowed.

"Me too," Charles told her, then reached over and patted her hand.

The gate slammed open and the bull came charging out. Destiny didn't have time to think about the consequences of mingling with mortals when she wasn't planning to steal their souls. No, her attention was fixed on the arena, the furious bull, and Chance as he gripped a rope in one hand. His other arm was high in the air. Destiny wanted to yell at him to hold on with both hands, but she doubted he would hear.

"Ohmigod, where did you meet this guy? He's some kind of hot!"

"LeAnn!" She was supposed to be giving moral support, not drooling over Chance.

"Oh, sorry." She cleared her throat. "He only has to stay on eight seconds. Everything will be fine."

"Yee-haw!" Charles flung off his hat and waved it in the air. "That's a real cowboy for sure! Ride 'em, young fella!"

"Give me strength," Destiny muttered.

It would only last eight seconds. Not long. Then everything would be fine.

The raging bull twisted and turned, kicking up dirt and creating clouds of dust. Chance was sweating, his lips pressed together as he anticipated each move the bull made. The crowd cheered. Any second now she was going to puke. Everything didn't look fine. Not one bit!

And eight seconds was a hell of a long time!

The buzzer sounded.

She breathed a sigh of relief.

The bull continued to twist and spin.

"The buzzer sounded," Destiny said. "Why isn't it over?"

Charles looked at her and shrugged. "The darn bulls never pay attention." He guffawed at his own humor.

"That's not funny."

"Sorry." He had the grace to look duly chastised.

Chance suddenly jumped off the bull and landed on the ground. It was over. Finally! Except the bull turned, with evil in his eyes. The enraged beast dug his hoof into the loose dirt, stirring up more dust. Then, like thunder crashing across the sky, the bull's hooves pounded the dirt as he charged Chance.

Without missing a beat, Chance ran toward her and the fence. He took the fence in front of her in one leap. The bull ground to a stop as Chance levered himself onto the metal walkway.

He was laughing when he took the metal steps two at a time, then grabbed her up in his arms.

His mouth found hers and she forgot all about the fact she would've aged ten years if she was alive. She lost herself in his kiss, oblivious to the crowd's applause. Why did being with him feel so right?

"Were you worried?" he asked when he ended the kiss.

"You know damn well I was worried." She frowned at him.

When he grinned, she couldn't help but forgive him. How could she not when he made her world feel brighter?

Someone cleared his throat, and Destiny remembered LeAnn and Charles. Chance definitely had the power to make her forget about everything except him.

"These are my—my neighbors, LeAnn and Charles." Hell, how did she introduce them? They weren't really friends or anything. She just couldn't get rid of them.

"Hi, LeAnn, Charles." Chance drawled, his arm still around Destiny.

LeAnn didn't say anything, only stared.

Charles stood a little taller. "Mighty fine ridin' there, young man." His expression turned sad. "I always wanted to be a cowboy, but by the time I decided what I wanted to do with my life, it was too late. Now I just go to rodeos and cheer the cowboys on."

Chance stuck his hand out. Charles looked at it for a moment, then grasped it. "And we're glad there are people in the stands to cheer for us." Chance told him as Charles enthusiastically pumped his hand. "Helps us stay on the bull a little longer."

"You can count on me."

Destiny glanced toward LeAnn who was still slackjawed. She nudged LeAnn.

"Oh yes, it's nice to meet you, too." LeAnn's face turned a bright red. "Uh, we'll leave you two alone. Charles, I'm really thirsty. How about if I buy us an ice-cold lemonade?"

"A gentleman never lets a pretty woman pay. Got my social security check on Monday, so I'll be doing the buyin'." He crooked his arm and winked at Destiny. LeAnn slipped her arm through Charles's and they left.

Destiny only shook her head as LeAnn and Charles left. Her attention was drawn elsewhere when Chance squeezed her waist.

"I think I like that you were worried," Chance said.

She returned his smile. How could any day be more perfect? Just as suddenly as the thought crossed her mind, dark clouds blocked the warmth of the sun's rays. A shiver of foreboding ran down her spine. She looked at the sky. An omen? Maybe so.

Would Chance still look at her as though she was someone special if he knew the truth? Would he still care that she worried about him?

Would Chance still want to be with her if he knew she murdered her lover?

Chapter 9

CHANCE WATCHED DESTINY FROM the corner of his eye. She was happy for a little while. He knew she made a concentrated effort to forget who she was and why the demons had sent her back.

He clamped his lips together. But then she'd apparently remembered. Once more, she brought up her protective shield. He wasn't ready for that to happen.

He grabbed her hand and pulled her along with him. There was something else he wanted to buy her.

"Where are we going?" she asked.

"You'll see." He hurried down the stairs. Most of the booths were closing as the rodeo came to an end, but he knew there was one that would still be open.

Nevaeh's booth looked pretty much like all the rest. Same weather-worn, wooden front, as if it had been around for a hundred years or more, and in fact it had. Her booth only appeared when someone needed something special. Like now.

Nevaeh's smile was a little wistful and a little sad when they stopped in front of her booth. Not that many years had passed since she lost the battle, and the soul of a man she cared deeply for. Her lover chose the wrong path. She was unable to save him.

"What is this booth?" Destiny asked as she nervously glanced around. She hugged her waist as if she was afraid she might brush against something and, thereby, be tainted.

"They're angels," he told her. The whole booth was filled with them.

Angel ornaments, angels to place above the bed so the person would have sweet dreams. Old angels, baby angels, flirty angels; necklaces, bracelets, and rings; angels with soft, furry wings, and angels praying.

"Why are we here?" Destiny nervously looked around. "It smells funny."

"Don't you like angels?" he asked.

"Umm… I'm not a fan."

"The aroma is a mixture of different flowers," Nevaeh explained. "Honeysuckle, roses, and many others that complement each other." She studied Destiny, then said, "Angels can give peace when your heart is troubled." Her words were as soft as a whisper on a breeze.

"I'm not troubled."

Nevaeh continued as if Destiny hadn't spoken. "I'm sorry life has been so difficult for you."

"My life is not difficult." Destiny turned to Chance. "Can we go?"

"I just need to buy something, then I promise we'll leave. Nevaeh makes all her own stuff. It's very special." He dragged her forward to a shelf where jewelry was displayed and chose an angel necklace. It was perfect. "We'll take this one."

Nevaeh smiled. "A good choice."

He paid for his purchase, then moved behind Destiny, undoing the clasp on the necklace as he did. He slipped the chain around her neck and fastened it before she could offer a protest.

"The charm has special properties," Nevaeh told her. "Whenever you're in need of anything, just hold tight to the angel and he'll be there for you."

Destiny fingered the charm with a grimace. "I don't really believe in that kind of stuff."

Chance tucked the angel between her breasts. "No one has to know except me and you." He felt her tremble just before he moved his hand away.

She hesitated before finally nodding.

"Take care, Nevaeh."

They left the store, strolling through the streets. The day was drawing to a close. People were moving to their vehicles. Some started loading their horses in trailers.

Destiny brought the necklace out and fingered the charm. Chance felt a tingle along his spine.

"Nevaeh seems very nice," Destiny casually commented. "But sad."

"Not long ago she lost someone she was very close to."

"I'm sorry. I know how that feels."

She suddenly looked afraid she'd opened up too much and clamped her lips together.

"Nevaeh may seem quite fragile, but she's the most resilient person I know."

"She's quite beautiful. Almost looks like an angel herself."

He dropped an arm across her shoulder. "I think you're even more beautiful."

She turned her face up to him. "Now you're lying."

Her words faded. His focus locked on her mouth. He couldn't resist and dropped what was supposed to be a quick kiss on her lips but damn, she was so delectable. He turned slightly until she was wrapped in his arms and deepened the kiss. His tongue explored her mouth, stroking her tongue, tasting her. She was sexy and hot all at once. How could any man not give up his soul for her?

His senses returned as quickly as if someone had hit him with a bolt of electricity. He ended the kiss, but pulled her close as they started walking again. He wasn't just any man. He was immortal, and he wouldn't lose his soul to her or to any demon.

"I've enjoyed spending the day with you," he told her. That was the truth. He had, and he felt as if he'd gained precious ground.

"All good things must come to an end," she said on a sigh.

"Not if you don't want them to." He didn't look at her, but held his breath.

"I've enjoyed today, but it's almost over. We all have to face our own realities."

Maybe this was the opening he'd needed. "What would you do if you could change your world? Make it something better?"

When she didn't answer, he glanced down. She raised her gaze to his and Chance saw a wealth of sadness. Life must have dealt her some pretty hard blows for there to be so much dejection in that one look.

"My world will never be more than it is right now."

"But if it could be?" he pressed.

"I think I like my life the way it is. I wouldn't ask for anything more. You're in it, what more could I want?" She suddenly gave a shaky laugh and looked around desperately.

She was so beautiful. For a moment, she'd faltered. He could tell by the look in her eyes that she was having second thoughts about becoming a demon. For Chance, time was running out. He had to keep chipping at her armor; only if he broke through could he set her soul free.

Free?

The ground beneath his feet rocked at the thought that even though he could save her soul, he would never be able to see her again. That was one of the rules that couldn't be broken. Even if he saved them, he had to let them go. No matter what the cost.

But she was his for the moment, and he planned to make the most of it. He hurried to catch up, grabbing her by the waist and lifting her into the air. Her screams quickly turned to laughter. And when they were on his motorcycle, their hats secured in the saddle-bags, her arms wrapped tightly around him, he knew he wanted to make this day last forever.

He gripped the handlebars a little tighter. The temptation to make love to her was getting more difficult. God, he had to step away, get control once again. He was too vulnerable.

It didn't help that the drive seemed excruciatingly long. Her hands were soft and warm as they wrapped around his waist. He imagined how they would feel on other areas of his body. Ah hell, what would it hurt to make love to Destiny? Damn it, Chance knew he would be lost if he did.

He expelled a deep breath when he finally pulled to a stop in front of the apartment building where she was staying. He kept the motor purring as she climbed off.

"Come up for a while." Her words were husky with need.

He pulled her close, then slipped a hand behind her neck. Their lips met in a searing kiss. She tasted hot and full of promise, and he never wanted anyone more than he wanted her right now. It took a supreme effort on his part to let her go.

"There's someplace I need to be, but I'll be back." He got her hat out, then handed it to her.

She frowned, but nodded her head. "I'll hold you to that." She stepped up on the sidewalk. "Thanks for the hat, and the necklace." She placed the hat at an angle on her head. He realized temptation never looked so good.

She was going to be the death of him if he wasn't careful. He gunned the motor, then took off. When he was around the corner, he closed his eyes. When he opened them, he was driving down a dirt road. The air was brisk and clean. No smog or city noises there. And finally he breathed a sigh of relief because he knew he was safe from Destiny's charms.

If it wasn't for a killer hard-on, he'd feel pretty good that he hadn't fucked up.

But it was there, and it wasn't going away any time soon. His damn jeans were cutting into him. And he was sore as hell. What made him want to ride that crazy-assed bull in the first place? But then he already knew. He wanted to impress Destiny. It worked. Chance had a feeling she could make him do quite a few things if he wasn't careful.

What the hell was happening to him? Up until then, his life was pretty good. Not perfect, but not bad. He had Hunter, Dillon, and Ryder, who were more like brothers than friends. But there seemed to be something missing, and he didn't know why he felt so restless.

He slowed, pulling to a stop in front of the ranch. A bit of paradise on earth. At least, as close as any of them could ever hope to get. He killed the engine and glanced around as he climbed off the bike. Until this moment, he'd always been happy to return.

He raked a hand through his hair, grabbed his hat from the saddlebag, and settled it on his head. Instead of going inside, he strode to the barn. Every step he took, he remembered Destiny asking him to come up to her apartment. He forced the images to the back of his mind. She was tearing him up inside and he was discovering there wasn't a whole lot he could do about it. Chance saddled his mount. They raced across the range, over hills, but he couldn't outrun the pictures in his mind. When he stood naked in front of the small pond, he imagined himself sinking inside her hot body, his cock caressed by her heat.

He closed his eyes and dove in, but the water was warm. *Hell, the pool would have been better*, he thought when he surfaced. He still had a killer hard-on, and he still felt dissatisfied.

Why? No one could ask for more than what he had. Immortality was a gift to be treasured. He'd accumulated more wealth than he could spend. But he knew it wasn't enough anymore. Maybe he'd just lived too many centuries, but there *was* something missing in his life. A quiet voice inside his head told him that it wasn't something, but someone.

This assignment was proving more difficult than he'd anticipated. He never got emotionally involved. He never made love to his assignments, either. When they were gone from his life, it didn't bother him so much. Emotional detachment.

He climbed out of the pond, dripping water everywhere, and

jerked on his clothes. The ride back to the ranch was slower, his energy spent. The late afternoon sun beat down on him as he headed home, and as much as he'd like to believe he cleared his mind, his thoughts still returned to Destiny.

By the time he got to the barn, he was dry and still confused. He unsaddled his horse, gave her a brisk rubdown, an extra square of hay, then made his way to the house.

This assignment would be over soon, then he would take a long break. Hang out with the guys. Leave saving souls to them for a while. Sometimes it was difficult not answering calls for help, but he might not have a choice. Not if he wanted to keep his own sanity, his soul, intact.

The ranch seemed eerily quiet as Chance went inside. Nothing new since the house was so big. They were closer than most families, but they still liked their privacy. The size of the ranch gave them everything they needed.

They'd each added their own ideas to the plan. Chance liked the dark, hand-scraped wooden floors. They had the rich smell of wood. With Ryder, it was the attention to detail. Dillon chose the layout. Hunter wanted the fireplace. The hearth was large enough for two grown men to stand inside. He never went small scale. Everything had to be larger than life.

Chance ambled over, standing in front of the cold stone. Summer was too hot for a fire, but come winter, oak logs would crackle and burn, giving off a welcome warmth.

Fire could be enticing to someone as vulnerable as Destiny. All at once, the flames could be powerful and strong, but she didn't see the destruction they could create too. And she hadn't felt the burn. She hadn't felt the pain. The demons were careful not to let the new recruits see the dark side. They were gullible and wanted to believe the demons.

If he couldn't save Destiny, she would feel more pain than she ever thought possible. His gut clenched at the thought of what she would suffer. From past experience, changing someone's mind was not easy. If he moved too fast, he could lose her.

Chance didn't want to think about what would happen if she lost her soul. The thought alone tore him up inside. He drew in a long breath and glanced around, needing to be with someone other than himself.

Where were the others? Rec room? He closed his eyes. He didn't sense anyone there. They weren't on a mission. They never liked to save more than one soul at a time. They could be answering prayers. That was always a nice change from the more difficult assignments. There were so many people who needed so many things.

He moved away from the hearth and made his way up the wooden steps as his energy drained and fatigue set in. He'd rest for a while, gather his strength.

"You look like you're deep in thought," Ryder spoke. His voice broke the silence like a cannon exploding.

Chance stumbled on the next step and had to grab the railing to keep from falling. Ryder scared the holy hell out of him! For a moment, he thought a demon had found his way to the ranch. Not that he really thought one ever would. They were too careful for that.

"Make some kind of noise when you come into a room," Chance grumbled.

"I did, but you didn't hear me." Ryder's forehead wrinkled. "Where have you been?"

"I took Destiny to the rodeo."

Ryder stopped at the bottom of the staircase and leaned against the banister. "I once met a cute little cowgirl at the rodeo. A saucy little number, I think her name was Tammy Sue—"

Chance held up his hands, annoyed that Ryder never seemed to take anything too seriously. "Please, I'm not in the mood to hear about another one of your conquests."

Ryder looked offended. "I saved her soul."

"You fucked her."

Ryder grinned roguishly. "That too."

"I don't know how you do it."

"Do what?"

"Stay emotionally detached. Don't you feel any kind of connection?"

Ryder was thoughtful for a moment. "Not really. I'm doing them a service, and they're reciprocating. It all evens out." He shook his head. "Your problem is that you're afraid of making some kind of connection, so you don't have sex with them."

"I guess that makes you a callous bastard." Chance immediately regretted his words. They'd been friends a long time and Ryder wasn't the cause of all his frustration. "I'm sorry."

Ryder turned serious. "This girl is getting to you. You can walk away."

Chance raked his fingers through his hair. "No, I can't." He studied Ryder. "How do you turn the emotions off?"

Ryder shrugged. "I miss them. But then someone else comes along. The problem I have is that I envy them."

Ryder surprised Chance, and he wanted to know more. "Let's talk." He motioned toward the two sofas that were in front of the fireplace. Chance walked down the few steps. They took a seat, stretching their feet in front of them

"Why would you envy anyone?" Chance asked. "We have everything here." He looked around. Paintings by Charles Marion Russell hung on several of the walls. One of his bronze sculptures graced a side table. Each room had at least one hand-knotted Persian rug on the floor. The furniture had been painstakingly crafted from Agarwood. No detail had gone unnoticed.

"It's not enough," Ryder said.

Chance raised his eyebrows. "What else do you need?"

"I've been studying mortals over the years. Haven't you noticed how most of them live life to the fullest?" Ryder's face took on an excited glow as he delved deeper into the subject. "They all love the challenge life gives them."

"All of them?" Chance raised his eyebrows. Not some of the ones he'd helped. They'd been on the brink of suicide. Ready to end their pain and suffering. If he hadn't come along when he did, they would have been lost to the dark side forever.

Ryder pulled his legs in and leaned forward. "Okay, so maybe not all mortals love a challenge. But it's their resiliency that fascinates me. There are so many of them who face hardship time after time and they stay strong because they know they'll get past whatever is wrong. They fight for survival."

"And that's what you want? Hardship? The pain and agony that go along with it?"

"You're not grasping what I'm saying." Ryder frowned, shaking his head. "It's the struggle, the challenges in life that make them stronger. Their spirit is amazing."

"And sometimes it breaks them."

"Those are the ones who need us the most. The ones on the brink of giving up. They only need a little help to regain their faith in life."

"I still don't see your point. You save them, then you walk away. What more do you want?"

"I don't want to walk away." Ryder stared straight ahead as though he could see something Chance couldn't. "We're not given a choice though," he said quietly. "We were never asked what we wanted. So yeah, I guess we have to forget them and move on. There's no alternative, is there?"

Chance sighed. "No, I guess not." Ryder still looked troubled and Chance knew there was more that he wanted to say. "What alternative is there?"

Ryder was quiet for a moment. Chance wondered if he was going to continue, but he waited. That's what brothers did.

"I want to be mortal," Ryder finally told him.

Chance sucked in a breath, fear spreading over him. "You know that can never happen."

Ryder's lips thinned to a grim line. "But it can. You know as well as I do that there's a way to become mortal."

Chance jumped to his feet, striding closer to the cold fireplace. Ryder didn't mean it; he couldn't. He faced Ryder. His friend's serious expression worried him. Fear weaved through him at the thought of losing his friend.

"No, you can't. It's too risky, and for what? To feel what they feel? Don't be stupid!"

"But it can be done."

"You would risk losing your soul?"

Ryder leaned back against the cushions, wearily rubbing a hand over his forehead. "No, I wouldn't risk my soul. It's just that sometimes I want more."

Chance breathed a sigh of relief. "I understand wanting more. I feel it sometimes, too."

"The assignment. I'm sorry. I've talked about my wishes and not given a thought to what you're going through. Are you gaining ground with the demon?"

"She's not a demon. She thinks she wants to be one," he defended Destiny.

It was Ryder's turn to look worried. "You're not getting too close to this girl, are you?"

"No, I worry about them all," he lied. Chance knew he was letting Destiny get under his skin. This assignment would be difficult to walk away from, but he didn't want to think about that possibility. God, he only hoped it wouldn't come to that.

"We're here for you if you need us to intervene."

"I know." He smiled at Ryder. They couldn't be any closer if they'd been twins. "I think I'll go to bed. It's been a long day."

Ryder nodded.

Leaving Destiny that afternoon was difficult. Sometimes when he was around her, she made him feel things he never felt before. Would he be able to save her? Or would he be the one in danger of losing his soul?

He trudged up the stairs and down the hall to his room. As close as the four of them were, they all still had their own problems, their own secrets, and they each faced their own demons in one way or another.

He walked inside the bathroom, tossed his hat on the counter, and removed his clothes. It had been a good day. Destiny enjoyed herself, too. He was glad he gave her that.

After pulling on a pair of thin pajama bottoms and a T-shirt, he went back to the other room, but he was still restless. What the hell was happening to him? He strode to the window, gazing out at the night. The stars were bright, the moon high in the sky. He wished he could show Destiny the beauty of his world. Show her there was more to life than the one that had been shoved down her throat.

He knew about the foster homes, the beatings, and some of the other stuff she had suffered. The nephilim were able to catch glimpses of what their assignment's life was like.

They never got the full picture, just bits and pieces, but what Chance saw of Destiny's past wasn't pretty. The more he was around her, the closer he got to her, the more he was able to see, but still it was only fragments.

Destiny hadn't stood a chance having anything close to a normal life. Her mother fell in love with a man who didn't want kids. She'd had to make a choice. Her daughter or him. She chose the man.

He saw that much of Destiny's life, but he knew he had to see more if he was going to save her. It was dangerous, but he had to know.

Give me strength, he silently prayed, then began to speak the ancient words. A fog swirled around him, growing thicker as the air grew so heavy he could barely breathe. But he didn't stop. He had to know everything.

And then he no longer stood in his room. He looked around. He was inside a grocery store. People passed by him, not seeing him. He didn't expect them to since he wasn't really part of their world.

Then he saw a little girl dressed in a ragged, torn blue coat that looked as if it had been salvaged from a dumpster. A woman stood near her.

The woman glanced nervously around, then knelt beside the little girl. "I'm so sorry, sweetheart, but mommy has to go." She brushed away a tear that rolled down her face. "You see, he doesn't want a kid."

"Mommy?"

"No, no, now don't get upset. I'll be back. I just have to convince Ray how good you are." She gave the girl a lopsided smile. "I do love you, Destiny, and if your father hadn't walked out on us, we'd all be together." She clamped her lips together. "It's his fault. Not mine. Always remember that. Just… just wait here, okay?"

Destiny nodded, her eyes big and round.

The woman straightened, then looked furtively around the store before hurrying away.

Destiny's fear washed over Chance in waves, making his gut twist. The woman climbed inside a late-model car, throwing her arms around the dark-haired man sitting behind the steering wheel. She was laughing as it pulled away. Her mother had told her to wait, so she did.

Mommy was coming back, wasn't she?

Chance watched through Destiny's eyes as she scanned the store looking for just a glimpse of her mother's black coat. When the customers began to dwindle, she hid beneath a table of oranges.

The heat was turned down to save on electricity, the doors locked, and Destiny was alone.

Mommy?

No one answered in the darkness.

She had to pee so badly. She couldn't hold it any longer.

The cold seeped past her thin coat. Mommy would come back to get her because she loved her. She'd said so.

The next morning, the lights came back on. The heat was turned up. Still she shivered, unable to get warm.

Someone grabbed her arm and pulled her from her hiding spot. Thief, they called her. They said she stank. She tried to tell them her mommy was coming back. Someone laughed and said it was no wonder she dumped a kid that smelled as bad as her.

Mommy?

Chance gritted his teeth as he relived that day with Destiny. She was only a kid. Just six years old. Who the hell abandoned their own kid?

He gripped the edge of the window, taking deep breaths as he reined in the emotional trauma Destiny had gone through. Her pain almost overwhelmed him.

Maybe that's why they were given only bits and pieces of their assignments' lives. To receive it all at once would be more than the mortal side of him could bear. It was as though he felt her pain tenfold. If he wasn't careful, her emotions could destroy him.

Chance knew there were several foster homes, but he didn't see too far into that part of her life. One foster mother regularly beat Destiny. No one gave her a chance.

"Damn them! Damn them all," Chance swore. "She was just a kid."

What had happened after that? After she'd gotten older. There were too many missing pieces. He looked out the window, as if he could find his answers in the stars above.

Why did a demon think Destiny's soul would be easy prey?

And why did Destiny think there was no other path for her to take?

He stepped away from the window and walked to the double doors that led to his balcony. Once outside, the crisp, clean air cleared his senses. He had to watch the rest of her life. He had to see what else had happened.

"Give me strength, Father," he prayed and closed his eyes. He raised his arms toward the heavens above and let the images come to him as he once again spoke the ancient words that would take him back in time.

He watched her life as if it played on fast-forward. Each foster home was worse than the last. She had no friends. No one to hold and comfort her.

She changed from the scared little girl and survived any way she could. She became hard. She didn't care about anyone, not even herself.

Destiny's foster mother slapped her across the face. Chance jerked back as if he was struck. In truth, he would've taken the blow if he could have.

Destiny ran from the house. Through the dirty back streets. Scared, alone, but determined to find something different. Like a movie, Chance watched her life play out. Her pain became his pain.

Older kids took her in. Rejects. Throwaways who learned to survive any way they could. Destiny found her home, but it was the wrong kind. She only thought they cared for her, but how could they when they couldn't even care about themselves?

Years were swept away until a man swaggered into Chance's line of vision. Immediately Chance tensed, even though he knew it was just a vision of what had already happened.

But Destiny was hungry for the affection he tossed her way, like bones to a starving dog. Chance was pretty sure the guy knew it, too.

Drugs, sex, alcohol. She shoplifted for the creep. She did whatever he asked. It wasn't enough. He began to beat her. She cried. She begged.

The man laughed.

Destiny's boyfriend raised his arm one more time. Chance felt the guy's fist slam into her face, felt the blood spurt from her nose.

You bastard, you won't hit me again. Never again!

Chance felt the weight of the gun in his hand—in Destiny's. It was almost as if he pulled the trigger, smelled the acrid smoke, heard the thump when the bullet hit the creep in the center of his chest.

The gun landed on the floor with a loud clunk. Destiny realized what she did and desperately scanned the room for a way to escape. She had to get the hell out of there! She had to run. His friends would hunt her down.

She opened the door and stumbled from the room, slamming into a hard chest. They surrounded her.

"Stupid cunt!" they yelled.

A fist slammed into her face, blood spurted from her mouth.

Mommy? Where are you? Why didn't you come back?

Another fist pounded her face.

I waited, Mommy.

The darkness closed in around her.

Someone whispered in her ear, "I can make the pain go away forever. I can give you everything you've ever wanted."

"Yes, take away the pain," she whimpered.

Chance gasped as the vision was swiftly swept away. He went to his knees, trying desperately to fill his starving lungs with air. He'd taken Destiny's pain and made it his own, he'd felt the demon's breath on his face, burning him, and it sucked the life from him. He couldn't breathe, couldn't draw in enough oxygen.

He shouldn't have let her life play out that far. It had been too much. The nephilim were never supposed to hear the bargain made with the Devil.

Never.

Too much.

It was too much.

Suffocating darkness closed in around him.

Chapter 10

DESTINY STARTED TO STEP inside the elevator, but hesitated when she saw Beulah. Oh hell, the mortal demon. Beulah glared at her. Destiny glared back as she stepped inside. The old battle-axe wore a shapeless, dark blue dress and heavy combat boots. At least that's what they looked like to Destiny. They were so ugly she couldn't look at them very long without causing eye strain.

"I guess *he* bought you that necklace." Beulah sneered. "It doesn't quite fit with your image."

Destiny absently reached up and fingered the angel necklace as the elevator doors closed and the tired box began to ascend. It was a good thing Beulah was the one to see the little angel that dangled from the chain, rather than a demon spotting it. She shuddered to think what would happen if one of them saw her wearing the necklace. Just to be on the safe side, she tucked it back inside her shirt.

"As a matter of fact, Chance did buy me the necklace, and the hat."

"Services rendered?"

Destiny smiled sweetly. "And I'm very good at it." On the inside, her gut twisted. She'd met Beulah's kind before. She probably went to church faithfully every Sunday and on Wednesday nights. She would be holier-than-thou until she left the sanctity of God's house, then she would find fault with everyone except herself.

"You'd best be getting on your knees and prayin'."

"Oh, I get on my knees, but I'm not praying."

"I never!" she sputtered, drawing herself up to her full height of five feet four inches.

Destiny raised an eyebrow. "That's pretty obvious. I doubt any man would ever look twice at you."

Something flashed in Beulah's eyes. Pain? For a moment, Destiny regretted her words.

"You're going to Hell!" Beulah ranted.

The elevator ground to a stop. It was a good thing because Destiny couldn't stop laughing, and Beulah's face was turning redder by the second. What would Beulah say if Destiny told her she was already there?

But Destiny held her words as she stepped off the elevator. What purpose would it serve to tell Beulah the truth? Before Destiny reached her apartment, LeAnn came out of Charles's apartment. He was right behind her.

"You're back early," LeAnn said.

"Thought you and that young fella would still be together, the way you was hangin' on to each other," Charles said as he stepped into the hallway.

Beulah snorted, glaring at LeAnn.

"What did I do?" LeAnn asked with surprise as she encountered Beulah's anger.

"You used to be a good girl, LeAnn West. Now here you are, seen leaving a man's apartment who's old enough to be your grand-father! Shame on you!"

Charles frowned. "I ain't dead yet."

"And I was only getting some stew started cooking," LeAnn defended herself. "If he doesn't start eating, he's going to dry up and blow away in the first wind that comes along."

Beulah pursed her lips. "I just bet you were cooking up some-thing, but it wasn't stew!"

"She ain't lyin', Beulah." He let out a frustrated sigh. "She even told me how to make it thick by adding powdered brown gravy mix."

Beulah grimaced. "That isn't cooking."

"You think you can do better?"

"I know so." She squared her shoulders.

Charles opened his door a little wider and waved an arm. "Then have at it, woman. Lord knows I can't cook."

"I'm only helping you because if I don't, you're liable to be corrupted and since you're getting up in years, I won't have it on my conscience that you went the opposite way of heaven on account of me keeping you from acting a fool around young girls." Without a glance in their direction, she waltzed into his apartment. At the last minute, she turned. "But don't go getting any ideas that I'm easy." She turned on her heel and didn't look back again.

Charles winked. "She's a feisty old broad, but she sure can cook." He quickly followed Beulah, shutting his door.

"Leave the door open! I won't have anyone talking about me being loose!"

The door opened again, and Charles grinned at them. "She may be ornery as sin, but I sure do like a woman who takes charge."

"Charles, get in here!"

When he hurried away, LeAnn turned and looked at Destiny. "Gross."

"I'm confused." What would a nice guy like Charles see in an old hag like Beulah?"

LeAnn chuckled as she looped her arm inside Destiny's. "I'll tell you the whole story over a cup of coffee."

It wasn't a good idea, but the thought of going back to her empty apartment held no appeal whatsoever. She would only think about Chance and wonder why he left her. Was there something wrong with her? Why did he always leave?

Her decision made, she walked with LeAnn. The minute she

stepped inside LeAnn's apartment, she felt better. There was something warm and cozy about the over-stuffed furniture with doilies draped across the back. Destiny couldn't help herself; she stared. It was so LeAnn.

"I know what you're thinking," LeAnn said with a grimace. "Suzy Homemaker."

"Huh?"

"When I'm nervous, I crochet. I don't even care for the silly things, but I can't seem to stop. It's like an epidemic. My mother taught me how to crochet."

"I like them," Destiny told her.

LeAnn's eyebrows shot up. "Really?"

"Really." Destiny wondered why she lied. Doilies reminded her of something she had never had: a real home.

LeAnn smiled. "I'll get the coffee started. Make yourself comfortable." She left the room.

Destiny wandered around, picking up trinkets then setting them down. She stopped at a picture. *This must be LeAnn's family.* She picked up the picture. LeAnn resembled her mother, a pretty woman smiling at her husband. LeAnn, on the other hand, had such a look of adoration on her face as she stared at her brother. Why did bad things have to happen to good people? She set the picture down when she heard LeAnn returning and quickly sat on one end of the sofa.

"I hope you like hazelnut coffee."

"I don't know. I've never had it before."

"Boy, you're really missing out on a lot of stuff."

Once they were comfortable and they each had a cup of coffee, LeAnn began her tale. "From what I've heard, Beulah was married once."

Now Destiny was really shocked. "Who would have her?" She took a sip of her coffee and decided she liked the taste of hazelnut.

"Exactly. But from what I heard, Beulah was desperate to get married because she cared for her ailing parents and hadn't had time to date. After they passed, she didn't want anyone calling her an old maid. She said she was going to marry the first man who asked her, and so she did. Only problem was, he was two weeks out of prison. A real ass. She didn't know that. Her parents left her pretty well off. Had their own laundry and all. They had Beulah late in life and died when she was twenty-five."

"Twenty-five is not old."

"I agree, but apparently back then they were already putting her on the proverbial shelf for spinsters."

"So what happened?"

"He bilked her out of every last cent she had, then ran off with a younger, prettier woman. Beulah started letting herself go after that. I heard she swore no man would ever take advantage of her again."

Oh hell, that put a whole new spin on everything. Destiny absolutely did not want to feel sorry for the old hag, but for a moment she pictured another Beulah. A young woman desperate not to feel so alone.

"And she's in love with Charles." LeAnn set her cup on a coaster. "And he likes her, too, but I think Beulah's afraid to take a chance."

"If I was Charles, I think I would be the one more afraid."

LeAnn chuckled. "Yeah, that's what I kinda thought."

"The coffee was good." Destiny set her cup on a coaster and came to her feet. The room suddenly began to close in on her and she had to get away.

"Do you have to leave?" LeAnn stood. "I could fix us something to eat."

Destiny was tempted, but the feeling quickly passed. LeAnn was a mortal and she couldn't afford entanglements of any kind. "I have some things I need to do."

"Well, here, I don't want you to leave empty-handed." She hurried to a chest sitting on the floor in one corner of the room. She knelt down and opened the lid, bringing something out. When she hurried back, she placed a doily in Destiny's hand. "Here, I want you to have this."

"Oh, I couldn't." She opened the soft white star shaped design. It was exquisite.

"I insist." LeAnn smiled.

Destiny reached toward her, then pulled back at the last second. "Thanks," she spoke gruffly and hurried out of the apartment. No one had ever given her anything except trouble and today she'd already gotten three gifts. Her eyes misted as she hurried to her apartment.

Just as she got to the door, Charles's door opened and Beulah stepped out. Destiny tried to picture the other woman as someone who was desperate for love.

"What are you staring at?" she growled.

Okay, the picture just wasn't going to form. "Not a damn thing." She opened her door and stepped inside, closing it firmly behind her. "Old battle-axe," she grumbled.

Chapter 11

CHANCE VAGUELY HEARD VOICES, but they seemed to be coming from a long way off.

"Is he going to be okay?" Hunter asked, concern lacing his words. "He's been out for a long time."

"Of course he's going to be all right," Ryder told him, but he didn't sound so sure.

"What happened?" Dillon grated out.

"We all know what happened," Ryder said grimly.

"Yeah, we do." Dillon sighed. "He's too close to this assignment. She got to him. He had to know more, to see more."

"He shouldn't have watched her life play out. Fool! He knows how dangerous it can be. We're only supposed to see pieces of their lives. All of it at once can kill us," Hunter said.

Chance felt like crap as the world slowly began to emerge through the darkness of where he'd been. The droning voices didn't help.

As always, Dillon, Ryder, and Hunter came to the rescue. They must have sensed he was in trouble. Chance wondered if they would leave if he didn't open his eyes. No, he knew that wouldn't happen. They were too much like mother hens.

"I'm okay," he wearily told them as he opened his eyes. It took a few seconds for him to focus. When he could see clearly, he almost closed them again. He was in deep shit. All three looked at him as though they were about to permanently put him out of his misery.

He should've pretended to be out. At least then they were concerned for his well-being. Now they looked as though they wanted to kill him.

Ah hell, he knew he deserved whatever they gave him. He'd stayed too long in Destiny's past. He might as well bring it right out in the open before they did. "I know I should've stopped the vision before I did."

"Ya think!" Hunter said, losing his cool. He glared at Chance.

Hunter, in all his gruffness, was probably the caretaker in their ragtag group. He didn't like it when one of them was in trouble, either. The guy really needed to take a class on anger management.

"I didn't think Destiny's life would be as bad as it was," he admitted. "Yeah, I knew she had it rough, but I didn't realize just how rough." Even now he could feel the remnants of the beating those men had given her.

"Walk away," Dillon told him in all seriousness. "Just walk away. If it was that bad, you're probably not going to save her anyway."

Walk away? The idea had never crossed Chance's mind. He shook his head. "Can't do it. I've got to at least try to save her soul."

"Why?" Ryder asked. "What makes this one so special? You've dealt with past lives that were horrible and kept your emotions intact."

Rather than answer right away, Chance started to get up. When he wobbled just a little, Hunter grudgingly stuck out his hand. Chance gratefully grasped it. Hunter hauled Chance to his feet with little effort, then pushed him into the nearest chair. Chance landed with an *oomph*. The guy had some serious strength.

"Chance, why this one? Why her?" Ryder asked, reminding Chance that he didn't answer the question.

Chance shook his head. He didn't know. He wasn't sure. There was just something about her that wouldn't let him give up.

"Destiny was never given a choice in life," he finally began as he tried to explain. "Everything was shoved down her throat. Her mother left her to fend for herself, leaving her in a grocery store. It was as though she had a dark cloud over her from the very beginning."

Once more the pain threatened to engulf him as Destiny's fear came flooding back. He drew in a deep breath, then exhaled before continuing.

"Her mother threw her away like she was trash. A string of lousy foster homes followed." He shook his head. "Even when she ran away, she ended up in a worse place."

Chance's words trailed off and the images flashed before his eyes again. He forced the pain to stay buried. No, he was in control. It was more like looking at quick pictures of what her life had been.

Dillon touched his arm, bringing Chance back to the present. "Stay with us, buddy."

"Yeah, I'm still here." Chance forced the images to the far recesses of his mind. "Everyone should be given a choice in life. If we choose the wrong path, well, it's our fault and we have to find a way to undo what went wrong. Destiny never had a choice. I want to give her one."

"You want her to choose between becoming a demon or being reborn," Hunter said.

Chance nodded. "Yeah, I want her to have that choice."

Ryder walked to the window and looked out. "Demons can be pretty persuasive," he said without turning around.

"The bastards promise the wannabes whatever the demons think they want to hear," Hunter ground out. "But they don't tell them that until after they've been cast into the fires of Hell. Once they come out, the only thing they want is to reap death and destruction wherever they can."

"But trying to convince the wannabes that the demons are lying isn't always easy when they're promising them temptations beyond their imagination." Dillon frowned as he took a seat in the other chair, stretching his legs in front of him. "It won't be easy to sway

Destiny. The only thing you can offer her is reliving her life, without a guarantee that it will turn out any better."

"I know, but I'm going to try."

"Time is running out," Hunter reminded him.

"I know that, too," Chance said. "But I can't give up."

The room grew deathly quiet. The silence stretched.

"You can do it," Ryder said, breaking the quiet as he turned from the window. Everyone looked at him; he shrugged. His grin bordered on wicked. "We're nephilim. Our fathers were angels who mated with some of the most beautiful mortal women ever created by God. You still have a few days. Besides, we'll have your back from here on out. Seduce the hell out of her—pun intended."

The tension from a moment ago was broken as the others laughed.

Chance and Ryder shared a look between them. His friend knew he wouldn't give up. Ryder had his back from there on out. They all did.

"If you want me to share some of my seduction skills with you," Ryder began on a lighter note, only to be met with groans from the others. Ryder's forehead wrinkled. "What? My mentors were some of the greatest lovers ever born. Don Juan himself bragged about my skill. The ladies fall at my feet. They love me."

Dillon and Hunter started walking toward the door, moaning as they went.

"It's getting too deep in here," Hunter groused.

"Maybe we'd better put on some boots so we don't step in all the bullshit." Dillon snickered.

Ryder's frown deepened. "Yeah, yeah, but you guys just wish you had one tenth of my finesse with the ladies." He followed them to the door, but turned before leaving the room. "You coming? We can shoot some pool or something. Have a few beers, get your mind off—everything."

Chance shook his head. "I'm tired. I think I'll just go to bed." When Ryder still looked unsure, Chance added, "I'll be okay."

"We're here if you need us."

"I know."

Ryder closed the door behind him.

Chance closed his eyes, resting his head against the back of the chair. He hadn't told them everything. God help him. Destiny had killed someone. It would be difficult to redeem her soul.

If the truth were told, Chance wasn't sure he wouldn't have done the very same thing. The bastard would've killed her eventually, then moved on to his next victim. He needed killing.

So yeah, Destiny was worth saving.

Except Chance had a fight on his hands. The demon schemed to steal Destiny's soul from the moment her mother had walked out of the store. Why? What was it about Destiny that made the demon want her so much?

Chance shook his head. Not that the reason mattered. Right now she still belonged to the demon. Unless Chance could change her mind, and he only had a few days left.

It would help if he knew what demon had purchased her soul, but he'd only heard his voice. It sounded familiar, but he couldn't be sure which demon struck the bargain. If it was a lesser one, stealing her back wouldn't be so difficult. On the other hand, if the demon was a little more experienced, Chance might have a problem.

No, he wouldn't think negative thoughts. He would save her. He had to. His sanity depended on it. Chance didn't want to examine why this assignment was so important to him. Why Destiny was so important to him.

Ah, Destiny. Just the thought of her eased the stress that flowed through him. He knew he was in danger of losing more than he bargained for with her, but he couldn't stop himself. She was like a potent drug running through his veins and he knew he had to have more of her.

He glanced at the clock. Almost midnight. Time slipped away and darkness moved across the land. Destiny would probably be asleep. Maybe even dreaming about him.

He gripped the sides of the chair as he pictured her, the covers kicked off, completely naked. Yeah, she probably didn't wear anything to bed. His dick sprang to life and he groaned at the image that brought to mind.

He needed to stop thinking like that! She was driving him to the brink of madness. He pushed out of the chair and opened the double doors, then stepped out to the balcony. The blast of cold air that greeted him did nothing to cool his ardor. He didn't think taking a cold shower would help either.

What would it hurt to watch her while she slept? The temptation couldn't be nearly as bad as when she was awake. He only wanted to make sure she was all right. Destiny wouldn't even know he was there.

He glanced around as guilt flooded through him. The others wouldn't like him going to her so soon after visiting her past. He'd be careful, and he would only stay a few minutes. He only wanted to look at her. That wasn't the same thing, and he felt stronger with each passing minute.

He promised himself he would only stay a little while.

Chance closed his eyes. When he opened them, he was standing at the end of her bed. A few seconds passed before his eyes adjusted, and when they did he felt a keen sense of disappointment. She wasn't in bed…

The bathroom door suddenly opened and there she was, framed by the soft glow of light that was behind her.

And she was completely naked.

And he was in so much trouble.

Chapter 12

DESTINY SMILED. CHANCE RETURNED after all. And she was never as glad for her aversion to clothes as she was right now, at this very moment, as she stood completely, utterly naked in front of him.

Her gaze lowered.

The guy wore only a white T-shirt and a thin pair of white bottoms that didn't hide his killer hard-on. Styles had really changed since she was alive and had become a hell of a lot more casual. Chance almost looked as though he wore his pajamas.

And how did he get inside the apartment? She could've sworn she locked the door. Not that she cared. No, she was much more concerned with keeping him from leaving.

"I'm glad you came back," she said softly.

His gaze moved over her naked body, then locked on a spot below her waist. "I can't stay." His voice cracked and he cleared his throat to try again. "I mean, I have to be somewhere." His eyes didn't move.

She slid one hand over her hip before lightly brushing her nails through the curls at the juncture of her legs.

He groaned.

Destiny smiled. It was going to be her night. She wasn't sure why he returned. Had he thought she would be asleep? Vulnerable? Did he think he would give her pleasure without giving her what she desired most of all?

Boy, did he screw up, because that was not going to happen.

Oh, he would give her pleasure; she would not be denied having him inside her.

"You're in pain," she said as she slowly drifted toward him. "But I can make you feel so much better."

She stopped a hairsbreadth from him.

He swallowed hard.

Oh baby, it was going to get a whole lot harder for him. She leaned just a little closer, letting her breasts brush his T-shirt, then licked her tongue across his lips. She felt the shudder that rippled over him.

When he would have kissed her, she quickly moved back a step. If he thought she would be susceptible to his advances, he was right. But she wasn't about to let him have the upper hand. Not for even a second. She would gain nothing because he'd take control.

She had his number.

Instead, she grabbed the hem of his T-shirt and tugged it upward and over his head, which wasn't easy because he was taller, but she managed, then quickly stepped back again.

She bit back her groan. He was sexy and beautiful. The guy had some serious muscles and the broadest shoulders she ever saw on a man. She lightly ran her fingernails across his chest, across his nipples.

Chance grabbed her hand. "You don't know what you're doing," he rasped out.

"Oh, I know exactly what I'm doing. Tonight, you won't deny me."

"This could be dangerous." He stared into her eyes and for a second she felt a bit of apprehension, but it quickly faded.

"I hope it's real dangerous."

Not daring to even breathe, she pushed down his bottoms in one move. Her body tingled to life. His dick was long and thick. She licked her lips. Oh yeah, all the parts were there and they looked to be in good working order.

"Destiny, you can't."

Oh yes she could. And she would.

But as much as she wanted to feel him sliding inside her, she wanted to taste him even more. Before he could protest, she knelt in front of him. Her fingers wrapped around him. His dick jumped in her hand. She was taking control.

She ran her thumb over the soft tip, sliding through the drop of moisture there.

Chance groaned before reaching down to grasp under her arms, but all he accomplished was bringing his dick closer to her face, closer to her mouth.

She did what came naturally.

Destiny sucked him inside.

Chance gasped, his hold loosening.

She swirled her tongue around and over the tip of his penis, sucking just a little. He tasted good, and it felt so right to have him inside her mouth. She sucked him in a little deeper. His hands moved higher and began to massage the top of her head in the same motion as she was massaging his dick with her tongue.

"Oh, that feels so good," he moaned. "I've dreamed of you sucking my dick."

And yet he still held back from making love to her. Why?

It didn't matter. He was here now, and that was all that mattered. Soon he would bury himself inside her.

She grasped his butt, bringing him closer still and taking more of him. Sweet! She massaged his ass, using one finger to stroke his anus. He tightened, then relaxed when she went no further.

His hips began to rock and she knew he was close to having an orgasm. She wanted to drain him, except she wanted to feel him inside her even more.

Slowly, she moved her mouth but slid one hand around to continue the up and down motion with her hand, lightly squeezing. She glanced at his face. His eyes were closed, lost in the sensations she created.

Perfect.

She moved to her feet, wrapped one arm around his neck, one leg over his hip. She positioned herself just right, guiding him toward her. When she was nearly there, his eyes flew open in panic.

She moved quickly, sliding over him. His dick slipped inside the heat of her body. She gasped when he entered. It was better than she imagined. She moved her other leg over his hip, her other arm around his neck, locking him in place as he sank deeper inside her. He was thick and hard and it felt so right.

For a moment, she couldn't move. She could barely breathe as her body began to tingle. The room came into focus and she knew she had to have more.

"Fuck me, Chance. Fuck me hard," she whispered close to his ear.

———

Chance hesitated. This was wrong. He never connected with an assignment. Not like this! He never fucked them!

Destiny wiggled against him. He sank a little farther inside her hot, wet pussy. Lights exploded around him as heat ripped through his body. Her heat.

God help him, he couldn't stop. He wanted her too much.

He grabbed her ass, tucking her in even tighter, then pulled out. She closed her eyes, arching her back. Her breasts were right in front of him. He leaned forward, sucking one inside his mouth, rolling his tongue over the nipple before releasing it. She cried out.

"Yes! Oh damn, don't stop."

"I don't plan to. Not now," he ground out.

He plunged inside her again. She clenched her inner muscles, squeezing him. He almost lost it. He sucked her other nipple into his mouth, scraping his tongue across the tight nub, then gently tugging with his teeth.

"Yes! More, give me more," she cried.

Something banged hard against the wall. "What the hell was that?" He paused.

"Demon," she gasped.

For a moment he couldn't breathe. There was a demon nearby? That went in the bad column.

"Demon. Neighbor. Battle-axe," she panted. "Same thing. Please, go back to what you were doing," she begged.

Destiny was greedy. He liked that about her, and as long as she wasn't talking about a real demon, Chance was happy to oblige. He sucked on her nipple, then released it and licked up her chest all the way to her neck, nuzzling the tender skin. "No, I won't stop this time. I've wanted to fuck you since the first time I saw you. I don't plan to stop now," he reaffirmed and realized what they were doing was right.

Chance tugged on her earlobe with his teeth, then swirled his tongue inside before licking down her neck again, then covering her mouth with his. She tasted so sweet. Like nectar from the gods.

He ended the kiss and moved forward until he had her braced against the wall, then plunged deeper.

In and out. In and out. Taking her closer to the edge, then pulling back.

She clenched and unclenched her muscles. He drove deeper and harder than he'd ever been with any woman. Destiny took every inch. He watched for signs that he might be hurting her and was amazed by the look of pure ecstasy on her face. In fact, she braced her hands on his shoulders so that she could wiggle in closer with each thrust.

"I can't hold back," he finally gasped.

"Then don't. I want you to fill me with your seed."

Her words were all it took. He plunged in harder and faster. In and out. In and out. Their bodies were moist with sweat. He plunged in again and again until she moaned, her body stiffening.

Her sounds of passion pushed him over the edge and his release came fast and hard.

He might have cried out—he wasn't sure—as lights exploded around him. He only cared about how soft she felt. How she fit perfectly against him.

And how he never wanted to let her go.

He rested his head against the wall then turned slightly, burying his face in her silky, black hair, breathing in her scent.

Ah fuck, he was in deep shit. This wasn't supposed to happen. He never let himself get close to an assignment.

Then why the fuck did it feel so right?

He opened his eyes and leaned back so he could look at her. Destiny's eyes were closed, her expression satisfied. Like a woman who was just loved, and loved well. She was so freakin' beautiful. That's when it hit him.

Destiny was never just an assignment. She was a part of him. Had always been a part of him.

And he was in danger of losing his soul.

Chapter 13

CHANCE LEANED ONE HAND against the wall and securely held Destiny against him. Her legs were still wrapped tightly around his waist as if she was reluctant to break the connection between them. Not that he wanted her to. He liked the way her body was pressed against his.

The sex had been fantastic, too, but damn, Chance had really screwed up the assignment. He made it a rule not to get emotionally attached. He clamped his lips together. That ruke had taken a flying leap.

A sick feeling began to churn inside his gut. Each of the nephilim had experienced loss at one time. There were souls they just couldn't save no matter how hard they tried. It took a lot out of them. It took a lot out of him. That was the reason he didn't have sex when he was on assignment. No emotional involvement on his part. At least to some extent.

But what if he couldn't save Destiny now that he made the connection with her? Yeah, he felt the bond forming between them. Chance knew that he might not be able to survive losing her. Hell, even thinking about the possibility of not saving her was eating him up on the inside.

"Why so quiet?" Destiny asked.

Startled, Chance moved slightly and looked into her eyes. "It's nothing." He pulled her closer, inhaling her scent, trying to commit everything about her to his memory.

"You're scaring me," she said. "Something is wrong. I can tell."

Was he that easy to read? Now he was starting to let down his guard. He would have to be more careful in the future. He looked at her again and attempted a smile. "Nothing is wrong."

Her eyes narrowed. "Are you sure you're not married?" She unwrapped her legs from around his waist, sliding her feet to the carpeted floor, and stood in front of him.

It was as if they were still connected. He should've known this would happen. He never let anyone get under his skin like he was letting Destiny.

Don't get close to anyone. That was his motto. If he didn't let an assignment get too close, he could never be hurt. Hell, he even held back from Dillon, Hunter, and Ryder.

"Chance?"

"No, I'm definitely not married." Maybe he should've said yes and ended the assignment. He'd never felt so freaking vulnerable.

He couldn't accept the alternative, though. Throw her to the demons? Demons who showed no mercy to the new recruits? No, it wasn't an option. At least not as far as he was concerned. "It's complicated."

"Gay?" She leaned back against the wall.

"Gay?"

"You know, you like other men except now you've fucked a woman. What would that make you? Bisexual?"

"No, I'm not gay." How the hell did this conversation start? He needed to get her mind off it before she dug a little deeper and asked questions that might be more difficult to answer. "So tell me about your neighbor."

Her eyebrows drew together.

"The one banging on the wall earlier."

The confusion left her face. "You really want to talk about Beulah?"

"No, you're right." There was only one other way he knew how to make her think about something else. Chance moved in closer, rubbing his thumbs across her nipples. Her eyes immediately drifted closed as she arched her back, silently begging for more.

She was sensuous and vibrant. And now she was no longer wondering why he was troubled. He could already feel her body heat enveloping him.

Hell, he didn't know why he should be worried. No, the only thing he was thinking about was how hard his dick was getting.

"Ever had sex in the shower?" he asked as he moved in closer and nuzzled her neck. "Ever had someone wash your back? Or down here?" He slid his hand downward, moving through her curls. They were still damp from their sex, and it was a hell of a turn-on.

"I want you again," he told her.

She reached for him, but he brushed her hand away.

She groaned.

He chuckled before pulling her into the bathroom. The room wasn't even a fraction of the size of his spacious bathroom. The shower-tub was a combo. There were no jets of pulsating water hitting him from all sides or dual showerheads. But she had bath gel, and that was all he needed to arouse her senses.

He turned on the water and as soon as it was warm, he stepped inside the small cubicle, holding his hand out for her to join him.

"There's not much room," she said.

"It'll be a tight fit, but you'll enjoy it."

Her smile was wicked. "It was already a tight fit and yes, I enjoyed it immensely."

He liked a woman with a sense of humor. But his laughter died when she eased inside, brushing her naked body against him. He couldn't stop his groan.

"I'm sorry, did I hurt you?" she asked innocently. "Want me to kiss it and make it better?"

His dick jerked, bumping against her belly. He closed his eyes, drawing in a deep breath. She was going to be the death of him—no, he didn't want to go there, either. Instead he opened his eyes and grabbed the shower gel, flipped the top open, then squeezed it over her breasts.

Destiny sucked air. "That's cold!"

"Don't worry, baby, I'll warm you up." He slid his hands over her, creating a trail of tiny bubbles. He lathered her breasts, squeezing each nipple between his thumbs and forefingers. "Is that better?"

"Oh, yes, much better. Except maybe I'm a little cold farther down." She raised one foot to the bathtub ledge, then let her leg fall open.

He couldn't breathe. Chance could only stare at her legs open wide and leaving nothing to the imagination.

"It's cold—right here." She reached down, sliding her fingers over her mound, then parted her labia.

The soap had made a trail between her legs and apparently made her slick. Her own touch must have created a friction of desire because she jerked her hand away, then blushed.

Ah, he liked that she wasn't so tough, so emotionless that she couldn't get embarrassed. It was a hell of a turn-on. He took her hand and put it back between her legs. "Don't stop. I like watching you pleasure yourself."

"But—"

He moved his fingers on top of hers. She moaned, leaning back against the shower wall, and continued the movement. Her eyes drifted closed. Her hips gently rocked. He reached over his shoulder and grabbed the showerhead. The hose was long. Long enough for his purpose.

He sprayed from a distance at first. Like a light summer rain. She bit her bottom lip. Chance moved to his knees in front of her, seeing each stroke of her fingers.

"I love watching you masturbate. It's fucking sexy as hell."

"I can't stop," she said, moving her fingers faster.

"I don't want you to." He looked at her face. She opened her eyes and met his gaze. "After you come, I'll wash you. I'll soap you, then I'll spray you with warm water. When you stop throbbing, when you rest for a bit, I want to suck your pussy. I want to run my tongue right where your fingers are now. I'm going to make you come again and again all night long."

Her ragged breathing filled the room. "Oh damn. Oh damn."

"Come for me, baby." He shoved the showerhead back into the holder, then used both hands to massage her thighs. When she began to tremble, he moved his hands to the cheeks of her ass. He began to squeeze and release. Squeeze and release.

And the whole time, he kept watching her fingers massage her pussy. He wanted to lick her, suck on her—oh hell, he wanted to fuck her so bad.

He swallowed hard. "That's it, baby, feel the heat build inside you. Harder now. Picture me sucking your pussy."

"Yes, yes, now. Oh fuck!" Her body tightened, her thighs quivering.

Her fingers slowed until she moved her hands to her thighs, digging her fingernails into the tender flesh. "Oh God, that was good," she rasped, her breathing ragged.

Chance couldn't help himself. He was so freaking close to her pussy. He buried his face in her curls, breathing in her musky scent. One lick, that was all he wanted, then he would let her rest.

One lick, one suck.

He drew her into his mouth and French-kissed her. His tongue lightly massaged as his fingers squeezed her ass.

"Oh man, I didn't think I could be ready again so soon, but oh damn, Chance. Please don't stop," she cried.

That was all the encouragement he needed.

He tickled with his tongue, then stroked and licked. He dragged his tongue over the lips of her pussy at the same time he inserted one finger inside her. Her hips shot forward. He loved giving her so much pleasure.

He moved his finger deeper inside. She was hot, her inner muscles clenching against his finger. He'd give her a lot more than his finger, but not yet.

He slid his finger out, then slipped his finger to her bottom, slowly circling before reaching the area he knew would give her even more pleasure. Her body tensed. He covered her with his mouth again and began to lightly suck.

Slowly. He wasn't in any hurry.

She relaxed once more, gently rocking her hips.

Chance knew it would take a while to build the fires inside her again, but he was prepared to take her higher than she'd ever been before.

He inserted his finger just a fraction, then stopped, letting her get used to it. She stiffened again, but he was ready. He drew her inside his mouth, sucking and stroking her with his tongue.

She melted.

He began to move his finger in and out of her anus.

"Chance, I… don't… Oh damn, the heat…"

Using his other hand, he opened her legs a little wider, then inserted a finger inside her.

"Please, oh please, don't stop. Oh fuck, it feels so amazing."

The ultimate fuck. Feeling her body react to what he was giving her was almost as good for him, but son of a bitch, he couldn't hold back much longer.

"Yes!"

He stood, legs trembling. Never had he wanted anyone as badly as he wanted Destiny right now. He grabbed her waist and lifted, then lowered her down on his throbbing cock. When he slid inside her, heat immediately surrounded him. He gasped, plunging deeper.

"Oh yeah, this is good," he breathed as he pulled out, then sank deeper. He grabbed her ass and brought her in closer.

She wrapped her arms around his neck, moving with each thrust so that he sank deeper still.

Long, steady strokes. Not too fast. Nice and slow.

"Faster," she gasped. "Oh, Chance, I can't stand any more."

"Neither can I, baby," he gasped, sinking deeper, moving faster.

"Hell yes!" she cried.

Her heat caressed him. When she began to tremble, he plunged deep inside her one more time then, with a roar, he came. A flood of heat washed through him. His world shook before exploding around him. He held her tight against his body as he gasped for air.

As everything slowly came back into focus, he knew it didn't matter that he fucked Destiny. That he went against everything he swore he would never let himself do because he would save her from the demons—he had to. That wasn't an option now. No, making love with her didn't matter because deep down, he knew it was right.

And the future?

He didn't want to think about the future. Or about letting Destiny go so she could be reborn. He would release her when the time came. When she was safe from the demons. He would because he knew he wouldn't have a choice.

Unbearable pain ripped through him. He held her a little tighter and buried his face in her hair as the water cascaded over them and, for the first time, cursed his father for creating him.

Chapter 14

DESTINY SNUGGLED AGAINST CHANCE with a sigh. They'd finally washed and then crawled into bed exhausted. She was sore but satisfied.

"I wish I'd met you a long time ago. Maybe things would have turned out differently," she said, then realized she'd voiced her thoughts.

Chance was mindlessly drawing circles on her back with his fingers, but his fingers stilled.

Why the hell did she say anything? It was too soon to tell him about Hell. What if she scared him off? Or worse, he thought she was a nutcase? She didn't want to lose what they had, not when she'd just found it.

"What do you mean?" he asked.

It was as though all the air was sucked out of her body and the blood rushed to her head. She closed her eyes tight, wanting to forget about why she was really there.

"Destiny, you can tell me anything."

The room stopped spinning, and the pounding inside her head quieted. He said she could tell him anything. Was he serious? Maybe he was ready to hear her out. To know everything about her.

Fear ran though her, turning the blood in her veins to ice. Her past rose in front of her. All the degradation, all that was bad about her. What if she lost him forever?

She moved until she could see his face, read his expression, but the only light came from the one they'd left on in the bathroom. His face was cast in shadows. She couldn't tell if he really meant what he said. She scooted back down in the bed and snuggled close to him instead, resting her head against his bare chest and listening to the rhythmic beat of his heart.

"It happened a long time ago." She drew in a heavy breath then slowly let it out.

"Tell me about it," he said softly.

Of course he wanted to know. He was curious about her. She squeezed her eyes shut, trying to block the past, but it wound through her mind like a slithering snake.

Why fight it? Chance wouldn't have stayed with her anyway, and she didn't want to force him to go with her to Hell by lying to him. Destiny finally realized what she sensed all along. Chance was a good person, and good people didn't belong with someone like her. Why not end it now?

"I've done some terrible things. I'm not who you think I am." Pain tore at her, ripping and stabbing her heart.

"Like what?" he asked.

Of course he wanted details. Everyone wanted to know her sordid history. They were shocked by what she'd done or what had been done to her. People only wanted to hear the bad stuff, and then they walked out of her life forever.

"I've been with a lot of men," she blurted.

"I've been with a lot of women. I hope you don't want a list. I'd much rather spend my time making love to you." He brushed his lips across the top of her head.

Tingles of pleasure ran up and down her spine. She was amazed that he could arouse her with one touch. But he still wasn't seeing the whole picture.

"I've cheated and lied. I've done drugs. I've stolen stuff. Once I even jacked a car because my boyfriend thought it was cool that I knew how. We went on a joyride and totaled the damn thing. Almost killed us both. I didn't just walk on the wild side, I lived it. I breathed it. It was as much a part of me as the blood that runs through my veins. I've even—" Her words came to an abrupt halt.

She couldn't say it. She couldn't tell him about Jack or the stuff he forced her to do, the beatings she suffered through or the fact that she killed him. The words just wouldn't come out.

"It's okay, Destiny. Everything will be okay."

No, it wouldn't be okay. Nothing would ever be okay again, but at least Chance didn't run away.

"Just hold me," she whispered.

"I'll hold you forever."

If only that was so. She wanted nothing more than to lie in his arms forever. Life was unfair, but death without Chance would be unbearable.

She closed her eyes and envisioned a life with him. Just the two of them. He said he would hold her forever, but would he give up his soul for her? Would he if it meant they could spend an eternity together?

"Chance, I—"

"Shh." He brushed the hair away from her face, stroking her cheek. "Sleep. Don't worry about anything. I'll take care of you."

Her eyes drifted closed. For the first time, she felt as though she was where she belonged. Morning would be soon enough to worry about everything else. She yawned as her eyes drifted closed and dreams transported her to a better place. A place where she and Chance were together and nothing could come between them.

Destiny stretched as she came awake, then cuddled her pillow. She sensed she was alone in bed. Was Chance still in the apartment?

She pushed the pillow away. It wasn't nearly as nice as Chance to snuggle against. She pushed up in bed, then shoved her hair out of her face. A sliver of light crept in through the window where the plastic blind was broken. She scanned the small bedroom.

No Chance.

She listened.

Nothing.

Destiny sat up, swinging her legs to the side of the bed.

"Oh good Lord!" She was so blasted sore.

As soon as she said the words, she cringed. It wasn't a good thing to even say Lord when one was a demon trainee.

That thought depressed her enough that she forgot about her pain.

Drat, she was having the best dream before she woke, too. Her life was different. All sunny and sweet. She dreamed that she grew up with parents who loved her. It was almost as if she had a guardian angel watching over her. She smiled. Her angel looked a lot like Chance.

Her smile turned wicked. Not that she would ever consider him angel material after what they did last night. Goose bumps popped up all over her body.

Speaking of which, where was the guy? Surely he didn't leave her again.

Just as suddenly as the thought entered her head, cold dread filled her. Had he started to think about what she told him and realized she had way too much baggage? Had he lied to her and left? Just like all the others in her life?

Destiny stood, then hurried to the bathroom. He wasn't there, either. She rushed to the other room. Empty. Her frown deepened as she made a quick inspection of the rest of the apartment.

Tears filled her eyes. She swiped them away with the back of her hand as she made her way to the kitchen.

"It doesn't matter that you left me, Chance. This isn't my first rodeo, cowboy! And I didn't care that much about you anyway. Nope, I only wanted your soul. You were only a quota to me!"

Nothing mattered. She'd been on her own long enough not to let anything get to her.

Then why did she hurt so much?

Destiny sucked back a sob as she stumbled into the kitchen. It wasn't fucking fair! Dammit! She swiped her hand over her eyes, but the blasted tears wouldn't stop.

She refused to care about Chance. She refused—

She spotted a note on top of a familiar white box sitting on the counter.

Well, hell.

She sniffed as she marched over and snatched it up at the same time she grabbed a napkin and blew her nose.

Morning Sweetheart.

A smile curved her lips. Chance didn't desert her.

Did he think of her as his sweetheart?

Just as quickly, the butterflies in her tummy transformed into dead moths and her smile turned downward. She never was anyone's sweetheart, only their doormat. Too many times someone used her to wipe their muddy boots.

But she skimmed over the rest of his note. He had somewhere he needed to be.

"That's a surprise," she mumbled.

She continued to read. Chance said he would see her later today.

She set the note down and opened the lid on the box. Chocolate doughnuts.

Humph!

As if she would wait around all day for him because he brought her doughnuts. Destiny had news for him—she waited for no man!

But oh, what a man! Her anger immediately vanished as her body began to awaken. She pulled out a doughnut, licking her tongue across the chocolate glaze. Yum. She'd like to glaze Chance with chocolate and lick him.

Oh hell, she was in so much trouble. Her body slumped against the counter. What if she couldn't convince him to give up his soul? Hell wouldn't be the same without him.

No, no, no! She refused to get emotionally tangled up with another man. They always screwed up her life. But Chance was different. She couldn't imagine him hurting her or lying to her like all the others. No, he was different.

But it had to be his choice. He had to willingly return with her. She didn't want it any other way.

The chiming doorbell brought Destiny out of her thoughts, which was good because she didn't want to dwell on the future. Maybe Chance was on the other side of the door. She shook her head. Probably not, though.

As she strolled through to the other room, she ran her hands down her body and immediately went from naked to clothed. She liked the feel of her tight-fitting jeans and the red halter top. She missed her jeans.

She opened the door. Destiny was right, not Chance. LeAnn was on the other side beaming. "I've got a gig," she squealed.

Destiny stepped back. "Is it contagious?"

LeAnn chuckled. "No, silly," she said as she strolled through the living room to the kitchen. "A singing gig." She grabbed the carafe from the coffee pot and took it to the sink where she filled it with water.

It amazed Destiny that the girl assumed they were best friends.

LeAnn dumped coffee into the paper filter she'd put in the holder, then poured the water into the bin. She flipped on the switch before turning around to face Destiny. Destiny assumed LeAnn would tell her about the gig.

She was wrong.

"Oh, you have doughnuts!" LeAnn hurried to the box and opened it, closing her eyes and inhaling deeply. "And they're chocolate. I really need chocolate." She brought the box to the table and sat in one of the chairs.

Help yourself, Destiny thought, but she really didn't mind. She liked LeAnn, even knowing a friendship between them wouldn't end well.

The doorbell rang. Destiny jumped. Chance? "I'll be right back." She hurried to the other room, then opened the door.

"Morning." Charles's voice boomed across the apartment.

"It's too early for company," she grumbled.

"What's that, you say? You gotta speak up."

She shook her head. "Nothing. Did you need something?" Or was he another person who wanted to ruin her morning?

"I'm all out of coffee. I thought maybe—" He stopped mid-sentence and sniffed. "I knew I'd pegged you for a coffee drinker. Black, right?" He didn't wait for her answer, but headed toward the kitchen.

"Just come on in. In fact, the whole apartment complex can join us for morning coffee." Destiny didn't care that sarcasm dripped from her words. But as she started to close the door, Beulah pushed her way inside.

"Was that Charles I saw? What's he doing in your apartment?" She eyed Destiny as though she thought Charles might be her next love victim.

"Yes, that was Charles, and before him, LeAnn. Would you like coffee and a doughnut, too?"

"Might as well since you kept me up most of the night yelling like a banshee in heat." She marched toward the kitchen.

"Great, just great." She started to close the door, but stopped at the last second and peered into the hallway, saw it was empty, then shut the door.

When she joined the others, Charles was pouring Beulah a cup of coffee and she was getting a doughnut out of the box.

"Sit and I'll tell you all about it." LeAnn practically squirmed in her seat.

Nervous energy?

"Tell her about what?" Charles asked.

Oh hell, why not. It certainly didn't look as though they would leave any time soon. Destiny took a seat across from her. LeAnn grabbed a doughnut and shoved half into her mouth.

"Dis iz good," she mumbled around the doughnut. "Imgonnasingatabar," she said.

Destiny raised her eyebrows, unable to decipher LeAnn's new language.

"She's lost it. Bound to happen the way she zips around like a bee in a field of blooming flowers," Beulah said before she opened her mouth wide, then apparently thought better of what she was about to do and took a dainty bite of the doughnut instead.

There was something different about Beulah. Destiny studied her for a moment before she realized what had changed. She didn't have the lip hairs and she'd plucked the mole hair, too. Her hair was done in a different style. Softer, more feminine. She was still dressed like a bag lady, though.

LeAnn laughed, then swallowed. "Sorry. I guess I'm nervous."

"Ya think?" Destiny asked, returning her attention to LeAnn.

"Spill the beans 'fore you bust, girl," Charles urged.

LeAnn grabbed Destiny's hand and squeezed. Destiny's first instinct was to pull away but she didn't, and suddenly she kind of liked LeAnn's touch. She realized that even though she didn't want it to happen, it had. LeAnn had become her friend.

Destiny mentally scoffed at the idea. They weren't friends. LeAnn was—what?

She studied the other woman as she began to talk about singing in some bar. LeAnn's eyes sparkled, and between sentences she laughed as though it was a dream come true. Her shot at breaking into the big time. At least it was one step in the right direction.

"Someone important could walk into the bar on a night I'm singing." LeAnn hugged her middle. "This could be it."

"Or not," Beulah said.

Destiny glared at her. "I'm happy for you," she told LeAnn and was surprised that she meant it. It would be great if LeAnn had the opportunity to do something with her life. Destiny regretted never having that chance.

"Wow, we can say we knew you when," Charles said.

"Or not," Beulah jabbed again.

Charles frowned. "Stop being so negative. Let the girl have her dreams."

"I'm just pointing out what could happen. Better to know up front, then disappointment doesn't hurt so much."

Charles rose to his feet. "Come on, old woman. Leave these girls to their talkin'. We'll bring the cups by later." He looked pointedly at Beulah.

She finally stood, eyeing the doughnut box. "I need the chocolate after last night." She grabbed another doughnut and hurried out of the room.

Charles was right on her heels. "And what exactly did you do last night that you need energy?"

Destiny didn't hear what Beulah said as the door shut behind them. Two down, one to go, and then blessed peace.

"If I make it big, I mean with my singing, you'll come with me. Won't you?"

Destiny couldn't stop her snort of laughter even if she tried, which she didn't. She couldn't help thinking about all the empty promises she'd heard in her lifetime, but she saw something in LeAnn's eyes that told Destiny the other woman was serious, and Destiny's laughter died.

"You barely know me," she told her.

"We're a lot alike, you and I." Her expression grew solemn. "I can't imagine you not going with me."

LeAnn said that now, but if she ever made it big she would change her mind. She would forget about Destiny. Not that it mattered; Destiny was dead, her life was over, and she had no place

among the living. It was a nice thought, though, and she was sure
LeAnn meant it.

"I need a refill." Destiny grabbed her cup and stood, moving to
the counter. It was hard for her to accept that LeAnn would actually
care for her.

"You'll come hear me sing, won't you?"

Destiny stilled, knowing her time left was getting shorter. "When?"

"Tonight. I know it's a Monday and there probably won't be
anyone there. It would be nice to have someone I know in the audience. The owner did say he knew someone who knew someone and
he would try to get them to come to the performance."

Destiny poured coffee into her cup and carried it back to the
table. "I wouldn't miss it for the world."

LeAnn breathed a sigh of relief. "Good! I was hoping you'd be
there." She blew across her coffee, then took a drink. After she set
her cup back on the table, she reached into the box of doughnuts and
took another one out. "I probably should stop eating these or I'll be
bigger than the stage."

"Chocolate is good for the soul," Destiny told her and took one
out for herself.

"Now that would make a good country song."

"Instead of drowning yourself in whiskey, you could write the
female version of drowning your sorrows in a box of chocolate."

LeAnn giggled. "I like that." Just as quickly, LeAnn sobered.
"Are you going to tell me about him?"

Destiny didn't have to ask what *him* she referred to. "I met him
in a bar." She took a drink of her coffee.

"That's it?"

What was she supposed to say? That she was only trying to steal
his soul? What would LeAnn think about her then? Instead, Destiny
shrugged. "It's a new relationship."

"New or not, the guy really likes you."

Destiny was about to take a bite of her doughnut, but paused. "Do you think so?"

"I know so." LeAnn happened to glance at the clock, then choked down the rest of her doughnut. "Crap, I've gotta run. I'm due at work in ten minutes."

She jumped up, downed a big swallow of coffee, but before LeAnn ran out she gave Destiny a quick hug. In the blink of an eye the other girl was gone. Destiny leaned back in her chair, smiling. Okay, so she liked LeAnn. What was the big deal?

She heard a noise in the other room and shook her head. LeAnn would forget her head if it wasn't tied on. Destiny came to her feet and strolled to the other room.

"What did you forget?"

Her smile disappeared when she spotted the man lounging on the sofa as he thumbed through one of the magazines she'd purchased.

"Vetis," she whispered, barely able to say his name.

Vetis looked up. His dark eyes moved slowly over her as he came to his feet. He had the build of a god, the sexy good looks of a man who knew how to please a woman, and the deadly charm of the Devil himself—except he wasn't a devil.

No, Vetis was a demon.

One of the most powerful.

One she never wanted to cross.

Chapter 15

CHANCE GALLOPED ACROSS THE land on his horse. The crisp morning air felt good. He could just as easily close his eyes and be at his destination, but sometimes it was the ride that made life more enjoyable.

Besides, he needed to clear his head. And there was something about feeling the wind rushing past that always gave him a thrill. No cares, no worries. It was just him and the horse.

Except no matter how fast he went this time, he couldn't outrun his demons. Damn, he broke his own rule and made love to Destiny.

He waited for the guilt, the anger at his weakness to emerge, but it didn't. The only thing that came to mind was how good it felt to pull her naked body against his, to plunge deep inside her hot body.

He groaned as his dick grew hard. He shifted on the saddle but it didn't ease his discomfort. Chance wanted to make love to her again.

Ah hell, he had to get his thoughts in order and plan what he would do next. Instead of giving in to temptation and returning to Destiny, he tugged on the reins and stopped his mount beside the barn. He wasn't ready to go inside and face the others just yet. At least not until he cleared Destiny from his mind. Instead, he strode around the corner toward the pool, but when he got there, her face still filled his thoughts, her body begged him to return and make love to her.

Please help me, he silently prayed as he began to strip out of his clothes, letting them fall to the pebbled surface in a heap. There was only one cure for getting Destiny off his mind so he could think straight.

He dove into the water.

When he surfaced Chance was gasping, his body one large goose bump. Damn, he didn't expect the water to be that freakin' cold! Shit! Fuck! What the hell was he thinking? But that was the problem, he wasn't thinking at all. In fact, he couldn't remember the last time he thought about anything other than making love to Destiny.

"What would possess a grown man to jump into frigid water?" Dillon asked, unable to keep the humor out of his voice.

Was nothing going right in his life? Chance's whole body shook like a grass skirt on a hula dancer. He turned and faced Dillon. "I f-f-fucked her," he said, trying to keep from shivering and having no luck.

One of Dillon's eyebrows shot up. "And what, now you're doing penance by freezing off your cock?"

"No, j-j-just trying not to think about f-f-fucking her again."

"Is it working?"

"N-n-n-nooo."

Laughter burst from Dillon as he scooped up Chance's clothes. "Then get out of there before you don't have anything left to fuck her with."

"G-g-g-good idea." He moved to the side, placed the palms of his hands on the side, and boosted himself out of the water, splashing water everywhere as he did.

Dillon dodged the droplets. "Hey, careful, that water's freezing."

"You d-d-don't have to tel-l-l-l me."

Dillon was still staring at Chance as he jerked on his clothes. Maybe his dick had frozen off and Dillon didn't want to be the one who gave him the bad news. Chance was too afraid to look. Finally, he had to know what the hell he was looking at. "What?" he growled.

Dillon shook his head. "Nothing. I was only thinking you look kind of like a big Smurf."

"Funny." Great. Dillon, with his usual matter-of-fact attitude, was pointing out the obvious. "If I get pneumonia, then you'll worry."

"Nah, we can't die. Well, at least not from doing something stupid like swimming in water which is well below freezing. If I were you, I would've turned the temperature up. You know Hunter likes the pool cold in the summer."

"I don't care what you would've done." Chance stomped back toward the rec room doors. "And keep this to yourself." If the others got wind of what he'd done, Chance would never live it down. Jumping into the freezing water just showed Chance exactly how much Destiny was screwing with his head.

"Of course I won't say a word," Dillon promised. "Why would you even think I would? We're practically brothers. I'm deeply hurt you would even imagine that I would."

Chance wasn't sure if he believed Dillon or not. The guy had been laughing at him a moment ago. He didn't have much choice, so he decided he wanted to stay on Dillon's good side. "I'm sorry. It's just that they would never let me live it down."

They walked the rest of the way in silence. Once inside, Chance went straight to his room, then stripped out of his clothes. He moved under the spray of a hot shower and finally started to thaw.

Jumping into the water was really dumb and it didn't solve his problem. He still wanted Destiny as much as he did before almost freezing his dick off.

What the hell was he going to do?

He planted his palms on the shower tiles and lowered his head, letting the water pour over him until the chill finally left, but then thoughts of Destiny returned.

She was going to be the death of him. He snapped the water off and stepped out of the shower, grabbing a warm towel off the heated rack.

He needed a plan. He had to try to convince Destiny there was another path than the one she chose. Surely he could manage that.

He glanced at the clock. It was still early morning. He'd grab something to eat then figure out what he was going to do. He only needed time to sort through everything.

The house was quiet as he went down the stairs. Where were the others? Chance didn't wonder long as he made his way toward the kitchen. The clanking of pans sounded like thunder during a bad storm. Being alone was out of the question. Not that he really felt like being by himself.

Hunter was scrambling eggs and Ryder was putting canned biscuits into the oven. No one would ever accuse them of being good cooks. And Dillon? He glanced up from placing sliced bacon in a skillet. Dillon's expression immediately went bland.

Chance's eyes narrowed. Dillon looked innocent. Too innocent. Chance didn't buy any of it for a second.

"You told them," he accused Dillon.

Dillon's eyes widened. "Told them what?"

Chance's gaze narrowed. Maybe he was wrong. "Nothing," he mumbled. "I'm starved," he said to change the subject.

"It'll be ready in a jiffy," Hunter said. "The biscuits were nearly frozen so they might take a bit to thaw."

"The OJ is nice and cold. Pour you a glass?" Ryder asked. "Unless you'd like something warmer."

Chance glared at Dillon.

"I didn't say a word," Dillon promised, then cast evil glances toward the other two men.

"And after we eat, we can all go for a swim. I hear the water is rejuvenating." Hunter snorted.

"Crap, I told you two not to say anything." Dillon slapped the skillet on the stove, then turned the burner on high.

Ryder grinned. "What did you expect us to do?" He met Chance's gaze. "I told you having sex with your assignment wouldn't be the end all. Now you'll be able to convince Destiny that demons only lie. Just tell her there's a better life waiting for her."

All three looked his way, waiting for a response. Chance pulled out a chair and sat with a deep sigh, finally giving in. "Yeah, maybe you're right."

"Of course we're right," Hunter said as he turned the burner off then carried the skillet of eggs to the table. He tossed a towel down then set the skillet on top.

There was a distinct odor coming from the skillet, and it wasn't tempting Chance to scoop some out on the plate Hunter shoved in front of him. Dillon turned off his burner, but at least placed the bacon on a chipped blue plate rather than leaving the strips in the skillet. He carried it to the table after opening a window to let the smoke out.

Chance took one look at the greasy, burnt bacon and decided he would skip the eggs and bacon. Biscuits would be plenty. He wasn't that hungry anyway.

Ryder opened the oven and grabbed a potholder. He juggled the pan before turning the biscuits onto a plate and brought them to the table. But when he pulled one biscuit away from the others, a glob of dough stretched all the way to his plate before breaking in two and snapping back.

"Maybe I should've left them in a little longer," Ryder mumbled. "They're brown on top, though."

"I told you two that everything you fix is always undercooked," Hunter groused.

Dillon snorted as he spooned up some eggs then dropped the burnt mess back in the skillet. "Do you think you might overcook things a little?"

Hunter's eyebrows veed. "It's healthier. Kills all the germs."

"And taste," Chance, Ryder, and Dillon grumbled in unison.

"Tell me what you really think." Hunter glared at them.

Before a battle broke out about who cooked worse than the other, Chance spoke up. "I think Mama Paula's."

Hunter's fuse snuffed out and his expression turned dreamy. "Mama Paula is definitely an angel when it comes to cooking."

Ryder and Dillon nodded in agreement.

Anyone would think they would have learned to cook over the centuries, but none of them ever took the time to open a cookbook. Why should they when there were plenty of places to eat? But it didn't mean they gave up trying. Hunter said it relaxed him. How anyone could ever feel relaxed after burning food Chance would never understand. He, on the other hand, didn't even try.

They stood together then closed their eyes. In a few minutes, they were walking into Mama Paula's café. The sweet aroma of her cooking filled the place. Chance's stomach rumbled.

Maybe he wasn't coming up with a workable solution at that very moment, but he would. He had to, for his sake as well as Destiny's.

Chapter 16

VETIS TOSSED THE MAGAZINE to the coffee table where it hit with a loud whack that echoed through the small apartment. Cold chills ran up and down Destiny's spine. Vetis appeared calm and collected until she looked a little closer. Red sparks glinted in his eyes.

"I expected you back long before now." His voice was like glass breaking, the shards flying through the air and biting into her flesh.

She flinched.

No! They gave her a week. He wasn't supposed to be there. She twined her fingers together.

A long time ago, Vetis swore that he could take away her pain. And he made good on his promise. The pain stopped. Once he got her to Hell, he seduced her into believing she could have everything her heart desired.

But she didn't have everything. She barely had anything.

"Is something troubling you, my sweet?" He strolled toward her, stopping only a few inches away. He reached out and smoothed a wayward strand of hair behind her ear.

She flinched.

He smiled. His hand continued downward until he brushed his thumb across her nipple. She gasped as the fire of his touch burned her skin. When she jumped back, his eyes widened.

"What? You don't like it when I caress you? There was a time when you craved me to stroke you just this way, even begged me to make love to you. Now you cringe?"

"No," she quickly told him, afraid of his anger. "It burned a little, that's all."

"They say when one begins to see goodness in the world, a demon's touch will start to burn rather than offer warmth. Is that what's happening to you, Destiny?" He raised his eyebrows. "Has this world tempted you more than I can? Has a man tempted you?" His lips thinned.

For the first time, she felt fear for someone other than herself. If Vetis even thought she might care for someone more than him, he would destroy them.

She squared her shoulders. "No, of course I don't care about this world or anyone in it. I'm here for one reason only, to get my quota. I haven't lost sight of my goal." But even she could hear the difference in her voice. Had she begun to change without realizing it?

"You never have been one who could lie well." He shook his head. "How quickly you've forgotten what it was like. A pity that I will have to remind you." He moved fast, grabbing her hand and pulling her against him.

Fire licked at her skin, burning wherever he touched. She cried out in pain. He held her chin in a firm grip, then lowered his lips to hers. His tongue set fire to her mouth. Tears ran down her face.

Please, stop, she silently begged, but he continued his assault on her body. Touching, pressing against her, forcing her to accept him.

When she thought it would be the end of her existence, Vetis stopped his torture, moving away only far enough so he could stare into her face.

"You think this life is what you want?" he spat. "You've created a fantasy world that can never be! Look and see again what life gave to you." He moved his arm in a wide arc.

Like a movie theater, her past began to play across a large screen. She saw her mother walking away, leaving the store, and getting into a car with the man she'd been seeing. She never even looked back.

An invisible hand squeezed around Destiny's heart. "No, please," she begged, trying to close her eyes.

"Watch," Vetis growled, clamping a firm hand on her chin.

Tears filled her eyes as she saw herself waiting in the store—scared, lonely. But Mommy didn't come back.

Vetis forced her to keep watching. It made her sick to her stomach to see how low she had sunk. Why couldn't she have found Chance back then?

"See," Vetis whispered close to her ear. "None of those men loved you. Not one. They wanted only what you could give them."

A shudder swept over her. He was right, of course. No one had wanted her.

"See what your life became," he told her.

Jack said he would take care of her. She believed him. He said he loved her and she believed that, too.

He sent her out to shoplift, coercing her to earn money for the both of them. Jack told her this was what love was, and if she wanted to keep his she'd better do as she was told.

And so she did, because even a scrap of love was better than no love at all. But nothing was ever good enough for him. Jack began to slap her around. The slaps turned to a doubled fist. She cringed.

"No more," she whispered, trying to turn away from her life as it unfolded in front of her. "I don't want to see any more."

"This is all life can ever be for you. No one loved you, no one took care of you until I came along. I saved you. Me! No one else."

Her spine stiffened as she gritted her teeth, knowing she would have to face her past once again.

Life with Jack became too much to bear. The gun was in her hand. She pulled the trigger. The explosion made her ears ring, and the force of the gun kicked her against the wall. But she hadn't looked away.

Relief flooded through her when he gasped, grabbed his chest, and fell to the ground, blood staining the dingy carpet. He wouldn't hurt her again. Never again.

She didn't look away until he stopped breathing. It all happened in a matter of seconds, but time seemed to move in slow motion.

Then fear set in. They would come for her, his friends. She fumbled with the doorknob, finally getting the door open, but it was too late. Jack's friends had heard the gunshot. One of them hit her, then another. Over and over. The pain was too much.

Destiny tried to draw in a breath but she couldn't. Her battered and broken body felt as though it were on fire. She whimpered, but they didn't stop.

"I can make the pain go away," Vetis whispered again.

One of them kicked her. A bone broke. Their laughter filled her ears.

"We're gonna make you wish you were dead, bitch. Then we're gonna make your wish come true. Just not for a long time yet." He pulled her up by her hair and looked into her eyes. Destiny knew he meant what he said and they would keep her alive until they tired of torturing her.

"I can make it all go away," Vetis whispered.

A fist slammed into her stomach. She doubled up on the floor, gasping for each breath as she wrapped her arms around her middle. The pain blurred her vision but she saw him, this strange being that no one else could see. She saw the pity in his eyes.

"I'll end it. Just give me your soul to keep."

A booted foot landed hard against her back. Pain exploded through her body.

"Yes," she gasped. "Make it stop," she repeated the words from that night so long ago.

With one wave of his hand, the screen was gone. Vetis opened his arms and she willingly went into them, crying against his shoulder.

"You don't want that life again, do you?"

"No," she sobbed.

"It looks good at first," he soothed. "But that life only gave you pain. It would be no different now. Get your quota and come back to me. I have never hurt you."

"No, you haven't." But a shiver of apprehension traveled over her.

"One more soul, then I'll make you burn for me," he promised.

In a swirl of smoke, he was gone. Destiny stumbled to the sofa and dropped onto the cushioned seat. How could she have been so stupid to forget why she was here? Vetis took away her pain.

But she doubted him. Her gaze skittered around the room, searching. He was gone, only his presence lingered.

Oh damn, she still doubted him. It was as though she was seeing him in another light. As though the gold paint was rubbed off in places and the tarnish was becoming more visible.

How could she doubt him, though? Vetis kept his promise and took away the pain.

But deep down, she knew why the trust was no longer there. He promised her life would be good, but she was still waiting for everything he swore would be hers. Maybe it was all a lie.

No, she wouldn't think like that! Something in her life had to be real. Once she convinced Chance to return to Hell with her, she would have everything she ever dreamed of. Vetis wouldn't go back on his word. She was the one who had to fill her quota.

A new resolution filled her. She would have it all, and that included Chance. He wanted her. He wasn't able to resist her. She only had to convince him that they could have everything if only he would follow her back to Hell.

It was time to start playing for real. What man could resist the world if it was given to him on a silver platter?

She pushed off the sofa and scrubbed the tears from her face. She could do it, would do it.

After a quick shower, she dressed in a pair of tight-fitting jeans, sandals, and a body-hugging top. Still, he didn't show. The clock ticked down the seconds. By noon she was going stir crazy. Did he get what he wanted and move on to his next challenge?

Anger burned inside her. It wouldn't be the first time she was used. Damn, how could she have been so stupid as to believe in someone again?

Crap, she still needed another soul. What would happen if she went back empty-handed? A shiver ran down her spine at the thought of facing a court of demons. She heard about things like that happening and it wasn't something she planned to go through herself.

She would get her soul and return to Hell, and then everything would be better. Something stabbed at her heart when she thought about not seeing Chance ever again. But she had no choice, damn it! Never once in her life did she have a choice. Why should it be any different now?

She grabbed her purse, slinging the strap over her shoulder. Her steps were quick and jerky as she made her way out of the apartment. As she rounded the corner toward the elevator, she met Beulah.

Destiny stumbled, but quickly caught herself and stared at the other woman. Was she wearing makeup? She'd changed into a light blue top and black slacks. The clothes and makeup softened her appearance. A far cry from when Destiny first met her. Beulah looked almost like someone's grandmother.

"What are you staring at?" Beulah grumbled.

"Really?"

"A person has a right to try something different."

"Whatever." She was wasting time talking to her.

Destiny hurried down the hall, then stepped into the elevator and punched the main floor. The box moaned and groaned as it descended. What was she going to do? She had to find another soul to steal. She had pinned all her expectations on Chance, but he wasn't around. She couldn't just walk up to someone and ask them if they would like to go to Hell.

No, it took finesse and time to convince someone that it wasn't so bad to die. People were afraid of death. But time was running out for her.

The elevator came to a jarring stop. As soon as the doors opened, she hurried out. Destiny didn't waste any time leaving the building and striding down the street. She sized up every person she met as a possible candidate, but there was something wrong with each one.

A man who already looked angry at the world strode past, glaring at her. Evil oozed from his pores. Just to look at him made her skin crawl. She knew men like him. Way too many, in fact.

Destiny quickly turned her head and hurried past. No, the stranger wasn't a good candidate. Vetis would only laugh and say her efforts were amateurish at best.

Her gaze flitted from person to person as she pushed past people on their lunch breaks. She had to find someone. What would Vetis do to her if she returned empty-handed? No! She refused to think about the consequences. She raked her fingers through her hair, desperately searching the faces of people as she hurried down the sidewalk. Her heart pounded and her palms grew damp.

A cowboy stepped from a store that displayed boots, jeans, and hats behind a plate glass window. He might do. Fortyish, so not too old. When he was closer, the man politely tugged on the brim of his hat. "Howdy, ma'am." The sun glinted off his plain gold wedding band.

She nodded and hurried past, knowing she wouldn't be able to convince him Hell was better than what he had. The man had that comfortable, married look about him. She frowned. He probably married his freakin' high school sweetheart.

What about the more mature woman strolling toward her? Destiny quickly ruled her out. The woman had a diamond on her finger that had to be at least a couple of carats.

Just down the street, a woman parked a coughing minivan and

opened the creaking driver's door. Destiny walked nearer, slowed, then came to a stop.

"Beautiful day, isn't it?" The woman wore a tired smile as she carefully counted out change and put it in the parking meter. Her clothes were clean but beginning to show signs of wear.

Life could be so much better for this woman. She could have new clothes. Jewels. Anything her heart desired. Destiny studied her. Yes, she would do just fine. Surely she would want to leave her poor existence for something so much better. Vetis would be so proud of Destiny.

"Yes, it is a wonderful day." Destiny smiled, knowing she was about to meet her quota. The tension drained from her body. The woman would please Vetis. Destiny would be safe from his wrath.

As the woman opened the sliding side door, Destiny couldn't help feeling empty inside. She'd thought there was something special between her and Chance. That he would be the one to leave with her. She was wrong, of course. She never was a good judge of character, especially when it came to men.

But it didn't matter now. Soon it would all be a distant memory. Destiny squared her chin. Prepared to use all her charm to convince the woman that a better life awaited her.

But as the woman straightened, small hands wrapped around her neck. The toddler couldn't have been more than four. The little girl smiled, clutching her mother's hand when she stood her on the sidewalk.

The blood ran cold through Destiny's veins. The little girl suddenly broke free and hurled herself at Destiny, giggling and laughing. Destiny instinctively knelt down. The little girl threw her arms around Destiny's neck and hugged.

Destiny inhaled her little girl fragrance like it was an expensive perfume. She absorbed her pudgy softness. That was what it felt like to love something.

"Oh my, I'm so sorry. Melissa, what has Momma told you about this?" she said with a slow Texas drawl.

"Pretty," the child said.

The woman laughed. "Yes, she's very pretty. I'm so sorry. Melissa can be a handful."

"Not a problem," Destiny told her as she bowed her head and stumbled away. Tears filled her eyes. No, she couldn't take the woman. She just couldn't. Not and leave the child to fend for herself.

Destiny quickly moved farther down the street. Her gaze darted over the thinning crowd. What if she didn't find someone? Desperation weaved its way through her.

A young man with longish hair was walking toward her. Homeless? Maybe. He was dressed as badly as some of the kids she used to run with. His jeans were ragged and torn—obviously too big. They hung past his waist, boxer shorts showing. But clean.

Destiny couldn't tell.

Her move was calculated. When he passed, she casually dropped her purse. She vowed to take his soul if he snatched it up and ran, but no, he stooped and picked it up, then hurried to bring it back to her.

It wasn't working out. What the hell was she doing wrong? She was almost a demon.

After all she'd suffered through, she should be able to take anyone. She should be able to just say, screw them! Take their soul any way she could and finish what she'd started.

Then why couldn't she? Why was she finding it so difficult?

The crowd thinned until there was no one on the sidewalk. She absently reached up and fingered the necklace Chance had given her as panic began to set in.

Vetis was going to destroy her. A shudder wracked her body. She needed a place where she could plan a new strategy. Where she could gather her thoughts.

She rounded a corner. The bar loomed ahead. She glanced

around. Hell, even the bum was nowhere in sight. She quickened her pace until she was pushing on the door and stepped into the cool interior. Once inside, she glanced around—hoping, but no. She was the only one inside the bar other than the bartender.

If she wasn't so desperate to get her quota, she'd laugh. Her situation was pretty funny when she thought about it. Really, what kind of demon was she going to make if she couldn't even find one soul to steal?

She moved to the bar, sliding onto one of the stools. "A beer." Drowning her sorrows was sounding pretty good. Drink enough so she wouldn't have to think about her life—or her death.

The bartender uncapped a bottle and brought it to her. She pulled some money out of her purse and dropped the bills on the counter.

"The cowboy not with you?" he asked.

She was in the middle of taking a drink, but his voice startled her so that the liquid went down the wrong tube. She coughed, trying to catch her breath.

"Sorry about that," he said. "I was just making conversation."

Destiny eyed him, remembering that she first thought he might be a good candidate to seduce back to Hell. The guy was maybe in his mid-thirties and kind of cute.

"That's okay," she told him. When he started to move farther away, she quickly spoke up. "You know cowboys. Here one day and gone the next."

He stopped. "How's that?"

She shrugged, took another slow drink of her beer then set the bottle back on the bar. "You never know when they'll walk out of your life."

"Is that what he did?" The bartender ambled down to her end. "Did he leave you high and dry?"

"I don't know," she answered truthfully. Hell, she didn't know a whole lot about Chance when she thought about it. Only that he knew how to make love to her, and that was the problem. With Chance, it wasn't just sex. They'd made love. There was a connection between them, or so she thought.

The bartender shook his head. "Nope, I don't think he's that stupid. No man would intentionally walk away from you."

Hell, Destiny could tell him people had walked away from her all her life. None of that mattered, though. The guy was nice. Why bring up her sordid past?

"I'm Destiny," she said instead.

"I go by Duncan."

"Have you always bartended?"

He glanced around. "Until I earned enough money to put a hefty down payment on this place. It's not much. Me and the bank own it. Mostly the bank." He frowned. "I'd hoped the area might clean up a little. Maybe get some of the overflow from Billy Bob's. It hasn't happened yet."

She leaned an elbow on the counter and studied him. There was something about Duncan. A feeling she had. He came across as a good man. A fair man. Okay, so maybe she wouldn't be able to talk him into going back to Hell with her, but she liked him all the same. Besides, he was making her feel a little calmer.

"Someday this place will take off, though," he continued. "I can feel it in my bones." It was his turn to study her. "Have you ever felt like that? Where you just know what you're doing is right?"

She didn't meet his eyes. "No, I've never felt like that. I've learned not to trust my judgment so much anymore," she wryly told him before taking another drink. She always thought dreams were for losers. She'd stopped dreaming a long time ago.

He suddenly grinned. "Then you're still wandering around trying to find who you are. Someday you'll know exactly what you're meant to do and you won't let anyone stand in your way."

"Like you did with your bar?"

"Yeah."

"And what if I told you it was already too late for me?"

He snorted. "You're just a kid."

She raised her eyebrows.

His cheeks took on a rosy glow. "Okay, maybe more than a kid. And yeah, I've noticed you're sexy as hell, but sometimes you can be old and still not know what you want out of life. There's a time and a place for everything."

"And you think I'll find it someday?"

"If you don't give up and stop looking."

Destiny wouldn't tell him there was only one thing she wanted and that was to finish out her quota and go back to Hell. Duncan could continue to live his dream. She had no dreams in her future.

A sliver of light spilled into the bar. She looked up. Duncan grinned and nodded toward the door. "Looks like your cowboy is still hanging around."

Her heart pounded inside her chest. She slowly turned on the barstool. Damn, how could one man look so hot? He swaggered toward her, jeans riding low on his hips. The red T-shirt he wore hugged his muscular chest.

As he moved nearer, his gaze traveled over her, slowly stripping her out of her clothes. Her body responded to his heated gaze. Just as quickly, she realized she was on a mission.

She stood, meeting him halfway across the floor. "You left me."

"I had some place to go."

"I've heard that line before."

He reached out his hand.

She cocked an eyebrow.

"Come with me."

"Give me one good reason."

He leaned forward and whispered in her ear. "Because I think you're fucking hot and I need you more than I've ever needed anything in my life."

She closed her eyes, trying to block out the images running across her mind, knowing her time was growing short. He was chipping away at her days left on earth, robbing her seconds, stealing every breath she took.

"Come with me." He took her hand and squeezed.

"I can't," she whispered, but as he led her out of the bar, she didn't pull away.

The bright sunshine hit her in the face, causing her to blink. When her eyes adjusted, she noticed the bum on the corner. He was sitting on the sidewalk, leaning against a building, reading a book. He'd traded his bottle of booze for words on paper.

Had the world turned upside down? She shook her head and looked at Chance.

"Where are you taking me?" she asked as he led her to his motorcycle that was parked next to the curb.

"Does it matter?"

There was no more fight left inside her. She shook her head. "Not really." And she realized it didn't matter. Nothing did when she was with him. But as she slipped on the back of the cycle, she knew she had to try to convince Chance to return to Hell with her. Time was running out.

But taking him to Hell left a sour taste in her mouth. It was as if she would be condemning him to a life he wasn't meant to lead.

But no, she couldn't think like that. She would make it better.

Chapter 17

CHANCE TOOK THE CORNERS with ease on his motorcycle. Destiny's hands were snug around his waist, but not tight. She was starting to trust him more and more.

But something occurred between the time he left and the time he joined her at the bar. Whatever happened must have scared her pretty badly. When he took her hand in his, hers trembled and, for a moment, he saw the look of desperation in her eyes. It was as though all her confidence and energy were drained.

Only one thing could have caused it.

A demon.

Probably the one who'd convinced Destiny that life would be better if she gave up her soul. He clamped his lips together. Why the hell didn't she call out for help?

Just as quickly as the thought came, so did the answer. She didn't know the truth about him, and why pray when she had no faith? With everything that had happened in her life, why should she?

He didn't have the answers. None of the nephilim did. They tried to help, but sometimes people slipped through the cracks. There were more people in need of help than the angels and nephilim could handle. His chest tightened painfully. Why hadn't he known she needed his help?

He gripped the handlebars tighter. His lips formed a thin line when he pressed them together. Someone had blocked her need. Had it been angels? Or demons? Could he save her now?

Chance felt Destiny's sigh as she rested her cheek against his back, then her hands tightened around his waist, as though she was afraid he would disappear from her life. He only wished they could ride his motorcycle for all eternity. Outrun any demon who tried to steal her away from him or any angel who'd claim Chance had crossed the line.

But running away would never work. Destiny had to make the choice. Chance could only pray that it would be the right one. Wondering about the outcome was tearing him apart.

He turned down a road that led to a favorite spot of his. Only a few more miles, and then he pulled over near an old oak with gnarly branches. He'd planted the tree two hundred years before because he liked the stream that wound through the countryside. It was peaceful there.

"This is nice," Destiny said as she climbed off the bike. "How did you find it?"

He couldn't tell her that he was watching over a wagon train of pioneers on their way to build a new life, so instead he said, "How does anyone ever find something special?" He swung his leg over the bike.

She was so near, so breathtakingly beautiful. He had to touch her so he brushed some loose strands of hair behind her ear.

"You look up one day," he continued, "and there it is, right in front of you."

She leaned toward him for a moment then quickly moved back, as though she needed to put distance between them. He wondered what was going through her mind. And maybe he already knew.

If the demon who took her soul came around, he would have reminded her that she was back on earth for a reason. He would have put the fear of Satan in her once more, but in a way that made her feel like Hell was her only choice. The demon wouldn't let her slip through his fingers.

"What would you say if I told you that beauty could be yours forever?" She waved her arm to encompass the area. "All of this, all of the time."

He was right. Destiny was making her move. "And you? Would you be there, too?"

She visibly let out a deep breath as though she'd been holding it in, waiting to see if he might be willing to listen to what she had to say.

"Yes! I would be there, and you would be there, and we could have all eternity together."

He laughed.

She frowned. "You don't believe me."

There was only one way to take her mind off what she was there to do. He moved closer.

"I would like nothing more than to be with you forever." He lowered his mouth to hers, tasting the sweetness she offered. His tongue caressed, then lightly sucked. He caught her moan, but before he could go farther she pushed out of his arms. Her breathing was shaky and she trembled.

"You have a way of making me forget what I need to do," she mumbled.

"Do I?" he asked as he reached for the hem of his red T-shirt and pulled it over his head.

Her gaze locked on his chest. "Oh yeah, you make me forget a lot of things."

Okay, he hadn't exactly planned to do a striptease, but it was the only way he could get her mind off Hell. Not that he was too inconvenienced. Damn, he wanted to love her like there was no tomorrow. Make her forget everything but each other.

"I want to make love to you," he said. "Out here in the open."

"We need to talk." Her words were strained. She cleared her throat and tried again. "We need to talk about the future. Our future."

"Are you proposing?" He flexed his muscles.

"What?" Her gaze moved to his face, then she frowned. "No, I mean, not exactly. We just need to talk."

"You think so?" He tugged at the waistband of his jeans and the metal button slipped through the hole. Still watching her, he slid the zipper down. When his pants were undone, he toed off his boots, then pushed his jeans over his hips, over his thighs, down his legs.

"You're not making this easy," she said, but her gaze was locked below Chance's waist.

"You're making it hard," he said, not even attempting to keep the humorous note out of his voice.

"Not funny."

"You're right. It's uncomfortable as hell. Only you can end my suffering." He hooked his fingers in the waistband of his briefs.

Her respirations became more rapid. She bit her bottom lip when he pushed the cotton material down a couple of inches.

"Don't stop," she whimpered when he didn't move the briefs any farther. "Please."

He let the material snap back into place, the waistband snug against his hips once more.

"What?" Her eyes widened as her gaze jerked to his face.

Chance shook his head. "You have way too many clothes on."

"Too many—" She arched an eyebrow.

Damn, he loved when she looked put out, and right now her expression told him she was very put out. He'd figured out that she liked to call the shots. She wanted to be the one in charge and it bothered her that he always beat her at her own game.

Well, except one time, but how the hell was he to know she would be in the bathroom and not asleep in bed? He would give her the point for last night, but he planned to be the final victor in this game they played.

Chance would convince her that she could do her life over again. Start fresh, and he would make sure he personally watched over her.

Either that or he would make her forget and keep her with him longer than she was supposed to stay.

He frowned. Keeping a demon wannabe longer than they were supposed to stay was difficult. Next to impossible, in fact. Demons didn't take too kindly to losing a soul.

There were so many obstacles stacking up against him. Even if he freed her, he would lose her. A sick feeling swirled inside him. Could he let her go? Watch her from afar? All memory of a past life would be buried deep inside her.

She could never know he was there. He would have to see her grow up, start dating, fall in love with someone else.

"Chance?"

He forced his thoughts to return to the present. Destiny was looking at him with concern in her eyes. Damn it! He had to be more careful about hiding his thoughts.

Instead of thinking about what the future might hold, he decided to make every moment he had with Destiny more precious. Enough that it would last him for all eternity.

"Like I said," he told her. "You have way too many clothes on. I thought we had the same thing in mind." He reached for his pants. "Sorry, I guess you don't want to feel my touch, to have me taste you, to feel me buried deep inside you."

"Did I say anything about not wanting to make love?" she quickly asked.

He knew she couldn't see the smile that played around his lips, and he made sure it wasn't there when he straightened. "Then you do want to make love."

"You tell me." She pulled her top over her head and tossed it away from her. The only thing that was left was the tiny angel necklace that he'd bought her.

His dick throbbed. She wasn't wearing a bra. But then he'd already guessed as much at the bar. The images running through his head had been slowly and painfully killing him. But seeing her breasts again was even better. They were plump, with rosy nipples, ripe for his mouth. He made a move toward her. She held up her hands.

"You want to play striptease, then I'll play." She raised her arms, reaching for the sky. "I've never been naked outside. It feels wonderful."

Torture. Pure torture, but so damn sweet! She kicked off her sandals, wiggling her toes.

Ever so slowly, she moved her hips from side to side, like a snake charmer hypnotizing the trainer. Chance was mesmerized by her movements. He almost looked down to see if his dick was following the same motions but couldn't take his eyes off her.

"My jeans are rubbing against me. I'm getting really hot thinking about your mouth sucking on me."

He swallowed hard, thinking the same thing.

She pushed a button through the hole.

Her jeans weren't the kind that zipped. Nope. Chance noticed there were at least three more buttons. At this rate, his whole body would be mummified by the time she was naked.

She continued her seductive gyrations. Her hand moved away from her jeans and he groaned. She smiled softly at his discomfort. He was so going to make her pay later. But for now he couldn't do a damn thing except stare as her hands continued their upward trek.

"This feels good," she said as she ran her hands over her breasts. "My nipples are so sensitive." As if to prove her point, she tweaked them, then moaned. "I love when you suck on them. When your tongue scrapes across my nipples."

"Destiny," he croaked, not knowing how much more he could stand.

"I could get undressed a little faster if I had more motivation." She pointedly looked down.

Hell, if that was all it would take... He jerked his briefs off and tossed them away.

All her movements stopped as she stared at him. "Damn, you're fucking beautiful."

"Please," he moaned.

A wicked grin formed on her face as she slipped another button through the hole. "Do I tempt you?"

"You know you do a lot more than that."

"What if you could have me for all time?"

His gaze jerked to her face. Fuck! He didn't see that one coming. Destiny had managed to turn the tables. Now he was playing on her court.

He moved his hand down, grasping his dick, sliding his foreskin down then back up. "I want to plunge my cock inside your hot pussy. I want to stroke you."

Her hands stilled.

"But you still have your jeans on," he said.

She slipped two more buttons through the holes and shoved her pants downward, kicking them away from her. She wore a pale blue thong. He could see the shadow of her curls.

"You could… uh… have me all the time," she said as if she suddenly remembered her mission again, but there was no conviction in her words as temptation weaved around her like a sweet aroma.

He snaked his hand downward, letting the weight of his balls rest in his palm. "Take off your thong. I want to see all of you."

She visibly swallowed, then tugged the blue thong over her hips. Only the blue triangle of silky material covered what he longed to see. Then even that was gone as the thong fell to her ankles. She kicked it away, the movement giving him a glimpse of what lay beneath.

He closed the space between them. "You're beautiful." He took her in his arms. Her soft form pressed against him. His dick rubbed against her stomach. For a moment they just held tight, breathing in the other's essence. She smelled so sweet. Like honeysuckle and a light summer breeze.

He leaned back just enough so that he could look into her eyes. "Life can be good, Destiny. Life can be very good." He lowered his mouth, tasting her sweetness. She sighed and leaned in closer, her breasts pushing against his chest, her tight nipples poking him, silently begging him to suck on them. At the same time her tongue stroked his.

When he ended the kiss, she rose up on her toes and ran her tongue down the side of his neck. "I love the way you taste," she said. Her tongue swirled around one nipple, then she scraped across with her teeth.

Chance grasped her shoulders, then loosened his hold. She moved to his other nipple and teased it with her tongue. "You're right," she said, pausing for a moment. "Life can be very good. We could make love every day for all eternity."

Her fingers moved over his dick as if she played a musical instrument. She applied pressure in all the right places.

"There's something you don't know about me. I could make all of it happen. Imagine every dream coming true. All the riches you've ever wanted right there for the taking."

"Don't stop," he gasped.

"No, I won't ever stop. We can be together forever. We'll make sweet love all day long."

He was losing the battle. He could feel his soul slipping away. She took a half step away from him, apparently wanting to remind him exactly what he would have, but at the same time the sun burst from behind a cloud, the angel around her neck filled with light, almost blinding him.

Chance forced himself to reach up and grasp the tiny figure. His hand felt weighted down, as though another force worked against him. He lightly ran his finger over the wings. Power charged through him. He sucked in a quick breath and glanced around. Everything looked clearer and he remembered exactly why he was there. He had to save Destiny. To do less was unthinkable.

But the smile on her face said she thought she'd won his soul. Her expression quickly changed to shock when he began to stroke between her legs, then his fingers trailed through her curls.

"Chance—"

"Shh, sweetheart, shh. Just let the pleasure I give you sweep you away. Now is not the time to think, only to feel." His words were soft, hypnotizing.

Destiny's eyes drifted closed. Her movements slowed. He regretted that he couldn't see her eyes, but he liked the idea she would get so caught up in the pleasure he gave her. That alone was a heady sensation.

With a wave of his hand, he made sure the grass would feel like the softest carpet, then he eased her to the ground.

Her eyes opened as he lay beside her. She suddenly turned the tables again and pushed him onto his back, straddling his waist. "You're very good, but I know your game. You think to seduce me."

A lifetime of bad relationships, of people leaving her, had made her wary. Chance knew she wouldn't be an easy assignment. When her pussy cupped his dick as she sat on top of him, he knew she was dead serious about taking him to Hell with her.

As she began to rub against his cock, he wasn't sure who would come out the winner in the immortal game they played. Destiny thought she'd win by massaging against him, and damn, her movements felt fucking fantastic.

She'd better rethink her strategy. On a mortal, her tactics would probably work. But he'd been a nephilim a lot longer than she'd been at the holding station and he had a lot more experience. But he damn sure liked the way she teased him.

"Do you like that?" she asked with a little too much innocence as she lightly rubbed against him.

He rested his hands on her hips and began to massage. "You know I do."

"Leave with me, Chance. I can give you everything you've ever dreamed about."

He skimmed his fingers through her curls right before he said, "You think so?"

"Umm." She cleared her throat. "I… uh… know so."

He thumbed her labia open. She gasped. His dick jerked when he laid eyes on his prize.

"You're seducing me."

"Yeah, I am. Want me to stop?" he asked.

Her eyes were closed and she was biting her bottom lip. "No," she panted. "Please, don't stop."

"Good, because I never intended to."

Chance continued his assault on her body as he slipped one hand to her butt and inched her forward. Closer and closer to his face.

"Not this time," she managed to say right before she moved off him. In one swift motion, she was blowing softly on his dick. She paused for only a moment. "Damn, you're so big. Thick and long." As if to prove her words, she ran her tongue the length of him, licking, placing small kisses as she went.

Chance drew in a deep breath. His hips rose to meet her touch. His vision blurred as heat spread through his body. Fuck! She was good, and he could feel the battle changing course. He tried to break free. His hand rose to move her, but she had him blocked. His hand only landed on her ass.

Her ass?

He forced his vision to clear. When it did, he was looking at her sweet ass wiggling in invitation. Her legs were pressed together.

Destiny sucked him inside her mouth.

Ah damn, her mouth on his dick felt incredible. He could lie like this for all eternity and never get tired of the sensations running through him.

Think!

He moved his hand between her legs. She stilled, like a suspicious dog afraid that Chance was about to steal her bone when all he wanted to do was give her one. "Damn, your mouth is driving me insane. I can't think straight."

Her body relaxed. He rocked his hips, but at the same time he began to ease her legs apart. He began to stroke down the inside of her thighs, then up and down her slit. She kept up the movement, rocking her hips.

The timing had to be perfect.

He closed his eyes when she began to fondle his balls while she sucked on him. His head felt as though it would explode any second. He brought his hips up, wanting more, needing more.

Her light chuckle drifted up to him, reminding him of what he planned to do. The little demon wannabe thought she had him. He wasn't about to let that happen.

Chance moved her leg over him. Her pussy hovered near his face. He moved his arms so that her thighs spread wider, dropping her down, just a mere inch from his eager mouth.

"Not fair!" she said.

"Not at all," he said at the same time his tongue shot out and he licked her slit before drawing her into his mouth. She gasped, pressing against his face.

"Oh, ohhhh," she moaned as she rested her head against his dick.

He jerked. He was so freakin' sensitive and ready to explode.

Just when Chance thought he'd won the round, Destiny sucked him back inside her mouth. His body tightened, then relaxed. How fucking great was that? He had her pussy in his mouth and she was sucking on his dick.

She began to moan; he knew she was close to coming. He sucked harder, his tongue massaging her clit, scraping across her—back and forth until she cried out. Her body tightened, quivered.

Her mouth lost its hold on him. Chance rolled her onto her

back and scooted to his knees. One swipe of his fingers up her pussy and she cried out, breath coming in little gasps.

"This is just the beginning, baby." He knelt, licking, tasting her muskiness before he grabbed his dick, guiding it inside her. She arched her hips but he pulled back, wanting to make the moment last.

Her eyes fluttered open. "Fuck me."

Her words wrapped around him like a hot caress. He plunged inside her. An even hotter heat wrapped around him. Hot and moist, like jumping into a raging volcano, her body consumed him.

Deeper he went, until his dick was buried inside her. He grasped her hips, holding on, then pulling out almost all the way. She whimpered. No, he wasn't stopping, not now. He drove deep inside her once again.

"Yes, damn it. Harder! Faster! I want it all!"

He plunged inside her. Again and again. It was all he could do to take a breath as he stared down at her nakedness. She was so lost in the moment that she was rubbing her breasts, pulling at the nipples. He couldn't take his eyes off her.

Deeper. Harder. Faster.

The world became a blur as the heat built inside him. Her heat. Her fire. Nipping at his dick, setting it ablaze.

The passion inside him rose until he knew he had to have release. He vaguely heard her cry out, felt her body tighten again as trembles swept over him, rippling down his body.

His release came hard and fast. He growled like a lion that had found its mate. His body shook as his world exploded like a jigsaw puzzle, pieces scattering to the four winds.

Then he came back to earth, lying down beside Destiny. She curled into his embrace.

As his eyes drifted closed, he heard her whisper, "You have to leave with me. I can't face everything without you."

"I can set you free," he said, but by the sound of her light breathing, he didn't think she heard him. He pressed his lips to her hair, knowing he'd be damned if he would let Satan have her soul now.

Chapter 18

FOR A MOMENT, CHANCE didn't move. He just let the world come to him. Damn, he felt good. He stretched and yawned.

Had a man ever felt more relaxed than he did right now? More satisfied? Chance didn't think so. In all his years, he'd never met a woman quite like Destiny. One minute she was trying to steal his soul and the next—

He smiled.

Yeah, and in the next she was soft and gentle.

And hot. Yeah, she was some kind of hot.

And right now he needed to see her, to touch her, to pull her body against his. He rolled onto his side, intending to do just that.

Destiny wasn't there. He frowned as he scanned the area. Where was she? Everything looked the same. Nothing amiss. The motorcycle was near the tree, their clothes scattered about.

A cold fear of dread swept over him. Had the demon who owned her soul returned? No, the demon would have known soon enough that Chance was immortal and he would have struck while he had the chance. Nephilim were the demons' mortal enemies. And he'd been lax in his vigil.

That was crazy thinking. No demon took Destiny away. He was being paranoid.

A sound drew his attention. He glanced over his shoulder. Destiny came toward him, tiptoeing, carrying a tin can, and watching where she placed each foot. Water dripped from her hair. As the droplets fell on her body, the sun caught each one and made them look as though diamonds sparkled on her naked skin.

Chance quickly turned back around, knowing by the way she crept forward, that she was attempting to sneak up behind him. What was she plotting?

When she was closer, he swung around to scare her. She screamed and flung the can of water in his face. He coughed and sputtered.

Destiny screamed again, jumping back, and then laughed. "Oh no, I'm sorry. You scared me. I was supposed to scare you!"

He wiped his hand over his dripping face. "Then you're saying you meant to do that?"

Her eyebrows drew together. "Well, not exactly." She bit her bottom lip, but he could tell she was trying hard not to laugh.

"In other words, you meant to throw the water on me."

"No, just dump it over your head." She bit her bottom lip as she valiantly attempted to quell her laughter.

"I'll make you pay for that."

"You'll have to catch me first." She laughed as she took off running toward the narrow stream, splashing into the shallow water.

Chance took off after her. Man, the view was great. He liked the way her bottom bounced just a little as she ran, but when she stopped and turned back to face him, Chance was mesmerized. Her breasts were high and full, her nipples hard nubs from the coolness of the water. She had a small waist that flared to her softly rounded hips. Her stomach was flat. His gaze lowered to the damp curls at the juncture of her legs. His dick jerked as if it had a mind of its own. When Destiny was around, it pretty much did.

She waded to the middle of the narrow stream; the water barely reached her knees. "Join me," she said.

He had a feeling she didn't mean just in the water. No, she wanted him with her in Hell. But he couldn't stop his feet from closing the short distance that separated them. Once he stood in front of her, he reached to pull her closer.

"Go to Hell with me."

Chance could see she held her breath, waiting for his answer.

"I'd rather take you to Heaven."

Her eyebrows drew together. "I'm serious."

"So am I." He pulled her against him, lowering his mouth to hers. His kiss was deep, forceful, as he tried to erase all thoughts of Hell from her mind. He wanted to kiss her until she forgot why she was there. Then he wanted to tell her what it would feel like to be reborn. How her life could be so much different from what it had been. Then he would let her go.

Ah damnation! He didn't want to let her go. He wanted to keep her with him always. He wanted to be with her when he showed her another side to living.

But that wouldn't happen.

"I want to make love," he told her after he ended the kiss.

"There are things you don't know about me," she admitted.

"As there are things you don't know about me. But we have now, and we're together, and I want to make love to you."

She hesitated, then nodded. "I want you to make love to me."

"Open for me." His words were raspy. She didn't hesitate spreading her legs. He lifted her, then slowly lowered her until he slipped inside. The heat of her body wrapped around him. He sucked in a deep breath. For a moment, he couldn't move as he held her tight. He needed the connection. Needed to feel like he was a part of her, even knowing he couldn't make it last.

Chance didn't move. Instead, he absorbed her body into his. Every part of her became a part of him. He wanted her totally and completely etched in his mind forever. He didn't ask himself how he could feel so strongly about Destiny. He didn't ask because he was afraid of the answer, and to admit what he felt could destroy them both.

But after a moment, just being inside her wasn't enough. He moved until he was sitting in the water, Destiny on top of him.

Then, on a deep sigh, she began to move her body. Slowly. It was almost as if she knew why he wanted the connection between them. That it wasn't only about the sex. The intensity was still there, but muted as if she understood the importance of what they had.

Water splashed against them. It reached halfway up her abdomen. The water was clear. Her curls undulated beneath it, giving him erotic glimpses of her naked flesh. He rose to meet her movements. She sucked in a deep breath and leaned back just enough so the connection between them created a tighter fit.

Their gazes locked. He never wanted to look away. Forever would not be long enough to stare at the passion on her face. To see her need. Her desire.

He increased the tempo.

Her breathing came in little puffs. Her chest thrust forward. Her breasts bobbed with the motion of their lovemaking.

She suddenly cried out as release came. He watched her expression, not wanting to miss a thing. Wanting to imbed it in his memory banks forever.

She tightened her inner muscles. He gasped as he came. The very ground beneath him rocked as he released his seed inside her. She wrapped her arms around his neck. Her soft, feminine body pressed against him.

"I love you," she whispered.

Chance thought he might have heard wrong, but no, he didn't think so. Ah man, that wasn't supposed to happen. How could he convince her that she could be reborn again if she didn't want to leave him? He shouldn't have let what was between them go as far as it had. He should have talked to her about a new life days before when he didn't feel the connection.

She stilled. He knew she waited for him to say something, and that she held her breath.

"I love sex with you, too," he finally blurted.

Her body tensed.

Chance knew immediately he had said the wrong thing.

She quickly moved.

"Destiny." He reached for her, but she moved farther away.

"The sex is fantastic, isn't it?" She pasted a fake smile on her face. "I've never experienced anything quite like it." Her laugh was shaky. "We could have a lot of fun together. I mean for eternity."

He watched as she waded back to the bank and climbed out. "Don't do this," he said.

"Do what?" She raised her arms toward the sun as if she could draw from its energy.

God, she was beautiful, and she was desperately trying to find the words that would convince him that he should leave with her.

"We have to talk," he said. "There are things I need to tell you."

Her gaze met his. Chance wished he could wipe away her sadness. Where were the words he needed to say that would convince her to give up her idea of becoming a demon? He raked his fingers through his hair. He was afraid it wouldn't be a good time to bring up being reborn.

Something crossed her face that he couldn't read. She nodded. "You've given me a great time," she told him. "But I really do have... have somewhere to be. LeAnn, my friend, is singing tonight and I promised to be there for her."

"I'm not leaving you alone," he said a little more firmly. He would keep her close, make sure nothing happened to her. He would somehow convince her she could have more, and he would tell her what he was.

"Can we go back to the apartment?" she asked.

He finally gave in and nodded, but he wasn't leaving her.

As she started to dress, he moved out of the water and began to pull on his clothes. She was in no frame of mind to listen to him tell her about how much better life could be if she only trusted him.

He climbed on the motorcycle. The bike shifted when she moved behind him, but her weight didn't meld to his. When she put her arms around his waist, he felt the coldness of her touch, the distance she was putting between them. He felt as if he'd already lost her. It wasn't a feeling he liked.

The ride back to her apartment didn't take nearly as long as he hoped. Not long enough for him to feel her warmth. She climbed off but rather than just walking away, she surprised him by leaning over and kissing him on the lips.

"Thanks for today. I'll see you later?"

"I told you that I'm not leaving."

She looked startled for a moment, then surprise crossed her face. "Do you really mean that?"

"Yeah, I do." He turned the key that killed the engine. "I'll never be very far away from you." He'd always watch over her. Chance wouldn't let her slip through the cracks again.

A soft smile relaxed the tense lines. "Then go."

He shook his head. "I don't understand."

"I have a lot to do before tonight. LeAnn is my friend and I want to help her. I don't want you distracting me."

Chance didn't like the idea of leaving her on her own, but he didn't want to talk to her about being reborn in front of a dirty apartment building, either.

She let her hand slide down the side of his face. He captured it, turning it until the palm was up, then placed a kiss in the center. She shivered.

It was only a few hours until dusk and she still had time remaining before she had to return to Hell. There would be no reason for a demon to bother her. He would give her these few hours with her friend, but that was all. "Tonight?" he confirmed.

"Meet me at the bar where LeAnn will sing."

He nodded and she quickly gave him the address. As he pulled away from the curb, all was right in his world. He would convince her that she could have a better life. He would set her soul free.

He closed his eyes as he went around the corner. When he opened them, he was driving toward the ranch, but there was emptiness inside him that he'd never felt before.

When he set Destiny free, she would be out of his reach forever. He would be able to see her, but he could never be with her again. Her own personal guardian angel.

His gut twisted.

He pulled to a stop in front of the ranch and shut off the engine. For a moment he sat there as if something might occur to him that would change everything. But nothing did. He swung his leg over the side and strode toward the front door.

It was quiet in the house. He closed his eyes and could feel the hum. The others were in the rec room. He debated for a moment then went downstairs.

Hunter looked up from the television when Chance entered the room. He studied him then said, "We were beginning to worry."

"You okay?" Ryder casually asked, but his words were laced with concern.

"I'm fine, before you ask too, Dillon."

"I didn't say anything," Dillon said, then went behind the bar and opened the small refrigerator. He pulled out a beer. "Catch." He tossed the bottle.

Chance easily caught it and twisted off the cap. Foam spewed over the top, but he didn't care as he brought the bottle to his lips and greedily drank. It was cold and went down easy. He only hoped it would numb his senses for a little while.

"How'd it go today?" Ryder asked.

Hunter switched off the television and joined the others as they made their way to the sitting area. Black leather couches were flanked by two black end tables that were ringed from never having seen a coaster. An equally scarred coffee table worked well to prop their feet on. Nothing fancy, but they liked not having rules.

Chance knew to play it casual with them. If they had an inkling he'd fallen for Destiny, they would do whatever it took to keep him safe, even if it cost Destiny her soul.

So he shrugged. "I'm going to tell her exactly what I am tonight. I think she cares enough that I can convince her to be reborn." He began to relax as the reality of his words sank into his brain. He would save her soul. That was what really counted. As long as he could do that, he'd survive.

Chance could feel them studying him, so he took another drink of his beer then lowered the bottle to rest casually on his thigh. "So, what about the three of you? Anything going on?"

No one spoke. Chance was beginning to wonder if they were going to stare at him all night, but then Hunter cleared his throat.

"I got a cat out of a tree," Hunter said.

They stared at him for a moment then began to laugh, and the tension evaporated.

Hunter frowned. "What?"

"Think about what you just told us," Dillon said. He always rationalized everything. "Chance is fighting for someone's soul, and you got a cat out of a tree."

Hunter's frown deepened. "It was an old cat and it was stuck. I like cats. What's wrong with that?"

Chance hid his smile. "Nothing. Nothing at all." He knew not to look at Dillon and Ryder or they would all three start laughing and then Hunter would kick their asses. So instead he took another drink of beer.

"I don't have anything going on," Dillon finally added to the conversation.

A good thing, too. It was getting uncomfortable the way Hunter glared at them.

Ryder shrugged. "I answered a couple of prayers." He suddenly grinned. "And there was this cute little blond that wanted a pair of shoes really bad. They were gold with little sparkles all over the heels."

"And did she get them?" Dillon asked.

Ryder sighed. "Yes, but I have to admit she wanted me more."

The other three groaned as Ryder launched into very specific details on how he gave the young lady exactly what she wanted.

A lively conversation ensued about women. Chance let the other three carry the conversation as he finished his beer, then got up and got another one.

Before he rejoined the others, he leaned against the bar and watched their animated conversation. They were his family. The only family he'd ever really known. He loved them like brothers.

A cold premonition swept over him, but he shook it off. Nothing would go wrong tonight. Destiny would take what he offered. Her soul would be free. Anything else was unacceptable.

Chapter 19

DESTINY WATCHED UNTIL THE roar of Chance's bike disappeared around the corner, but she didn't go inside. Instead she went for a walk, hoping it would clear her head.

It didn't.

Maybe he didn't tell her that he loved her, but he still wanted to see her again, she rationalized. And he cared. A lot. But would it be enough? Her hands began to tremble. It just had to be.

Tonight she would tell him exactly what she was and then she would know exactly where she stood. It had to be tonight. Tomorrow night she would have to return even if she failed. A shudder swept over her. She had to convince Chance to leave with her. They were meant to be together, she could feel it all the way to her heart. A lot was riding on what Chance would do. He said he would never leave her.

She almost ran over Beulah when she rounded the corner. She was the last person Destiny needed to run into. When the woman started to speak, Destiny held up her hand. "I really don't want to hear it."

"I apologize," she blurted.

Had she heard right? "What?"

Beulah pursed her lips as if she'd just sucked on a lemon. "Charles said I can't let one man make me hate the world." She smoothed her hands down the front of her slacks.

"Really?" Was the world about to end?

"That doesn't mean you still don't need to be a little quieter when you have... have..."

"Sex?" Destiny supplied.

"Yes." She didn't meet Destiny's gaze.

"And why would you apologize just because Charles told you to?" Destiny couldn't see Beulah doing anyone's bidding.

"Because he said if I was going to be his wife, he didn't want me running off all his friends. So like I said, I'm sorry."

Destiny opened her mouth, but no words came out.

Beulah was frowning when she looked up. "What, you don't think a man could love me?"

"No, it's not that."

Beulah squared her shoulders. "I know I'm not much to look at." Her face suddenly softened, and Destiny finally saw a bit of what Charles must see. This was a softer side. "Charles is a good man. I've known him for years. He won't be like that other one. I've still got some of my money. He didn't get it all. Charles doesn't know it, but he's going to have that ranch he's always wanted. A small one, but maybe a horse or two, and a few head of cattle." She ran out of breath and her flood of words stopped abruptly.

"I think you'll make a great couple."

Beulah studied her for a moment. Maybe she wanted to make sure Destiny wasn't making fun of her. She apparently decided she wasn't.

"Thank you." She hurried away.

Destiny was at a loss for words. The sooner she was away from these mortals the better. She couldn't help feeling just a little happy for the old battle-axe, though.

Destiny was about to step inside the elevator when she heard a familiar voice call out to her. Great, another one.

"I'm terrified," LeAnn wailed. She waved her hands about, opened her mouth, then snapped it closed without saying a word.

"Of what?" Fear filled Destiny as she glanced around. Had a mugger chased LeAnn? It certainly wasn't the best part of town. Destiny did a quick head-to-toe check but found no dangling limbs. Not even a bruise.

"About tonight. I don't think I can do it."

Destiny breathed a sigh of relief as her heart slowed to a more normal rate. "Is that all?"

LeAnn's eyes widened as she marched into the elevator. "Is that all?" She snorted. "Believe me, that's plenty." She slumped against the back wall as though all her energy had just drained away.

"You really are scared," Destiny said.

LeAnn shook her head. "Nope, I'm way beyond scared." Her face crumpled. "What am I going to do?"

Destiny planted her hands on her hips as the elevator chugged its way upward. "You're going to stop talking like that right now, that's what you're going to do. You're a very good singer. This is your chance to shine and if you don't take it, I'll… I'll shove your head in the toilet."

LeAnn took a step back, forehead wrinkling. "Really?"

The girl was so gullible. "No, I wouldn't shove your head in the toilet."

LeAnn laughed, a bit shaky, but still a laugh. "I meant about you thinking that I'm a good singer. Not shoving my head in a toilet."

"Oh."

"Do you really think so?" LeAnn hurried on before Destiny could answer. "Don't lie to me. You can tell me the truth. I swear it won't hurt my feelings. I mean, I've watched *American Idol* and they've had some horrid singers, but their friends and family have been too nice and actually convinced them they could sing but they can't and I don't want to be like them." Her rambling stuttered to a stop.

What the hell was *American Idol*? LeAnn was making no sense whatsoever. It didn't matter. Destiny suddenly felt like an older sister and something inside her softened right then and there.

She placed her hands on LeAnn's shoulders and looked her right in the eyes. "I think you're one of the best singers I've heard in a long time and I've only heard a little of your amazing talent. You have what it takes—except for needing a little more confidence. You'll go far, but you have to believe in yourself."

"Believe in myself," she repeated.

Destiny nodded as the elevator came to a grinding stop.

"I can do that, I think." LeAnn nibbled on her bottom lip.

They stepped out of the elevator and walked toward Destiny's apartment, but once they were at the door LeAnn leaned against the wall and sighed, her expression dejected.

"No, I can't. That's why I've never made it to Nashville. I make plans, but that's as far as I get." Her short laugh was derisive. "I even have a folder of exactly what I need to do, all the way down to what bus I'll take and where I can find cheap rent. But I never leave." Tears swam in her eyes.

"Why?"

"I'm afraid of rejection." She chewed her bottom lip. "What if they don't like me?" she whispered.

"Not everyone will, but who cares about them?"

"I do."

Destiny paused before opening the door. "No, you don't. You only think you do. Those people don't matter. There will be people who don't like your way of singing, but it doesn't mean you're not still a good singer."

"I don't have anything to wear, either." She rubbed the tears out of her eyes and squared her shoulders as if she already had her mind made up. "I might as well just not show up."

"You will show up and yes, you do have something to wear."

LeAnn frowned. "No, I don't. Just worn jeans and a boring top.

I picked it up in a thrift shop. It has lots of stupid ruffles. A dumb purchase. The shirt is butt ugly. I have no style."

"You're beautiful and that's all that people will see. Besides, I found a suit the other day and thought about you. It's hanging in my closet. I was going to give it to you today so you might as well pick it up now."

She straightened. "Really?"

"Yes, really, now come inside and I'll give it to you." Okay, she hadn't bought the suit, but creating a killer outfit was no biggie. If it would get LeAnn on stage, even better.

Destiny opened the door, but when LeAnn began to talk again, she turned her attention back to her friend.

"I can't believe you bought me a suit to wear. No one has ever bought me anything. Well, not in a very long time, that is. And I think you're so stylish. You could have stepped out of a magazine." She came to an abrupt stop, her eyes growing round. "Oh, you have company."

Destiny's gaze jerked up. She froze as her stomach began to churn.

"There you are," Vetis said as he rose from the sofa. "I'd wondered where you went, but I can see you've been spending time with this lovely lady."

LeAnn blushed. "We met up in the elevator."

Vetis stopped in front of them, then reached for LeAnn's hand and placed a kiss on it. "Very lovely," he murmured as his gaze raked over her.

"Vetis, I wasn't expecting you again so soon." Destiny nervously looked at the demon.

When his eyes turned to her, she took a step back from the anger she saw. Something was terribly wrong. He was furious with her for some reason. What the hell did she do? And how could she make it better?

Vetis looked at LeAnn again, immediately turning on the charm. "Destiny didn't properly introduce us. I'm her cousin."

LeAnn frowned when she looked at Destiny. "I thought you grew up in foster homes?"

The fire burned brighter in his eyes, then cooled. "We found each other later in life. It's quite a touching story. I'd love to tell you all about it some time."

Destiny noticed Vetis didn't let go of LeAnn's hand. He was rubbing his thumb lightly back and forth over it. A new fear settled inside Destiny as she realized exactly what he was doing. Vetis was seducing LeAnn.

LeAnn shyly smiled, moving a little closer to the demon. "I'd like to hear all about how you found each other. I love stories with happy endings." Her eyes misted. "Will you be staying here for a while?"

"As long as it takes." He paused. "To tell you all about our reunion, that is."

"I'll just get the outfit," Destiny quickly said, but she wasn't sure LeAnn heard her.

Destiny practically ran to the bedroom. Once there, she closed her eyes as her knees went weak. *Oh please, don't let Vetis hurt her.* There was still so much that was innocent about LeAnn. She glanced up. But would anyone hear her plea? They never had in the past.

This time was different. Destiny was a lost cause, but not LeAnn. For Destiny, there was only one choice. That wasn't the case for LeAnn, if Vetis didn't interfere. Somehow she had to convince the demon that LeAnn wasn't worth his time.

But first she had to get LeAnn out of the apartment.

LeAnn had once *oohed* and *ahhed* over an outfit in one of Destiny's magazines. The first time she met her, in fact. They were going up in the elevator. Black jeans and a black fitted jacket that had black crystals on the lapels. A plain, black knit tee and black boots. It would have been too much black except there was a sexy little necklace in soft pink beads and heart-shaped crystal. LeAnn had said it was bling-bling and that every girl needed it.

Whatever.

The magazine had, thankfully, ended up on top of the dresser. Destiny grabbed it and quickly thumbed through until she got to the right page. With one sweep of her hand, she changed the outfit from being on a page to hanging on a hanger, the boots sitting on the floor.

She grabbed everything and hurried back to the other room. Vetis was lightly running his fingers up and down LeAnn's arm in a casual gesture, but Destiny knew better.

"Here you go," she called out.

LeAnn jumped, moving away from Vetis. His eyes narrowed, but Destiny didn't care. LeAnn was her friend. Her only one ever, and she wasn't about to let Vetis entice LeAnn to Hell. Not when the girl had a chance at more.

"No way!" LeAnn said, rushing to Destiny. "But how?"

"My cousin can do most anything she sets her mind to," Vetis said, then his eyes narrowed. "She only has to focus."

Destiny heard the double entendre and understood perfectly that he thought she wasn't focused on why she was there.

"Wait a minute." LeAnn snapped her fingers. "This is the exact suit I showed you the first day we met. It was in one of your magazines." She fingered the beads on the lapel. "How?"

"A thrift store."

"No way," she breathed, then squared her shoulders as her expression turned solemn. "I can't take it."

"And why not?" The girl could be so exasperating!

"It's far too nice to just give away."

"I can't wear it. You're shorter than me."

"But—"

"Either you take it or I'll toss it in the trash." She made a move to follow through with her threat.

"No! I'll take it!"

"Then you'd better hurry and get ready. This is your night to shine."

"It is." But before LeAnn took the hanger, she hugged Destiny.

For a moment Destiny couldn't move, then she returned the gesture. Her toes curled. She couldn't stop the warmth that spread over her like sweet maple syrup drizzling over fluffy pancakes. Destiny had never felt so strong a connection to another woman. They really could have been sisters.

In a heartbeat, LeAnn stepped away.

"Don't forget the boots." Destiny cleared her throat, blinking away the moisture in her eyes.

"Oh yeah." LeAnn smiled sheepishly. "It was nice meeting you," she shyly told Vetis. "I hope you'll be able to tell me all about how you found Destiny before you leave."

His smile was that of a snake about to strike its prey. "Oh, I can guarantee we'll meet again."

LeAnn blushed and hurried to the door. As soon as it closed behind her, Destiny turned to Vetis.

"Don't hurt her."

"Me? Hurt her? Have you lost faith in me so soon?"

She glanced away as he meandered closer. She knew better than to push him.

"You think you have it all figured out," he continued.

She squared her shoulders and met his gaze once again. "I know I don't have it all figured out, but I know LeAnn has more of a chance at living a good life than I ever did."

"And the man you've been fucking?" His words were silky smooth. "Do you have him figured out yet?"

Her heart stopped, then began to pound inside her chest. Vetis knew about Chance. That she'd made love to him. Her gut told her there was something terribly wrong.

"What do you mean?"

"Do you really think he will return to Hell with you? That you'll have your quota and the two of you will live happily ever after for all eternity?" He circled behind her, then stopped in front and ran his hand down the side of her face.

Destiny gritted her teeth at the burning pain he left on her skin. She wouldn't let him know how much his touch burned, but it was all she could do not to cry out. And beneath the pain, she wondered how he found out about Chance.

"Do you love him?" Vetis casually asked.

"Of course not," she lied.

"You probably think he loves you, too," he continued as if she agreed with him.

What did he know? His expression told her nothing as a sick feeling began to form in the pit of her stomach.

"I watched the two of you today," he ground out, but the whole time he smiled.

Fear so intense that she swayed swept over her. Please don't hurt Chance, she silently begged.

"I saw him plunge inside your body and the look of ecstasy on your face. I never saw that look of passion on your face when I fucked you," he snarled.

"No, it was only sex," she whimpered.

"Only sex?" he roared. "Is that why you told him that you loved him?"

"I'm sorry." Everything began to crumble around her. How could she have let her relationship with Chance go so far?

"You don't even know he's playing you for a fool."

She stilled, her heart falling to her feet.

No, this was just another game he played, but one look at his serious expression and she knew this was not a game he played. "What do you mean?"

"You've cast me aside for a nephilim, you stupid, stupid girl! An immortal!"

The room began to spin. Vetis lied! He lied!
Chance couldn't be immortal.

Chapter 20

VETIS SUDDENLY TRANSFORMED INTO something hideous. The horned monster standing in front of her bore no resemblance to the handsome demon who once seduced her. Dark red skin stretched across muscle and bone, the ligaments and tendons visible. The creature's eyes glowed yellow with black triangular slits.

Destiny's terror intensified. She stumbled back, wanting to run. Knowing there was nowhere she could hide.

In the blink of an eye, Vetis shifted back to the angry seducer. Handsome once again, but trembling with rage. He turned away, drawing in a deep breath, then faced her once more. Had she only imagined the change in his appearance? She knew the mind could play tricks on the eye when someone was consumed with fear.

Destiny ran a weary hand across her forehead, eyes closed. She wasn't sure what she saw. It happened too fast.

"Your lover is a nephilim. An immortal," he repeated.

Her hand dropped to her side. What game did Vetis play? "Nephilim?" She didn't know this word, but she did know Chance wasn't an immortal. He couldn't be. Wouldn't she have sensed it? He was a cowboy, nothing more.

"I see he hasn't mentioned any of this to you." He smirked.

She studied Vetis. There was something in his expression that said he wasn't lying. Ice crystals began to form inside her veins and around her heart.

Chance an immortal? Why didn't he tell her? No, it couldn't be true. They were lovers.

A niggle of doubt weaved its way through her. What did she really know about him? He wore a cowboy hat, so she assumed he was a cowboy.

What did he tell her about his life? Nothing whatsoever. He took her out, showed her a good time, but he wouldn't be the first man to have done that while all the time he had a different agenda.

They did have a good time. The sex was fantastic, but spending time with Chance was more than that. They were comfortable with each other. He took her to the rodeo, bought her a hat. They laughed. He risked his life when he rode the bull.

Or had he? Immortals didn't die.

Doubts flooded her. Did she only see what she wanted to see?

No, Vetis lied.

Destiny studied the demon. He was gloating. The sick feeling inside her grew. She knew without a doubt that what Vetis was about to tell her wouldn't be good, but it would be the truth.

"Angels came down from heaven and mated with mortal women," he explained as his eyes narrowed angrily. "See, and I bet you thought angels were pure and untarnished by the world," he spat. "No, they laid with these women, then the women bore their unholy children—nephilim. The brats like to think they're demigods." His satanic laughter filled the room. "And now one has seduced you."

"No." She put up a hand as if she could stop the words he flung toward her.

"No?" His lips thinned. "You still want to believe the best about him, don't you?"

"Chance didn't lie." She shook her head.

If she hoped for a sudden miracle, it didn't come. No, Vetis still stood in front of her, waiting for her to stop denying what was right in front of her.

The words Chance had uttered that afternoon came back to haunt her. *I'd rather take you to Heaven.*

She stumbled away from Vetis, sitting on the sofa with a hard thud. No, the demon lied. Vetis had been lying to her from the start. Hadn't he? Chance was all that was good in her world. He wouldn't lie to her. Not when she loved him so much.

Her hands began to shake. She held them, forcing the trembling to stop. The sick feeling inside her grew stronger.

"He wants to convince you that you can be reborn again. That you could be perfect." Vetis snorted. "As though that would ever happen!"

She dragged her gaze to his. "What?"

"You're not paying attention!" He closed his eyes for a moment, took a deep breath as though he barely held his temper in check, then looked at her once again as he began to explain. "He's going to tell you that he can give you another chance to relive your life by literally being born again."

"To live again?"

"Exactly!" he said as if she finally got a very important question correct. "Of course, there's no guarantee your life will be any different. Who's to say it wouldn't be exactly the same. Or worse."

"No, it's not true." She shook her head.

"Isn't it?"

She reached up, touching the necklace Chance had given her, but as her fingers ran over the angel wings, she quickly dropped the charm as if it had burned her.

An angel, of course.

He'd mentioned more than once how her life could be better. She thought she was seducing him, but he was the seducer. Again she let someone into her life, and that person lied to her.

"He was never planning to spend all of eternity with you." Vetis delivered his last blow. "As soon as you're reborn, the rules change for him. You can never be together. He'll move on to the next pathetic person whom he believes needs saving while you're left all alone once more to fend for yourself."

The couch sank as Vetis sat next to her. He opened his arms. She hesitated before going into them, letting him wrap her in his warm embrace. At least with Vetis she knew where she stood. He'd told her from the beginning that he wanted her soul. Chance lied about everything.

"I thought he would return to Hell with me," she whispered as the cold feeling moved over her.

"I know."

A tear slipped from the corner of her eye and trailed down her cheek. "He was never planning to go with me."

"No. Not even for a minute."

She sniffed. She was so stupid. She fell in love with an angel. How ironic. Didn't Chance know she belonged in Hell?

Chance. She sucked in a deep breath as reality set in completely. It was over. There would be no living an eternity with him. That's why he didn't tell her that he loved her. He'd only wanted to steal her soul. He'd used her like all the others.

She buried her face against Vetis's chest as pain ripped through her. She just wanted everything and everyone to go away.

"But you still have to meet your quota." Vetis's voice penetrated past the ache that buried itself deep inside her. "I won't be able to stop the others if you don't." He lightly stroked his hand up and down her back.

She stiffened in his arms as his words sank into her brain. "What do you mean?"

"The tribunal."

She closed her eyes tight as if she could will his words away. Everyone in Hell had heard of the tribunal. Demons who were almost as old as time. People said once you went before the council, you were already doomed. They always found the person guilty.

A shiver of dread swept over her. The rest was guessing on everyone's part, but she had a feeling all the things she heard might be pretty close to the truth, which scared her even more.

When Vetis continued, Destiny knew she had to listen.

"You will go before the tribunal. There are six of us in all. I'll be there, but I'm afraid they will join against me."

"What will they do?"

He patted her back. "You still have time to get your quota. Think of it this way, you'll be giving someone a chance at a brand new life where everything can be theirs. Dreams waiting to be fulfilled. Riches beyond their imagination. Who wouldn't want to trade their soul for all that?"

Except she had yet to see any of what he'd offered her in exchange for her soul. No, Destiny couldn't do it. She didn't have enough time to convince someone to return to Hell with her.

"I can't. I need a few more days. You could talk to them."

He shook his head. "I'm sorry. Our laws have been in place for centuries. I couldn't change them even for you, my love."

"What will they do if I fail?" she asked as she straightened from his arms.

Pity showed in his eyes. "They will cast you into the fires of Hell. There you will burn for all eternity, never dying. You will be driven insane by the pain, but it will always be with you."

Destiny sucked in a deep breath as she pushed out of his arms and jumped to her feet. She began to pace across the floor as images of constant pain filled her head. How would she be able to stand that kind of sustained torture? Fear trembled over her. She tamped down the hysteria building inside her. No, she wouldn't let it happen.

She suddenly stopped, turning to him, raising her chin. "Help me. You can if you want. You have to help me."

He opened his hands, palms up. "Why do you only call upon me when you're desperate," he shook his head, his eyes turning sad, "only to reject me when I'm no longer needed?"

He was right, and she felt his disappointment in her. She hurried over, knelt in front of him, and rested her head on his knees. "Forgive me," she cried.

"Shh, hush, sweet child." He patted her head. "How can I let them cast you into the fires when I love you so much?"

She raised her face, eyes swimming with tears. "You do?"

"I love all my children."

"You'll help me?"

"Just bring me LeAnn's soul and all will be right."

Chapter 21

CHANCE WENT INSIDE THE bar when he first arrived but didn't spot Destiny. The man he met at the rodeo, Charles Dickens, was sitting at a table with an odd-looking woman near the stage. He overheard the woman grumbling about everything from how the place stank, with which Chance agreed, to predicting that the night was going to hell in a handbag quicker than a speeding train filled with ex-cons.

The old cowboy seemed likable when he'd met him at the rodeo, but Chance didn't want to get into a conversation with him right then, and definitely not with the woman. He was more concerned about why Destiny wasn't there yet.

Chance stepped back outside. The fresh air was a vast improvement. The bar smelled like old booze, stale cigarette smoke, and unwashed bodies. A dark, dreary olive green color paint had been slapped on the walls. Nothing about the place tempted him to sit and enjoy a beer.

No one waited outside. There were a few cars driving down the road, people getting off work. Chance glanced at his watch. It was still early.

Maybe she was just running late.

Chance pushed on the door and went back inside. He hoped there was another entrance that he might have missed. His eyes adjusted to the dim light. The choking fog of stale cigarette smoke hovered above the twenty or so patrons who had decided to come out. But Destiny wasn't there.

A heavyset man lumbered up the three steps to a stage that wasn't much bigger than the bathroom in the apartment where Destiny was staying. A fat cigar protruded from one side of his mouth, the end glowing red when he puffed. His shirt might have been white at one time, but now it was a grease-splotched beige color.

The man stopped in front of a microphone perched on a rusted metal stand and hitched up his pants. "I'm the manager of this bar, so make sure you drink up. Can't stay in business if you don't. Besides, it's the cheapest booze in town."

"'Cause you water it down," someone yelled.

The handful of people laughed while the owner glared at them.

"You can leave if you don't like it," he growled and people quieted down. When no one stood up to leave, the owner plastered a smirk on his face. "That's what I thought."

The door to the bar opened. Chance looked hopeful, but a man walked in, looked around, then waved at a woman before he joined her.

"I even have someone to sing for you," the owner told the small crowd. "This here's—" His eyes narrowed when he looked toward a dark corner. "What's your name, girlie?"

"LeAnn West," came her whispered reply.

Where was Destiny?

"Welcome LeAnn onto the stage." He laughed. "She's real pretty, and cheap." He guffawed at his joke. "Free, actually."

As soon as the owner lumbered down the steps, LeAnn made her way to the stage. She had a guitar strap slung over her shoulder and was holding the instrument so tight that Chance thought it would crack any second.

Chance almost didn't recognize the girl he'd met at the rodeo. She was dressed to the nines in a black outfit with sequined lapels. A pink heart-shaped necklace captured the light and cast a rainbow of color around her. He'd bet his wings, if he had any, that Destiny was behind getting the outfit.

Not that it helped. LeAnn chewed her bottom lip as she searched the crowd. He knew she hunted for Destiny.

Oh, please, dear God, help me. I'm scared shitless. No, no, I didn't mean to say that. I meant to say I'm just really scared.

Her desperate prayer drifted to him. Chance knew he had to help her. He closed his eyes, wanting to give her the courage she prayed for, but he felt the invisible wall that rose in front of him.

His shoulders slumped as he opened his eyes and saw her fear again. Sometimes it was like that. There were some people they weren't meant to help and nothing they did could change the outcome. Some things were meant to be. It didn't mean he had to like it, though.

"I was expecting my friend." Her laugh cracked. "Something must've happened."

"You gonna sing or talk?" the manager yelled out.

Charles half stood as he turned in his seat. "You shut your trap or I'll be doing it for you."

The manager snapped his mouth shut and went back to wiping off the bar with a dirty rag. "It's my bar," he groused, but not loud enough Charles would've heard him.

LeAnn gripped the guitar even tighter, then defiantly raised her chin and drew in a deep breath, but as soon as she did her nose wrinkled in distaste. Chance had to give her credit for the quick recovery as she started to talk again.

"This is a song I wrote for my brother." She cleared her throat and began to strum the strings of the guitar.

Some of the people began to talk to each other. Laughter drifted from one of the tables. Chance wanted to yell at them to shut up, but he was afraid it would make LeAnn even more self-conscious.

"You were always the one I looked up to," she sang.

Her voice was soft, barely heard above the patrons who were talking and laughing a little louder now.

"Walking side by side."

Chance glared at the crowd as she continued to sing. They were rednecks who only cared if they had enough money to buy another beer.

A waitress waddled out with a longneck and slapped the bottle down on a scarred table. "Two-fifty." She stuck a dirty fingernail between her two front teeth, brought out whatever had been left over from her last meal, and wiped it on her skirt.

"Two-fifty? Whatever happened to happy hour?"

"Do I look happy?" she sneered.

He thrust a five toward her. "I want all my change, too."

"Cheap bastard," she muttered as she left.

Charles started to stand again, but the woman with him patted his hand and pointed toward LeAnn. Smart woman. If Charles started a brawl, it would only make the night worse for LeAnn.

Chance turned his attention back to LeAnn who was looking less sure of herself, but she struggled onward.

"You were the one I admired.
With hero worship in my eyes."

Someone dropped a quarter in the jukebox. Chance tensed as a record dropped into place. He couldn't take his eyes off the needle as it made its way across to the turnstile, then dropped in place. His gaze jerked back to LeAnn as a fast beat country song began to play.

A woman jumped up from her chair and began to dance in front of the stage. "Sorry, darlin', but this is real music! Yee-haw!"

The color drained from LeAnn's face. Her gaze flitted around the room and her bottom lip trembled. She hugged her guitar close to her chest and fled the stage. Her thoughts hit him hard and fast.

"Not good enough! Stupid, stupid, stupid! You'll never be anything, will never amount to anything!"

Chance reached a hand toward her as she ran past, but just as quickly he brought it back. She didn't even see him and it wouldn't have done any good if she had. It wasn't her time. Not right now.

"You stupid broad!" The woman with Charles stood up, marched over to the dancing woman, reared back her fist and knocked the fool out of her. The dazed woman found herself sitting on her ass in the middle of the dirty dance floor.

"That's my Beulah," Charles sang out. "Darlin', you're the woman I've been waiting for all my life." He grabbed her in a bear hug and planted a wet one on her lips. When he let her go, she quickly stepped back.

"Charles Dickens, we're in a public place." She smoothed her hands over her very proper, dark green dress. Anyone might think she was offended, but Chance saw the pleased look on her face before she quickly pulled on an affronted mask.

"That's exactly why I did it," Charles countered. "I want the world to know you're my gal."

Chance scanned the bar one more time. He still didn't have his answers. Where was Destiny?

—⁓—

When LeAnn ran out of the bar, the heat of the day slapped her in the face. Why did she even try? The bar was filthy and stank. It was a dump. A short burst of laughter erupted from her. If that was the best she could do, giving up might not be a bad idea.

She hurried to the street where her car was parked curbside. Tears blurred her vision. She jerked the strap off her shoulder, holding the guitar by the neck. For a moment, she pictured slamming the instrument against the sidewalk, but something stopped her at the last moment.

Her brother Ernie had given her the guitar. He'd been her best friend, bigger than life itself. As she unlocked the car door and climbed inside, she let the memories flood her mind.

Ernie grinning and patting her on the head when he gave her the instrument. "Someday you'll be a famous singer. You've already got talent."

He believed in her and taught her to play the instrument. Maybe he was only teasing, but she didn't think so at the time. She reached across to the passenger seat and stroked her hand over the smooth surface of the guitar. "Why couldn't I die with them?"

A tear slipped from the corner of her eye, then another. She'd had everything. A mom and dad who loved her and her big brother. The tears came faster. She didn't try to stop them, only wiped the back of her hand across her face.

Her chest began to ache and she could barely draw in a breath. "Oh God, why didn't you let me die, too?" Maybe there wasn't a God. You lived, then you died. That was it. Nothing else.

No, she wouldn't think like that. There had to be something more. They had to be waiting for her somewhere. She couldn't bear the thought of never seeing them again. She hugged her middle.

The pain drove deep inside her heart. Oh damn, she'd lost so much. She wanted to curl up and die. Let the world go on without her. There was nothing left. She had no one. Destiny didn't care enough to show up.

A sudden thought chilled LeAnn to the bone. What if Destiny was in an accident? Oh damn, how selfish could one person be? Here she was feeling sorry for herself and Destiny could be in a hospital somewhere dying. Some friend she was. She was more worried that she bombed tonight. Who cared about her old singing career anyway?

LeAnn started the car and pulled away from the curb. Where should she start looking? The hospitals? Her stomach churned. *Please, God, I know you didn't hear me tonight when I prayed for courage, and maybe some of my prayers have been all about me, but for just this one prayer, please keep Destiny from harm. Watch over her, Lord.*

LeAnn only hoped God would hear this prayer.

Chapter 22

"The door was unlocked," Chance said as he came into the living room. "Are you okay?"

Destiny looked up from where she was curled on the sofa. How could one man be so breathtakingly handsome? But then he wasn't just a man, was he?

And the door wasn't unlocked.

But then Chance was an angel. He could probably go anywhere he wanted. She uncurled her legs, but didn't bother getting up. "Have you been worried about me?"

His forehead furrowed. "You missed LeAnn's performance."

A niggle of guilt weaved through her. She had forgotten LeAnn was singing tonight. There was only one thought going through her mind: Chance betrayed her. Now the only way to redeem herself would be if she took the soul of the only person who had ever befriended her.

He started toward her, but she held up her hand. "You don't love me, do you?" she asked. She could see his hesitation as if he carefully chose his words.

"I care deeply for you."

"But you can't let yourself fall in love with me."

He expelled a deep breath. "No, I can't."

Her gaze raked over him. "You don't fuck like an angel." She laughed. "But you are a damn good lay."

"How did you find out?"

"Vetis told me," she absently replied.

He stiffened and some of the color left his face. "Vetis?" he asked, as if he might have heard wrong.

"Yes, Vetis. The demon who bought my soul, but you knew all that, didn't you?"

He shook his head. "No, I didn't know which demon it was."

"What difference does it make?" she spat. "You lied to me." She came to her feet. "Everything about you is a lie."

"What about you?" he fired back. "You don't know this demon. He's powerful and he's mean. Everything about him is a lie!"

"And you're not! I was ready to spend an eternity with you." She drew in a deep breath, reining in her anger as she looked at the man she had loved, damn it, still loved. "We could be together. It's not too late." Damn, she hated how she sounded, the begging note that had crept into her voice.

"Let me give you a new life," he said.

"How?"

"You can be reborn. It won't be easy breaking your contract with Vetis, but I'll do whatever it takes to keep you safe."

"Then what?"

"You would be born again. Just like I said. I would watch over you."

Didn't he know that being without him would be a hell all its own? Even if she didn't remember him, she would know something was missing in her life. But apparently he wouldn't have that same problem. She was just another notch on his halo.

"I would make sure your next life was better," he promised.

A cold chill of foreboding washed over her. "You know what my life was like?" She studied his face and saw the truth before he answered.

"I know about it," he said.

"Everything?"

"Yes."

For a brief moment she saw pity in his eyes before he masked it. She raised her chin. All this time he knew about her mother leaving her, the foster homes, living on the streets, that she'd murdered a man. The shame was almost too much to bear.

"Leave," she said.

"I can't."

"I'm not asking."

"You still need a soul."

"Don't you think I know that!"

"Let me help you."

She inched nearer until she was only a breath away. "Let me help you?" she repeated, running her hand down the side of his face, caressing his jaw. He leaned toward her, but stopped at the last second. Maybe all wasn't lost.

She raked her fingers over the front of his shirt, felt his nipples tighten. She flicked a fingernail across one. He groaned.

"Can you feel the heat? We could have this all the time."

"Don't." His words were gravelly, as if it took all he had inside him just to speak.

"All eternity. Just you and me."

"Vetis lied to you."

"He saved me from being beaten to death," she countered, her hand moving downward.

"You had no choice."

She rubbed her hand against him. He was already hard. "Go with me back to Hell."

He lowered his lips to hers, but right before his lips touched hers he said, "Let me give you a new life. A better life."

He pulled her tight against him. His lips molded to hers as his tongue thrust inside her mouth. Each tried to claim victory over the other in the kiss.

One minute they were in the apartment and the next, the evening breeze brushed across her skin. She pulled out of his arms. "Where are we?" she asked as she nervously looked around. They were on top of a hill, surrounded by the gently rolling countryside. She drew in a shaky breath and her senses were filled with the heady aroma of wildflowers.

Her short laugh bordered on hysterical. He was a nephilim, an immortal like herself, that's how he managed to transport them to another place. He probably had powers far greater than she could imagine. "Take me home." She put more distance between them.

"You have no home," he said as he ambled nearer.

"I do too." She wondered at this new game he played.

"What? Hell?" His laugh was bitter. "That's not a home. You'll only find pain and despair there."

She crossed her arms. "No, I found that on Earth when I was alive."

He stopped in front of her, then walked behind her. "Life can be sweet." He spoke close to her ear.

Destiny jumped as his warm breath caressed her cheek. "I like what I have now." His grimace made her take a step back.

With a sweep of his hand, the air around her grew so warm she could feel a trickle of sweat slide between her breasts and it was all she could do to take a deep breath.

"Is it too hot for you?" he asked as he made his way around to stand a few feet in front of her. "Better get used to it."

"I'm comfortable."

"You're sweating."

Two could play his game. "You're right. It is rather warm." She reached for the hem of her shirt and pulled it over her head, tossing it to the ground. "Oh, that's much better." She brought her hands up, letting her breasts fall into the palms of her hands.

If he wanted to play dirty, fine, but she knew all the tricks. She'd show him dirty. She took a step toward him, he took a step back.

"What's the matter? Afraid you might get burned?" she purred.

His eyes narrowed as he let his gaze rake down her body, then returned to meet her eyes. "Not on your life, sweetheart. Not when I'll be causing the heat."

He pulled off his shirt. The shadows of the setting sun played off his tanned muscles, making her mouth water. Damn, he was some kind of gorgeous. But when her gaze traveled back to his face, she could tell he thought he'd already won the game.

Not so.

"In Hell, we could be together for all eternity," she pressed as she slid the zipper down on her jeans. Her hands slid inside. She let her eyes drift closed and bit her bottom lip as her fingernails grazed her mound. "I'm so freakin' sensitive."

"Don't do this, Destiny. In Hell, we would burn until there was nothing left of the people we are now."

She opened her eyes and frowned, slipping her hands from her jeans. He really knew how to kill the mood. "You're wrong. Vetis promised I would have everything I've ever dreamed about." She slapped a hand to her chest. "Everything that was denied to me in life. I've earned it. I've more than paid my dues!"

"He lied! Everything he has ever told you has been a lie." Chance stepped closer.

She moved away from him, keeping him at a safe distance. "No, I don't believe you." Because if Vetis had conned her, then what was left? Nothing. Absolutely nothing. She couldn't relive her life. It was worse than any hell she might face.

"You'll be cast into the burning fires," he continued. "Only when all that was human is gone will you reach demon status, but by then you'll be so eaten away by the pain you've suffered, there will be nothing human left."

She stumbled back another step, shaking her head. "No."

His eyes were sad. "I'm telling you the truth."

"Just like when you told the truth about who you are?" She jutted her chin.

"I never lied."

"You didn't tell me you were a nephilim, either."

"Would you have stuck around if I had? Or would you have run away?"

She turned and grabbed her shirt off the ground when he moved closer, and slipped it over her head. "No, I won't listen to any more." He was wasting her time. "Return me to the apartment."

"So you can find another soul to steal?"

"Yes. You know why I'm here."

"Please don't."

She drew in a ragged breath. "I have no choice."

"Yes, you do."

She looked at him then. They could have been good together. But he didn't want to be with her for all eternity. He only wanted her soul. No one had ever wanted her. Not really.

"I want to leave now," she told him and saw something flicker in his eyes. He tried to quickly mask it, but the look had given him away. She saw the truth in his eyes. He was part angel, after all.

"You have to take me back, don't you?"

He sighed. "If that's what you want."

She pulled her shirt on. "It is."

He closed the distance between them, taking her in his arms. "Don't do this. Please don't."

She inhaled his scent, wanting to commit it to her memory. If he only knew how much she didn't want to step out of his arms, she would be more vulnerable to his promises than even he knew. But empty promises never got her anywhere. Her mother promised she would return, except she never did.

The string of social workers had promised Destiny that she would love her new foster parents. She didn't.

Jack promised to take care of her and love her forever, but he used her like all the rest. Now Chance was doing the same thing, and he was killing her all over again.

"Take me home."

She closed her eyes. Felt the earth move beneath her feet. When she opened them once again, she was back in her apartment, alone. Chance was gone. She could have dreamed the whole thing, except for the grass stains on her shirt.

And his scent that lingered in the room.

For one wild moment, she wanted to call him back, beg him to do whatever he wanted, but that would gain her nothing. She couldn't relive her life all over. And why would she even want to if he wasn't a part of it? A bitter laugh escaped. She was more afraid of living than she was of burning in Hell.

Someone pounded on the door.

Destiny jumped.

Had he returned? No, of course not. Chance wouldn't knock. He was an immortal. He could go wherever the hell he wanted.

She trudged to the door and opened it.

LeAnn stood on the other side; tear tracks had streaked through her once carefully applied makeup. Her hair was a mess, as though she'd raked her fingers through the blond curls more than once.

"Oh God, I thought you were killed or something." She stumbled inside, throwing her arms around Destiny and sobbing.

"I'm sorry," Destiny lamely told her as more guilt was dumped on her head. Of course LeAnn would think there had been an accident.

It was LeAnn's night to shine, and Destiny let her down. Earth was quickly becoming a nightmare. Vetis was right when he said she didn't belong there anymore. She only screwed everything up.

"I'm sorry I missed tonight. I swear I'll make it up to you." She drew in a deep breath.

"It doesn't matter now. I'm just glad you're all right."

"How did it go?" Destiny couldn't help asking.

"It was awful. Just awful. I was awful. I wanted to die."

"Come inside and tell me about it."

LeAnn sniffed before stepping away from Destiny and going to the sofa where she collapsed, hugging one of the cheap, decorative pillows to her chest. She began her tale of woe when Destiny sat on the other end.

"I looked for you, but you weren't there. Not that I could've missed you. Charles and Beulah were there, but it wasn't the same without you." She shook her head. "There were only a few other people in the bar, counting the owner. He was even more awful than the first time I spoke to him about singing at his bar. I guess I looked past who he was and only saw my chance to be a star. My big debut, yeah right."

"I'm sorry." Destiny would have thought the good ones in the world wouldn't have to suffer so much, but apparently that wasn't the case. LeAnn was definitely one of the good ones, and look what life did to her. A family snatched away, and then she was sent to live with relatives who didn't want her.

"It doesn't matter." LeAnn shrugged. "No one really cared if I was on stage or not. Then a guy put money in the jukebox and some bimbo jumped up and began to shake her booty when a fast country song started playing. They were more interested in her than me. Cheap hussy." She buried her face in the pillow.

LeAnn's chance at the big time had been a bust. Life sucked. Seemed as though neither one of them could catch a break. But Destiny could make it all better.

"How would you like to have everything you've ever dreamed about?"

"Did you win the lottery?" came her muffled reply.

People in the store were talking about the lottery when she bought her magazines. Wouldn't it be nice if life was that easy? Give the clerk a dollar, get a lottery ticket, and become an instant millionaire. There were no quick fixes in life, though. Death was another matter altogether.

"No, not the lottery, but almost as good."

LeAnn raised her head. Her eyes were big and blue and round

with innocence. An uneasy feeling crept over Destiny. Her gut told her to leave LeAnn alone. Find someone else. But Destiny's time had run out.

Chapter 23

"I BLEW IT," CHANCE told Ryder. "I let Destiny get away." He couldn't look at his friend as shame and regret filled him. "I don't know what to do next."

The sunset usually calmed him. The patio that looked out over the rolling hills dotted with tall oaks and mesquite trees was one of his favorite places. The full moon rose high in the sky and cast a soft glow over the land. When they first discovered the area, it was wild, free, untamed. But as the sun set and rose, the land came alive as if it was bathed in an artist's palette of warm hues. Burnt orange and deep blue would burst across the sky. The pioneers had called Texas "God's country." Chance thought they'd just might be right. The ambience never failed to calm him. Except today. Chance felt anything but calm right now.

"You were so sure you could save her. What happened?" Ryder sat in the chair across from him, handing Chance one of two beers, his eyes filled with sympathy. They had all been in his spot at one time or another, but it didn't lessen the pain they felt when a soul slipped through their fingers.

Chance gratefully took the bottle, then downed half the ice-cold liquid, wishing it would dull his senses, knowing it probably wouldn't. He set the beer on the table between them.

"Vetis is the demon who stole her soul," Chance told him.

Ryder was in the middle of raising his beer to his lips, but stopped and carefully set the bottle on the table between them.

"Walk away." His words were tight, as though he barely held his emotions in check. "Right now. This girl is lost to you. You can do nothing to save her soul."

"It's killing me," Chance admitted, but couldn't agree with Ryder about giving up. He only needed a plan. Right?

"No, it's not killing you because this is as far as it goes. You know better than to mess with Vetis. He's been around as long as we have."

"Could you walk away?" He met Ryder's gaze. "Could you commit Destiny to an eternity of torture? You know that's what will happen. Whether she meets her quota or not, she's doomed."

Ryder jumped to his feet. For a moment, he just stood there as if he didn't know what to say or do next. He finally shoved one hand deep into his front pocket, grabbed his beer with the other, and marched to the edge of the patio.

"You're my family," he finally said after a moment of silence, his voice cracking. "At least, the closest thing I've ever had to one. Our mothers knew each other. They were practically sisters. We grew up together." He faced Chance, his forehead creased with frustration. "Have you forgotten all that? How we played as children. How we both discovered we were nephilim at almost the same time. The powers that we started to acquire."

"How we were shunned by the village." Chance leaned back in his chair, feeling suddenly very tired. "We scared them. People who knew us all their lives. They blamed us for everything that went wrong. I think we even frightened our mothers."

Chance grabbed his beer and took a long drink. Damn, that had always bothered him. His own mother afraid of her child.

"Our mothers wept when they sent us away," Ryder reminded him. "They weren't afraid of us, but *for* us. They heard the grumbling amongst the village elders, too. We used our powers unwisely, showing off."

"We were barely twelve when they forced us to leave." And he and Ryder were terrified out of their minds. They were still kids.

"You know that it wasn't just about the villagers. Our mothers were trying to protect us from the demons who freely roamed the earth in those times. If one discovered us, our whole village would've been destroyed." He frowned. "We survived because our mothers sent us away. There were many nephilim who didn't."

And they never saw their mothers again. They were too afraid to return. The pain still lingered.

"I love Dillon and Hunter like brothers," Ryder continued. "But you and I both know the bond doesn't run as deep as it does between us. You would risk everything we have between us to save her?"

Chance saw the pain in Ryder's eyes. "You know how much you mean to me. We've been there for each other. But I love her too, and right now I need you to understand."

Ryder's shoulders sagged. "Vetis would like nothing more than to steal the soul of a nephilim. No demon has ever been able to do that. It would give him great power."

Chance shoved out of the chair. "Don't you think I've thought about all of this?" His frustration and anger rose to the surface. "After all is said and done, I might lose my soul and still not save her. I know that!"

He strode to the edge of the patio and stared up at the moon rising in the sky, knowing it might be his last one because he could do no less than face Vetis.

"I'll go with you," Ryder said.

"You can't. I have to do this alone. I won't risk anyone else. This is between me and the demon."

"You could try to convince her one more time."

"She won't listen. Destiny feels as though I betrayed her by not telling her the truth. She believed the demon's lies. Her mind is made up."

"She needs to take a soul back with her. Have you thought about that? Someone else might be at risk."

"There's no one. She doesn't have enough time. At least, I doubt one that the council of demons would approve." A sudden thought made his blood run cold. "Except for LeAnn."

Ryder's forehead wrinkled. "LeAnn?"

"A young girl that has apparently befriended Destiny. Destiny was supposed to hear her sing tonight."

"Isn't socializing against the rules if you're not trying to steal their soul? The demons are sticklers about that sort of thing. They think the wannabe demons will change their minds."

But Chance was afraid that was exactly what Destiny would do if she was desperate, and now that she didn't have his soul, she would be frantic. Vetis would have already told her she would have to face the tribunal. Destiny would think she was giving LeAnn everything she ever dreamed about when in fact she was committing her to an eternity of suffering.

"I have to go," Chance said.

Ryder clamped a hand on his arm. "Don't."

"I have no choice."

Ryder's expression was grim when he released Chance and nodded. Maybe Ryder figured he would do the exact same thing if their positions were reversed.

"Be careful."

For a moment they were kids again and the years, the centuries, fell away. Chance had left the cave where they found shelter that first night they were on their own, and went to look for food. It was in the early days, before they grew into their full powers. To save time, Ryder left in the opposite direction, both warning the other to be careful.

Chance ran into a young demon, but one with more experience than Chance. A demon who almost destroyed him. Through the years, they fought battles, neither winning, neither losing, but always too close to call a victory for either one. And each time, Chance had been amazed how the demon's powers grew stronger. Strong enough that he was wary about meeting him again. The demon was Vetis.

Chance knew without a doubt the demon was even more powerful, stronger, over the years since the last time they met. He wouldn't be so easy to escape this time, and Chance wasn't looking forward to facing him again.

"I'll be careful," he told Ryder and closed his eyes. The wind whipped past, then swirled around him before dying down to a soft breeze.

When he opened his eyes again, he was standing in Destiny's living room. He listened, but heard no sound alerting him to the fact that she was there.

Blood rushed through his veins causing a roaring inside his ears. Did she leave? Take LeAnn with her? His world tilted and he had to put a hand on the back of the sofa to steady himself.

As he regained his equilibrium, he caught a distinctive odor. His nose wrinkled in distaste. He quickly glanced around the room. "Show yourself, demon!"

"It's been a long time."

The voice came from behind him, but Chance didn't need to see the face to recognize who spoke. He turned, his gaze moving over the demon.

The man before him was handsome with dark hair, dark complexion, and wore a stylish black suit. A mortal would have envied his good looks, but Chance saw the fiery sparks in his eyes that bespoke the demon's true self.

"Hello, Vetis," Chance said. "You're looking different. Whose body did you steal?"

Fire flashed in the demon's eyes, then quickly vanished as he shrugged. "Someone who no longer needs it." He suddenly whirled in a circle and transformed into the demon he was.

Chance took an involuntary step back and the demon laughed. Chance forgot how Vetis really looked. The demon preferred a handsome body over the cloven-hoofed, misshapen form.

"Yes, I admit I'm quite scary to look upon, the better to frighten small children and the unwary, my dear." He cackled at his reference to *The Big Bad Wolf.* "But alas, so much harder to seduce the souls I need when I look like this." He waved a clawed hand in front of himself, moving with a disjointed gait around the room.

"I've seen you in many disguises."

"That you have. We go a long way back, you and I."

"Are we going to talk about old times?" Chance cocked an eyebrow.

"Why rehash the past? Still, we would have made a great team. Think about how good we could have been together." He cocked his head to the side and studied Chance. "We still could."

Chance always knew Vetis wanted him to join forces. "I don't destroy lives."

"Why? Out of some sense of loyalty? Your father left you to fend for yourself. I almost defeated you when you were young. Did he rush to save his son? No. The angels don't care about any of the nephilim."

Vetis swung his arm wide. Three women appeared, dancing in front of Chance wearing transparent scarves that hid nothing of their lush bodies. They swayed in front of him, beckoning him to come closer. When one reached toward him, Chance grabbed her wrist and shook his head. The woman pouted her perfectly painted red lips.

Vetis clapped and they quickly turned toward him, their master. They laughed as they danced past Chance and moved on either side of Vetis. Two of the girls kissed. The third one dropped down in front of Vetis, rubbing her face and hands up and down his legs, opening her mouth, silently begging for more, not caring that she seduced a monster.

"They're very beautiful." Vetis patted the girl on the head. "You could have one, or all if you prefer. These lovelies are like nothing you've ever been with before."

"Your tricks won't work on me," Chance told him.

Vetis hissed, waving his arms. The women's screams echoed through the room as the demon sent them back to the fiery depths of Hell. "You would condemn them?" he accused.

Chance shook his head. "No, *you* would. I had nothing to do with it."

Vetis suddenly smiled as he transformed back into his human body. "But there is one you might give your soul for." His words were silky smooth.

Chance moved to the sofa and sat down. He only hoped he looked as casual as he pretended to feel. Vetis would destroy Destiny just to make Chance suffer. "You win some back," Chance shrugged. "And some you don't," he told the demon. "You know that as well as I."

"But you fucked this one." His eyes narrowed. "You've never fucked them in the past. Maybe you care more than you're willing to admit."

"You mean there are rules to the games we play?" He shook his head. "No, I fucked her because I wanted to. Sure, I would have liked to save her soul, but it doesn't look as if that will happen." He studied the demon. "Are you ready to take my castoffs?"

Vetis hissed. "She was mine first. I bought her soul."

Chance sat forward. "No, you stole it. You lied to Destiny. What did you expect her to do when those men would have beaten her to death?"

"True, but I've never claimed to be anything but what I am." He laughed. "You tried to seduce her soul away." He raised his eyebrows. "That doesn't say a whole lot for how good a lover you are, now does it? But I think you lie. You care more about her than you're willing to admit."

"Let this one go." Chance slowly came to his feet. They were playing games again. They both wanted Destiny. They both knew it.

"I think not, old friend. She still amuses me."

"And if she doesn't get her quota?"

"She'll no longer be of any use to me. I'll cast her into the fires of Hell without a second thought."

Chance charged, but Vetis disappeared in the blink of an eye, laughter trailing after him. Damn him! Chance wanted to wrap his hands around the demon's throat and squeeze the immortality out of him.

"Her time is running out. What will you do?" Vetis's words were soft, quickly fading. "Who will you save, nephilim? Her or yourself?"

"Damn you, Vetis!"

"You forget. I already am." And then he was gone.

Chance paced the tiny living room. He had to think. Come up with a plan to set Destiny free. He raked his fingers through his hair as sweat formed on his brow.

What would he do if it came down to it? Would he give his soul to set Destiny free? Vetis would make the trade.

His gut clenched at the thought of burning in Hell for all eternity. Vetis would take great pleasure in watching him suffer. For some reason, the demon hated him with an intensity that surprised Chance.

And if he didn't make the exchange?

No, the alternative was unacceptable. Destiny would be consumed with pain forever. Ah no, he couldn't let that happen. He would do whatever it took to save her.

Chance closed his eyes, but before he could travel he was surrounded by bright chains that quickly looped around him, weaving over and under like golden snakes.

"No!" His voice boomed throughout the apartment. "Release me!"

Three shapes began to take form in front of him, undistinguishable at first, but he knew them. Ryder, Dillon, and Hunter emerged from the mists.

"Let me go to her," Chance begged as his frustration threatened to choke him.

Sadly, Ryder shook his head. "You know we can't do that. We agreed a long time ago not to let an assignment destroy one of us. That's exactly where you are headed."

"I have to save her. Don't you see?"

Dillon's mouth was set in a grim line. "If you save her, Vetis will take you instead. It's the only way he'll let her go. We can't let that happen."

"We agreed!" Hunter's voice joined in.

"Then I am already dead." Chance dropped to his knees as his energy drained. He knew he wouldn't be able to survive a day without Destiny, let alone an eternity.

Chapter 24

"I CAN'T DO IT," LeAnn said, her face turning a sickly gray color. "You're asking too much."

Destiny gritted her teeth, reminding herself that she had no choice, and LeAnn was making this all way too difficult! "If you don't, then what I'm giving up will be all for naught!"

LeAnn frowned. "What are you talking about?" Her eyes narrowed as she studied Destiny. "What are you not telling me?"

"Nothing," Destiny quickly told her. "It's just that I want the best for you."

"But this might not be the best thing for me," LeAnn sadly shook her head. "And I don't think I'm worth this much trouble."

Destiny was going to kill the girl. Absolutely fucking kill her! No, she only needed to convince LeAnn this was the only solution.

Now, deep breath.

And exhale. *Whoosh.*

Better.

She looked up as a man and woman walked past, then went inside The Stompin' Ground bar. The place was packed, but then Destiny had made sure it would be. She looked at LeAnn again.

"If you don't go up on that stage when Duncan introduces you, then you'll be throwing away your opportunity for everything you've dreamed about." Her words were calm and soothing.

"But—"

"No buts!" Destiny stomped her foot and glared at LeAnn.

LeAnn hung her head. "If you could've seen me earlier tonight, you wouldn't be trying to talk me into this. I was a dismal failure."

Destiny grabbed LeAnn's shoulders and gave her a gentle shake. "It wasn't you. From everything you've told me, that place was a dive. This time will be better. I promise."

Besides, Destiny had made sure there would be a record producer who would just happen to make a wrong turn and get lost on his way to Billy Bob's. And if Destiny's timing was on the mark, then he would walk inside the bar in the middle of LeAnn's performance to ask for directions. Getting a man to ask for directions would be a feat in and of itself.

And LeAnn stood here and argued?

Grrr!

Deep breath.

Exhale. *Whoosh.*

Better.

She couldn't make the producer fall in love with LeAnn's voice, but Destiny would at least be giving her a chance, except the window of opportunity was quickly closing.

"Please, do it for me." Destiny begged, holding her breath. "I know I let you down once, but I swear, this time I won't."

LeAnn glanced toward the bar, conflicting emotions warring across her face.

"You know it's your dream. Can you walk away from it? Forever?"

"I'm scared."

"I'll be with you." For as long as she could. Destiny hoped it would be long enough.

"Okay, okay, I'll do it. Just stop badgering me."

The tension finally eased inside Destiny. "Great. Let's go." She grabbed LeAnn's hand and began pulling her toward the bar, but LeAnn wasn't budging. "What?"

"We're just going to meet the owner, right?"

"No, you'll be singing tonight."

She shook her head. "I don't have my guitar."

"There's a band. You won't need it."

"A band! What about rehearsal?"

"No time." Then more firmly. "You promised."

"Fine! I just don't know why you're being so persistent or why it has to be tonight."

For a teeny-tiny moment, Destiny thought about throwing fire beneath her friend's feet, but that might be a little hard to explain. Thankfully she didn't have to, as LeAnn reluctantly moved forward.

Once inside the bar though, LeAnn pulled against her hand. Destiny could feel the trembles that flowed over LeAnn and felt some of the other woman's fear.

"I swear it will be okay. You have a fantastic voice. Look, Charles and Beulah are already here."

LeAnn groaned. "To see me crash and burn again."

Charles and Beulah turned as if they knew they were being talked about. They got up and hurried over.

"This is a lot better place," Charles told her. "You'll do fine here."

Beulah's usually pursed lips softened to a smile. "You have a beautiful voice, dear. You'll have the whole town talking before this night is over. It's not going to be like the last time."

"And if it is, my Beulah will kick their asses," Charles said, then grinned.

"I told you that was an accident."

"Yeah, your fist landed against her jaw."

"Well, she had it coming." Beulah straightened, smoothing the front of her green dress with the palms of her hands. "We'd best get back to our table so LeAnn can get ready."

"Nice dress," Destiny commented.

Beulah preened. Funny, Destiny didn't think the woman had it in her to preen.

"I was getting tired of the dreary. It's not like I'm always going to a funeral or anything." She shrugged. "And maybe it's past time I started living."

"I can't do this," LeAnn muttered.

Great, here we go again!

"You must be LeAnn," Duncan said as he joined them.

Destiny glanced over her shoulder. Thank goodness, reinforcement. "Duncan, hi. This is the friend I was telling you about."

"You're Duncan?" LeAnn asked.

"And you're hot." His gaze slowly roamed over LeAnn, then met her eyes once again. "Destiny told me you could sing, but she didn't tell me just how beautiful a singer I would be getting. My bar dims in comparison."

"Thank you." She blushed to the roots of her hair, smiling shyly.

Destiny looked between the two of them. Who would've thought? This might work out even better than she hoped. But then she always knew the guy had potential.

"You don't know how I sound. You might not like my voice," LeAnn said.

"She sounds great," Destiny jumped in. LeAnn was too damn modest for her own good.

"You've only heard a few notes!"

"But they were really good notes."

"I'd love to introduce you if you're ready."

"She's ready." Destiny was still holding LeAnn's hand and could feel her begin to shake.

"Right now? I need a few minutes, or maybe tomorrow night would be better." LeAnn shook her head. "I don't think I could stand to flop twice in one night."

Destiny wasn't about to let LeAnn's nerves destroy everything she'd pulled together just for tonight and in such a short amount of time. Besides, Destiny knew that she wouldn't get another opportunity to help her friend.

"Now, it has to be now," Destiny urged.

"Please, do it for me," Duncan said, taking her hand.

"I… I…" She couldn't seem to look away from his mesmerizing eyes.

Destiny decided to strike while she could. "Go introduce her."

"You got it," Duncan said, but kissed LeAnn's hand before he released it, and then walked toward the stage.

"I'm not ready," LeAnn frantically whispered.

"Yes, you are."

Duncan jumped to the stage in one smooth leap, rather than taking the two steps on the side, and then made a motion for the band to stop playing. As soon as the room was quiet, he grinned at Destiny and LeAnn. Destiny forgot just how cute the guy was, in a good ol' boy, country way. He and LeAnn would make a perfect couple.

"I can't do this," LeAnn whispered.

"Yes, you can." Destiny slipped behind her and maneuvered her toward the side of the stage as Duncan began his introduction.

"It's my great pleasure to introduce a brand-new voice on the country music scene. Y'all give her a warm welcome because this little lady's star will soon be on the rise."

"Oh God," LeAnn moaned.

Duncan moved to the steps and held out his hand. Destiny bit her bottom lip. A second passed, then two. LeAnn grudgingly took his hand.

Destiny let go. She knew then what it felt like for mothers to send their children out into the world for the very first time because that was exactly what she felt right now.

But rather than rush to the stage and shield LeAnn from the hardships life might toss her way, Destiny did what all mothers know to do: she stepped back into the shadows and prayed LeAnn had the courage to follow her dreams, to be the person she was meant to be.

LeAnn moved to the microphone as Duncan left the stage. Her trembling hands grabbed the microphone stand. It jerked to the side. She grabbed it tighter, and a shaky laugh erupted from her. "I guess I'm just a little nervous."

The crowd was silent.

Her sigh came over the microphone. "Maybe a whole lot nervous." She looked around until her gaze found Destiny.

Destiny smiled and nodded.

"I wrote a song about my brother. Actually, I've written a lot of songs, but this one is my favorite, and I've never gotten the chance to sing it for anyone. Well, not all of it at once."

She turned slightly toward the band and began to hum the tune. There were two guitar players and a drummer. One of the guitar players began to strum. LeAnn smiled and nodded. The other guitar player joined in, then the drummer.

"Yeah, just like that. Nice and easy. That's the way my brother was. Nothing seemed to bother him. He was my hero and I was the little sister who tagged after him." She looked out over the crowd. "Any of you have brothers or sisters that you tagged after?"

Destiny looked around. Nearly everyone nodded their heads and smiled. The door opened and a sliver of light crept in. A man who looked totally lost glanced around, giving LeAnn a cursory look before he moved toward the bar. Duncan took his place behind the counter again, but was intently watching LeAnn.

Destiny smiled. Everything was going according to plan.

LeAnn began to sing, her voice as pure as an angel.

You were the one I cherished most,
Walking side by side.
You were the one that I admired
With hero worship in my eyes.

There was a short pause. The room was so quiet that you could hear a pin drop.

> *But no one told me heroes die.*
> *But no one told me heroes die.*

LeAnn closed her eyes and began to hum. She didn't see the tears that formed in people's eyes. Or the men who were suddenly reaching for their beers just to have something to do. Then she began to sing again.

> *You taught me to ride my bike,*
> *You threw me in the pond.*
> *That was when I learned to swim,*
> *When we formed the bond.*
> *But no one told me heroes die*
> *No one told me heroes die*
>
> *Although you're not with me now*
> *I never walk alone.*
> *These are the memories we still share,*
> *Since the angels called you home.*
> *Heroes only die if you let them go,*
> *Never let them go.*

Destiny sniffed. LeAnn really had a fantastic voice. Either way, her plan couldn't have worked out any better if she did say so herself. She focused on LeAnn as she finished.

LeAnn looked at the band and gave a little nod.

> *Never let them go.*

Her words trailed off, her voice cracking on the last note. The band stopped playing except for one guitar that slowly faded.

The room was silent, then pandemonium erupted. Everyone jumped to their feet clapping their hands. A few of the women openly cried. LeAnn looked at Destiny and smiled as a tear slid down her cheek. She quickly wiped it away.

"More, more, more!" the crowd shouted.

Charles and Beulah were on their feet clapping with the rest of the patrons.

LeAnn spoke briefly with the band, then began to sing a lively tune. The producer was still standing at the bar. He began a frantic search in his pockets before pulling out a cell phone.

Duncan nodded at Destiny, then grinned.

"I guess you feel pretty proud of yourself," Vetis said behind her.

Destiny jumped as though someone had stuck a hot poker deep in her heart. So this was it then. Vetis would exact retribution for her actions. But then, nothing really mattered anymore. Eternity would be the same as life. Why should she have expected anything less?

She turned and faced the demon. "I do feel proud of myself."

Anger, like a match being struck, flared in his eyes. "I'll make you regret not giving me her soul."

She shook her head, looking over her shoulder at LeAnn. A tender smile curved her lips. LeAnn was singing another ballad and everyone was on the edge of their seats, enthralled with her voice.

"How could I regret this? She has a chance at living a normal life." Her gaze moved to Duncan, who was totally entranced with LeAnn's performance. "She has a chance at having someone love her."

"I loved *you*!" he ground out.

She met his fiery gaze. "That isn't love."

"I saved you!"

"Because you wanted my soul."

Heat filled the space around her. She gasped as it singed her skin. The room grew dark. LeAnn's voice faded.

A hot wind whipped around Destiny, tearing at her clothes. She shook with fear and tried to tell herself that she did the right thing, but it didn't feel right when she was so scared.

Everything grew still, and she felt the ground beneath her feet once again. She kept her eyes tightly closed, unable to look at where Vetis had brought her.

"Any regrets now?" he taunted.

She drew in a deep breath, but the air burned her lungs. *Please help me be strong*, she silently prayed.

"No one will hear your prayers in Hell." He grabbed her throat and squeezed. "Chance can't save you now!"

Her eyes flew open. She was in a dark cave, flames licking up the sides of the walls. The horned monster she briefly thought she saw at the apartment stood in front of her. No skin covered the red, leathery muscle and ligament that stretched taut across his face. The creature's eyes glowed piercing yellow.

She took a step back, screaming.

The creature threw back his head and laughed. "So now you fear me?" Vetis's voice came out of the hideous monster. "This is my true form. That of a demon." He turned in a circle and the Vetis she knew was back. "Or do you prefer the human body I stole? He no longer needed it. No, he's still burning in Hell!" He shook his head. "A shame because I rather liked him. He made a great lover. Just as you did. But there will always be others."

"Why are you doing this to me?"

"Not to you. To him. I want his soul and you were supposed to bring it to me! But he almost took yours! You failed!"

Destiny stared as Vetis began to pace the cave.

"It was never you. But I knew he would try to save you. The two of you were perfectly matched."

"Why Chance?"

He tilted his head and stared at her, insanity shining from his eyes. "Everything played out as I planned," he said as if he hadn't heard her question. "You never once guessed how I orchestrated your life."

"What do you mean?"

He tapped his head. "Think! Remember the man your mother left with?"

Destiny closed her eyes for a moment and let the years slip away. She'd moved to the window of the grocery store just as her mother climbed into the car. The man turned and looked directly at Destiny. It was as if a veil lifted and she looked right at Vetis. The man was different, but the eyes were the same.

Her eyes flew open. She took a step back. "It was you! You seduced my mother."

Vetis smiled. "Your mother was a stupid slut. Sexy, though. It was a shame I had to kill her before she would give me her soul. She actually had second thoughts and wanted to return to her daughter. I couldn't let that happen."

Destiny flew at him. He only grabbed her arms before she could pummel his smiling face. "I hate you!" Through the tears, she saw his face distort and become the foster mother who beat her, then once again and she looked at Jack. She shook her head. "No, I killed you."

"You would do anything for me, wouldn't you? Anything I asked. I tossed you a few scraps of love and you were like putty in my hands." He frowned. "I knew it wouldn't last, though."

"You let me shoot you."

"It stung like a son of a bitch, too."

"Why me?"

"I told you, so I could get to him." He exhaled a deep breath. "But you failed to bring him to me. Stupid girl."

He waved his arm and steel doors appeared behind him. The rusty hinges creaked open.

"Where's your nephilim now? It would seem he has thrown you away, too." His eyes narrowed. "In fact, no one ever really loved you, did they? Your mother certainly fell into my arms, and my bed quick enough."

"Shut up!" He was wrong. Chance loved her. LeAnn loved her. And her mother would've come back for her.

"Come along. It's time to face the tribunal."

Fear kept her feet from moving forward. There was only one verdict they would give her and she knew it. They would find her guilty. She'd burn forever.

Oh, screw it!

She glared at Vetis, raising her chin. "Go to hell." Even though she was pretty sure she was going to throw up, she walked toward the doors.

Screw him. Screw them all.

His mocking laughter followed behind her. "But didn't you know? We're already there."

She didn't care that he mocked her. She'd lost Chance, the only man she ever loved, and she'd lost the only friend she ever had, but at least they were safe. She'd done one good thing in her life: Destiny gave LeAnn an opportunity to succeed.

As they went into the chamber, fire licked at her feet. It felt as though she walked over hot coals, but she was determined not to cry out. She kept her head held high even though she shook on the inside. She refused to let them see her fear.

There was a long table that sat higher than she was tall, so that she had to tilt her head back to look at the five demons she faced. Vetis joined them.

They were just as ugly and scary as he was. Suddenly she didn't feel quite so brave.

"One soul, that was all you had to take." An ugly-ass demon stared down at her.

"But no, you felt pity for the mortal woman and you let the nephilim slip through your fingers," another said.

"He would have been a rare prize to bring us," one more said. "You let the half angel, half mortal seduce you," he spat.

"You could have had it all," Vetis told her.

She wanted to yell at him that what he offered wasn't good enough. Not when it would have cost LeAnn her soul. And she was glad Chance escaped as well. Vetis lied.

But she kept quiet.

"Do we have a verdict?" one demon asked.

She cocked an eyebrow. "This is a trial?"

"Silence!" one screamed and his breath sent down waves of heat.

Destiny's mouth snapped closed. The trial was a travesty of justice. Did she really think they might treat her fairly?

"Guilty." The demon pointed a long bony finger down at her.

She flinched.

One after another, the demons pronounced their verdicts.

"You shall burn in the fires of Hell for all eternity," one loudly proclaimed.

Destiny expected no less. She only hoped the knowledge that she prevented the same thing from happening to her friend would sustain her through the pain and agony.

Chapter 25

CHANCE HAD SPENT HIS energy trying to break the bonds that held him. He knew it was no use trying to get loose, but the knowledge didn't stop him from trying after the three nephilim had left him to vent his anguish on a silent room.

Ryder suddenly appeared. "It's over." He squared his shoulders as though he carried a heavy burden and he didn't want to buckle under the weight. "She's been found guilty by the tribunal."

For a moment Chance couldn't breathe. He felt as though all the air was sucked out of his lungs. Then his world began to crumble as the significance of Ryder's words sank into his brain.

"The verdict?" Although Chance already knew Ryder's answer, he had to ask. The demons never deviated from a guilty verdict. They loved to watch their victims squirm. Still, he had to hear Ryder say the words.

Ryder's expression turned grim. "She will be cast into the fires of Hell."

He clamped his lips together as anger burned through him. His information had to be wrong. Vetis had cared about Destiny. Chance saw it in his eyes.

"You know that for a fact?" Chance asked.

Vetis wouldn't destroy her. Then why bring her in front of the tribunal? Vetis had to know what would happen. Maybe he knew how much Chance would be tortured by the news. For some reason the demon had always hated him. Over the centuries, they had too many confrontations, with neither one able to claim victory.

"I have it from a good source," Ryder continued. "She went immediately before the judges."

"No, it's not true!" Chance struggled against the chains that bound him. "She took LeAnn. She made her quota. They wouldn't completely destroy her. Vetis wouldn't have gone that far." Not even for some insane idea that he could exact revenge on Chance. He enjoyed the game they played too much to end it this way.

Ryder was silent for a moment before waving his arm. The silken chains that bound Chance disappeared. "You can't save her. I'm sorry."

If Ryder was lying, he wouldn't have released him. He would have been afraid of what Chance might do to gain Destiny's freedom.

Chance studied his friend. Ryder's mouth was set in a grim line. He spoke the truth. Destiny was lost to him. Vetis would torture her for all eternity.

No! Chance wouldn't let himself believe there was no hope. Ryder lied! He had to be lying. *Oh God, let him be lying.*

Chance grabbed Ryder by the shoulders and forced his friend to look him in the eyes. "Vetis wouldn't bring her in front of the tribunal if she made her quota. What is it you're not telling me?"

When Ryder hesitated, dread weaved its way through Chance. "She didn't make her quota." Pity shone in Ryder's eyes.

Chance stumbled back as though he'd been hit with a sledgehammer. "LeAnn was an innocent. I saw how much she worshipped Destiny. The girl would have followed her anywhere. Even to Hell."

"Destiny worked the situation so the girl would have a future. It happened tonight. At the bar where you met Destiny. LeAnn sang there. Destiny made sure a record producer got lost and ended up going inside the bar while LeAnn was singing. She was offered a contract. Destiny fixed everything so Vetis wouldn't have an opportunity to steal her soul."

"Idiot. Vetis would have been furious that she let two souls slip through her fingers. She would be condemned to burn for all eternity. Didn't she know that?"

"I believe she did."

"Why, then?"

He shrugged. "I think because she cared for the girl as much as the girl cared for her. It's as you said, Destiny wasn't given an opportunity in life to love. When she found a chance in death, she grabbed it."

Chance dropped to the sofa, rubbing his forehead as though he could wipe away the vision of Destiny burning in Hell forever. The cost was too great. How could she have sacrificed everything?

"There's nothing you can do," Ryder quietly told him.

"Isn't there?"

Ryder's lips pressed together to form a thin line. "Damn it, Chance, you can't do anything now and you know it."

"And what do you think I would do?"

"We both know exactly what you were thinking. You would trade your soul for hers. The higher ups wouldn't allow it. They would stop you before you stepped one foot in Hell."

"No, they wouldn't. They don't care about us." He snorted with disgust. "Our fathers have never cared."

Chance regretted his words as soon as he saw the hurt on his friend's face. Ryder was the more emotional of the four nephilim. Even though he liked to pretend he was cavalier about everything, Ryder was the one who could hurt the most.

Chance raked his fingers through his hair. "You're right, of course. I would be stopped." He didn't believe his lies, and he had a feeling neither did Ryder, but Chance would pretend. He was good at pretending.

"There really is nothing you can do," Ryder said.

Chance nodded. "I know. But damn, it hurts so much."

"It always does when an assignment doesn't go our way, but there's still nothing we can do."

"Knowing doesn't make it easier."

"Let's go for a beer or something. Hunter and Dillon are waiting for us in the rec room back at the ranch. You can't be alone right now."

Yeah, Chance knew they wouldn't be far away, and they wouldn't want him to be alone to dwell on what happened. He did the same when they had a bad experience.

"No, yeah, okay. It might get my mind off losing Destiny. I need something to help me forget. I almost let this assignment destroy me."

"I know, but we made a pact a long time ago that we would stick together. Help each other through the rough times. You'll heal. We always do."

"Sometimes I wish we didn't," Chance said.

"I know what you mean, buddy."

Chance glanced down at the clothes he wore. "I left some things here. I'll just take a quick shower first. I stink after being around Vetis."

Ryder didn't look like he trusted Chance, but he finally nodded.

"There's a DVD in the player," he casually told him, hoping Destiny didn't change it. "You can watch it while I clean up."

"Sure, why not, but don't take too long." Ryder made himself comfortable on the sofa as Chance turned and left the room.

In other words, Ryder would be timing him. If Chance took too long, he'd check to see if he was okay. That's what they did, they looked out for each other. They always had.

Chance turned back once before walking out of the room. The title of the XXX-rated movie that Destiny played so she could seduce him flashed across the screen. His lips lifted just slightly as he remembered that night and how proud Destiny had been with her seduction setup.

Chance's attention moved back to Ryder. Sadness welled inside him. He would miss his friend. He would miss all the nephilim. They were brothers and had been with each other a very long time.

But he loved Destiny with all his heart and he couldn't let her suffer for the rest of eternity, no matter what it cost him.

As soon as he was in the bedroom, he shut the door. Ryder was right, it wouldn't be easy going to Hell.

He closed his eyes. Nothing happened at first, and he wondered if it would. He clamped his lips together and concentrated.

Air rushed past. Voices came to him, swirling around fast and furious. Chance gritted his teeth. He began to make out the words.

"You are forbidden in this place!"

The wind pummeled his body with such force he was afraid the skin would be shredded from his body, but still he held on.

"I have to go to her."

"She is dead to you!"

"She gave up everything for her friend."

"A demon owns her soul! Are you willing to sacrifice yours?"

"Yes!"

The wind volume decreased and there came a deep sigh of air. Chance felt the pain that swirled around him and lowered his head. Who was this being behind the voice? He didn't know. Chance only wished he hadn't caused so much sadness in him.

"Then so be it."

Chance knew he'd crossed over, but at what cost?

The direction of the wind changed once again. Not as strong as before, but just as deadly. He could feel the burning heat as he was sucked farther and farther down into the bowels of the Earth.

He opened his eyes when his feet landed with a thud on the hot ground below. The landing was so jarring that it knocked him to his knees, and the air was so thick it was all he could do to stand straight again.

So this was Hell. The cave walls were black as night, crying tears of blood. The fires whipped around Chance, shooting up the sides of the cave. Sweat began to bead his forehead. He drew in a breath, the heat burning his lungs, the smell of fire and brimstone so strong it made his stomach churn.

Hell was even more dismal than he'd imagined.

"Now how did I know you would show up here?" Vetis spoke from behind him, then chuckled.

Chance squared his shoulders and faced the demon. "You're a good guesser?" His words dripped with sarcasm. "Where's Destiny?"

Chapter 26

"DESTINY IS SAFE." VETIS smiled, then added, "For now."

Chance didn't let Vetis see the relief he felt. He'd been afraid he might be too late, but he had to slip away from Ryder rather than rush out. He could risk his own life but not that of his friend, and Ryder would have followed. By the time Ryder decided to check on Chance, the bargain would be struck.

"Where is she?" Chance asked once more.

"Locked away. Why, don't you trust me?"

"No."

"Then see for yourself."

Vetis waved his hand and a room appeared before them. Destiny huddled in a corner, tears streaking her face. There were flames all around her, but none touched her skin.

Chance knew with one flick of Vetis's wrist the flames would start to devour her, very slowly, one inch at a time. When there was nothing left, she would be reborn from the ashes and her torture would start all over again.

The heat from the fire was intense enough that Chance could see she was terrified thinking about what would come next. The demons were good at playing mind games. They loved watching their victims suffer.

Chance reached toward her. He wanted to tell Destiny that everything would be okay, that he wouldn't let her suffer, but he knew what he looked at was only an illusion. Vetis wouldn't let him get that close to her.

"Let her go." Chance's words dropped like stones on a hard surface.

Vetis waved his arm and the image disappeared. "And what are you willing to exchange for the girl's soul? She is a beauty, you know, and I really hate to part with something so precious."

Vetis snapped his fingers and a chair appeared. It was made of volcanic rock and trimmed in gold. He snapped his fingers again and a servant girl, head bowed, appeared with a drink on a silver platter. He took the jewel-encrusted cup.

The servant glanced toward Chance and was rewarded with a casual flick of Vetis's wrist that shot flames over the girl. She screamed in pain, dropping her platter.

"Enough!" Chance bellowed.

"Oh, I do apologize. Would you like something to drink? The heat can be quite unbearable if one isn't used to it."

The girl dropped to the floor, crying for forgiveness.

Vetis chuckled, then doused the girl in water before motioning for her to leave as if he hadn't done anything at all. The girl kept her head bowed low and rushed away.

"Stop playing your cruel games. What do you want?"

Vetis leaned back in the chair, taking a drink of the cool liquid. "Why, your soul, of course. I've waited a long time to get it."

Chance had known his soul would be the price. "And you'll let Destiny go free?" he asked.

"I might."

"What else could you possibly want?" Chance roared.

Vetis threw the cup away. It hit the wall of the cave and bounced to the ground with a loud clank. "I want to beat you. I don't just want your soul. No, that would be too easy. I want to battle you. I want you to know I'm the victor. We need to finish it!"

Chance felt as if he'd been hit in the stomach and all the wind knocked out of him. He drew in a deep breath and chose his next words carefully.

"Of course you would like to battle here." He swung his arm wide. "You would have the advantage. We both know your powers are greater than mine when you're in Hell. It wouldn't be a fair fight unless we're above ground, but if that's what it would take for you to let Destiny go, then so be it. I don't give a damn."

"The fight will be fair!" Vetis's voice echoed in the chamber. "We will meet as equals, but it's my skill that will give me the advantage, nothing more. Then your soul will be mine! Are you ready to burn in Hell for all eternity over a woman?"

"Who says I'll lose?"

Vetis took a step toward him and Chance thought he might have pushed him too far. Demons weren't known to play by the rules, even when they were their rules.

"Then choose a neutral place," he told the demon.

Vetis smiled, his eyes showing a measure of victory already. "The place the four of you created. What did you call it? The Old West? Your retreat? Immortals playing Cowboys and Indians. You defeated holograms, but can you defeat the real thing?" Vetis gloated.

The demon was craftier than Chance had guessed. They thought they were safe at the place they created. Were they just as vulnerable on the ranch? At their apartments? Or had hiding in plain sight confused the demons?

"Another decade and I would have discovered the other places where you hide."

Chance breathed a sigh of relief. The others would be safe, no matter what happened to him. "Then let the battle begin, but first let Destiny go. I want her freed."

Vetis studied Chance, then shrugged. "It matters naught to me. I've never cared that much for her. I didn't want you to have her, though."

"Why not?"

Vetis curled his lip. "You've never guessed. It amazes me that the nephilim can be so clueless." He laughed. "But then, none of the angels who sired nephilim have ever cared for their offspring. Your father never warned you about me."

As hot and suffocating as the air around him was, Chance felt a cold chill ripple over him. "What do you know about our fathers?"

"I know everything about them, especially yours. He is, after all, my brother."

Chance cringed at the thought of this vile creature being his uncle. "You lie!"

"Not about this, nephew. My brother and I chose different paths." He spat on the ground, then glared at Chance. "We could have ruled the world together, conquered anyone who stood in our way. Together we would have been invincible."

Vetis's eyes were wild as his gaze bounced off the cave walls, as though he searched for something that was not there.

"Everything was at our fingertips," he continued, and with each word his voice became more shrill. "Anything we could have ever imagined would have been ours for the taking. But the demons didn't want just one brother. It was a package deal." He began to pace.

Chance waited for him to continue. He had to know the whole story and he knew Vetis would tell him.

"They cast me into the fires of Hell. I stayed there for more than a century."

His body shook as he turned back to Chance, but it was as if he looked at someone else.

"Can you even imagine the pain I suffered because you denied me, brother? The burning fires that tore off my flesh? But now I have your son!" His head turned upward, his maniacal laughter filling the room.

Chance didn't dare breathe as he waited for the demon's tirade to end. It didn't take long. The wild gleam left his eyes and his shoulders slumped.

He frowned, looking back at Chance once more. "I loved my

brother dearly, but he destroyed the bond between us," Vetis continued, squaring his shoulders and glaring at Chance. "Now I will destroy his son. My brother will feel a measure of the pain I've had to live with."

This was exactly the opportunity Chance needed. "Free the girl first."

"And if I don't?"

"Then there will be no battle."

"I could kill you now."

Chance shrugged. "You could."

Vetis frowned.

Chance pushed his point home. "You'll lose if we fight. You do realize I'm younger and stronger."

Vetis growled, but waved his arm. "She's at the place the four of you created. Are you done making demands?"

"Let it begin."

Chance closed his eyes. The air pressed against him on all sides. Coils of fire whipped around him as if they would keep him in Hell. For a moment he wondered if Vetis might have lied and this was a mind game. Chance wouldn't put it past him.

But as before, he heard the voice but couldn't make out the words this time. The sound was soothing. His fears were immediately calmed.

Once again, Chance felt the ground beneath his feet. He opened his eyes at the same time that he was knocked off his feet by a force that slammed into his chest.

"I thought you'd be better than this." Vetis stood nearby in demon form. "At least make the battle interesting and try to fight back." He smirked as he stood on cloven hooves, his arms flapping up and down as if he might fly away, but he only taunted.

"Do you think to scare me with your ugly-ass demon form?"

Vetis glowered, his anger building.

Chance didn't give the demon time to think about what he should try next. He came to his feet, charging toward Vetis with a roar.

Vetis was taken off guard. The demon didn't move quite fast enough. Chance barreled into him. Vetis expelled a whoosh of air and was sent tumbling back.

The demon recovered quickly and moved to a safer distance. "Did you think that would hurt me?" Vetis spat, but he was breathing hard. "I've endured much more than you could ever deliver!" He reared his arm back and released a ball of flame. Chance barely moved out of the way in time; even so the fire scorched his skin, the acrid smell stung his nostrils.

The demon ran into the woods, darting behind a tree. Chance followed.

"You charge into the woods like an enraged bull. Do you think to beat me with brute force?" he called out. "You won't win because you think with your heart rather than your head. Your father was the same way. He gave up all the riches of the world for his idealistic views."

"At least he believed in something. What do you believe in?"

"Winning."

Vetis's words came from the right. Chance darted, then swerved as another ball of flame shot toward him. It smashed against a tree, instantly burning it to the ground until only ashes remained.

It could've been him. Chance knew he had to be more alert if he was going to save Destiny. Vetis battled as much in a game of wits as he did with his powers.

"That was close," Chance told him.

Vetis laughed, apparently thinking he would have an easy victory. Chanced planned to set him straight.

"Did you ever fight my father?" Chance asked.

"Always."

"But you never won, did you? Isn't that what you're angry about? That you never beat him?"

Vetis stepped from behind a tree, arm back to throw another ball of flame, but Chance was ready for him. He threw a bolt of lightning at the demon. It shattered against a tree, sending volts of electricity at the demon. Vetis yelled, ducking behind a tree.

"Maybe I'll beat you, too."

"Never!"

"I wouldn't be so sure about it," Chance goaded.

Silence.

Chance wondered if the demon had run away. A new fear washed over him. How could he save Destiny if he didn't know where Vetis hid her? Was she really on the island? The demon could've lied about that.

There was a rustle to his left. Chance breathed a sigh of relief and moved to his right. Vetis hadn't left.

"I thought you might have fled," Chance told him.

"You shouldn't think. It might get you in trouble," Vetis spoke from behind him.

Chance whirled around, but Vetis was faster. He pulled a flaming sword from the air and lunged toward Chance. He moved, but not fast enough. The sword plunged into his side. He gasped.

Vetis moved closer, twisting the metal. "Does it hurt, nephew?" He bared long, pointed teeth, his fetid breath filling the air around Chance. Vetis jerked the sword out of Chance and moved back.

Chance glanced down at his wound. Blood streamed from his side. He was almost consumed by the burning pain. He looked up at Vetis.

"Didn't you know that you can't heal from a demon's sword?"

Vetis lunged again, but this time Chance moved away from the sword's edge.

"You can run, but I will find you and finish it!"

Chance closed his eyes, then reached into the air and brought out a golden sword. When he stepped from behind the tree, he faced the demon with a glint of determination in his eyes.

"I won't run, demon, but I will kill you."

Vetis was startled enough that he lost the advantage. Chance moved fast, even with his bleeding wound. He thrust hard and caught Vetis in the thigh.

"What about you, Vetis, will you heal when I wound you?" He stepped back, but saw the fear in Vetis's eyes and had his answer. So the demon could be killed, and from the look on his face Vetis saw his own destruction.

Chance raised his sword high, ready to end the game they played, but Vetis' next words stopped him cold.

"You might find it difficult to fight me if you're busy trying to save the woman you love."

Cold chills ran down Chance's spine. "We had a bargain, demon! What have you done with her?"

"A bargain? With a demon? A bit of an oxymoron if you ask me." His laughter was like glass falling to a tiled floor and shattering on impact. "Demons don't honor bargains," he sneered.

"Where's Destiny!"

"I'm only fulfilling the verdict handed down by the tribunal. She's burning. Don't you hear her cries?"

Chance cocked his head to the side, listening. Destiny's screams of pain reached his ears.

"Destiny, where are you?" He whirled around, searching.

"You can't help her."

Chance grabbed a nearby tree as his legs suddenly went weak. Her screams tore at him, ripping him to shreds.

"She's lost to you forever, nephilim! You'll never be able to save her now."

He closed his eyes, could feel her touching the angel necklace he'd bought her. The fire rose up around her, burning her skin.

And in that moment he knew where Vetis had hidden her.

Without stopping to think about what he was doing, he ran

forward, leaping over the trees, over the lake the nephilim had created so long ago. The closer he got, the louder her cries became. Then the fires were there in front of him.

Chance had never entered by himself. To do so would be certain death. No one could make it out alone. But he had no choice.

He stepped into the fire. The flames licked his flesh, burning his skin. "Destiny," he yelled over the popping and hissing.

"Chance!"

He trudged toward her voice, fighting his way through the fire until she was there before him. He wrapped his arms around her, trying to shield her as much as he could, taking the brunt of the heat.

"I'm sorry. So sorry. I didn't want you to suffer, too," she cried. "Oh damn, it hurts so much."

"I know, but we'll find our way out." He gritted his teeth as flames scraped down his back. For a moment he couldn't move, then he inched forward, making sure that Destiny was with him all the way.

"You won't find your way out." Vetis's words cut through the hissing flames. "I have beaten you."

"Never!"

"Stubborn, just like your father. You might as well give up and accept your fate."

Destiny whimpered.

"Everything will be okay," he whispered close to her ear. But after only a few moments, Chance knew there wasn't much hope of escaping the flames. Each step he took only led deeper into the fire. Somehow Vetis had trapped them both. They were doomed.

"I love you," he told Destiny. "More than life itself."

"I love you, too." She rested her head against his chest, more than likely guessing the truth, knowing there was no hope. The odor of burning flesh surrounded him. Already the pain was unbearable.

A hand clamped down on his shoulder. Chance turned.

"Don't give up yet, brother," Ryder yelled above the crackling fire. He turned. Gripping his hand was Dillon, and with Dillon was Hunter.

Chance couldn't speak as emotions welled inside him. Of course they wouldn't let him face a demon alone. They were brothers, not by blood but by the bond they'd formed over the centuries.

Chance held Destiny close and together they forged their way out of the fire. When they stepped from the fire, rain showered down on their heads. Chance dropped to his knees, consumed by weakness. He held Destiny close, letting the rain once again heal his scars and ease his pain, until he was whole except for the wound Vetis had inflicted, but even that had been cauterized by the fire.

Chance should have known the others watched over him, as they had done for centuries. He was safe. Destiny was safe. He'd never let the demons have her!

"You're free, my love," he told her as he glanced down. Her scars healed, but there was no breath left in her. His world crumbled as he pulled her lifeless body against his chest.

"No!" he cried. "You cannot take her from me!"

"She's dead," Vetis scoffed. "Haven't you realized yet that I own her soul?" He held up a glass bottle with bright colors swirling inside.

"Give her back. We had a bargain!"

"Never!" Vetis shot back. "Only when I have your soul will I open the bottle and free hers."

Chance gently laid Destiny on the ground and stood.

"Don't do it, Chance," Ryder told him.

"You can't," Dillon and Hunter chimed in.

"I'll do whatever it takes." Chance squared his shoulders.

"Fool!" Vetis told him, but then he smiled. "You're just as stupid as your father. He fell in love with a mortal woman and was banned from returning to Earth. He could have had his family if he would have changed allegiances. He chose to give you up instead, and now you're mine!"

Chance raised his chin. "First, let her go."

"You want to spend all eternity with her?" Vetis laughed.

"Free her," he quietly told the demon. "Free her and you can have me."

"Then let it be done." Vetis threw the vessel that held Destiny's soul. The bottle crashed against a tree. The vapor inside swirled in the air before coming to rest on Destiny.

Destiny inhaled a deep breath. Her eyes fluttered open, her gaze fearful, then softening when it landed on Chance. "You saved me."

His own smile was bittersweet. "Always know that I have loved you since the moment we first met." Chance turned to Vetis. "End it," he growled.

Chapter 27

Vetis howled with glee. "I have won!"

Ryder glared at the demon and stepped forward, Dillon and Hunter at his side. Before they could take more than a couple of steps, Chance stepped in front of them.

"We made a bargain," he told them.

"A bargain with a demon," Hunter spat. "We won't let him take you."

"Her soul or yours?" Vetis said. In his hand was a bottle just like the one he broke to set Destiny's soul free.

"No!" Destiny cried as she struggled to her feet and rushed to Chance's side. She clung to his arm, her eyes filled with tears. "What have you done?"

"I've set you free. Hunter, Dillon, and Ryder will take care of you. No one will ever hurt you again."

She suddenly pushed away from him. "And you think that is supposed to make me feel better? My life was messed up from the start." She shook her head. "I won't let you take my place in Hell."

"You have no choice. His soul belongs to me!" Vetis stretched his arm toward Chance.

Chance gasped as he felt the demon's power reach inside him. He dropped to his knees as his life force began to leave his body. His world grew bleak and dark. From a distance, he heard Destiny cry out.

"God forgive me, but I had no choice," he whispered.

The clouds above split apart and a burst of blinding light crashed to earth. The ground shook beneath their feet.

"No!" Vetis shouted to the heavens. "You have no right!"

With Vetis's attention diverted, Chance's soul was released. He gasped, his knees growing weak. Ryder grabbed him on one side, Destiny on the other as they supported him.

He looked around. "What happened?"

Vetis slouched to the ground, his body trembling as he tried to cover his head. "You're not allowed," he whined.

Chance stilled as the light crept over the ground, settling on Vetis. The demon cried out as if he'd been burned.

"What have you done, Brother?" came a voice from the heavens.

Brother? Chance searched the sky until finally the beams of light came together and an angel drifted slowly to earth. He was the most beautiful man Chance had ever seen. The angel was larger than life.

He wore a white robe and there were golden sandals on his feet. His face was lined and there were streaks of gray in his dark hair. But the gentleness Chance saw on the angel's face brought tears to his eyes.

Chance knew him, even though he'd never met him before now. This was not a man who would ever forget his child. This was his father, and he'd felt his presence before but hadn't known the intense feeling of love had come from him. Chance thought his father hadn't cared, but he'd been there all the time.

"You owe me, Jacob!" Vetis snarled, drawing everyone's attention back to him.

"I owe you nothing." Jacob sadly shook his head.

Vetis glared at his brother. "You left me to burn in the fires of Hell!"

Chance felt his father's deep sadness. His emotions ran so deep that Chance ached all the way to his soul.

"It wasn't I who caused your downfall, Brother. You chose the wrong path, even after I begged you to stay."

Vetis crept behind a tree, crouching low as if he was afraid of the aura surrounding the angel. "We had nothing! Only crumbs."

"We had everything. You never saw the perfection of our world."

"You gave up your wife, your child!"

"But I have my wife back, and someday, when the time is right, Chance will join us. We'll live the rest of eternity together."

"But I have your son's soul!" Vetis reminded him.

"You never had his soul." A tear fell from Jacob's eye. "I can't save you, Brother."

"Do you still think I want to be saved?" He stood, coming from behind the tree, proud of his demon form. "I am who I am!" His gaze darted over the others until it landed on Destiny. "And she will return with me as well!"

Chance grabbed Destiny, pulling her against his side. "Never!"

His father's light moved to surround all four nephilim and Destiny. Chance gasped as the beauty filled him with an unbelievable peace and joy.

"The girl no longer belongs to you. She redeemed herself many times over."

"She gave her soul to Satan!"

The angel shook his head. "No, she gave up her soul so that she could protect a friend, then again to protect my son. Her soul is no longer yours to take."

"We had a bargain. What do you say to that? You can't go against the rules. You know that as well as I."

"But I haven't," Jacob told him.

"You're trying to trick me."

Chance looked at his father, wondering what he was up to. His father looked at him and smiled.

"A deal was made that if a person not yet a demon were to stay on Earth for one week and one day, their soul would be returned from whence it came." He looked at the sky as the sun began to rise on the horizon. "It has been one week and one day. Her soul no longer belongs to you."

"I took her to Hell!"

"No, you created an image to bring my son to you. She never returned to Hell. There was no tribunal. It was only a lure to steal something that didn't belong to you. But you forgot about the passage of time while you fought with Chance."

Vetis yelled and shook his fist. "You cheated! This isn't over, Brother!" Before anyone could blink, Vetis reared back his arm and threw a deadly bolt of lightning straight toward Chance's heart.

Chance shoved Destiny out of the way, bracing for the death blow, but a golden shield shot up in front of him. The bolt of lightning hit with such force that it ricocheted off the shield and shot back toward Vetis. Before the demon could even move, the bolt plunged into his chest.

Vetis stumbled back, hands grasping the bolt of lightning. In stunned surprise, he looked up. "You have killed your own brother? Flesh of your flesh?"

Jacob sadly shook his head. "No, I would not harm you, Vetis. It is by your own hand that you die."

Vetis reached toward Jacob. "Then I am free at last?"

Jacob cast a warm light over Vetis and he transformed from demon to a man with similar features of his angel brother. "Yes, you are now free." A tear dropped from Jacob's eye, landing on Vetis. His body dissolved into a mist and was no more.

Chance closed his eyes, brushing his lips against the top of Destiny's head. He felt as if he'd aged ten lifetimes.

"You'll have to let her go," his father said as he turned toward his son.

Destiny stiffened in his arms. "I won't be born again," she said, stepping away from Chance.

Chance wanted to pull her back against him and protect her

from his father. Angels were notorious for their tempers if someone pushed them a little too much. What the hell was she thinking?

"Destiny, we don't have a choice," he told her. "I'll make sure your next life is better than your last. I swear."

"As my guardian angel?"

"Yes. I'll watch over you."

"It ain't happenin', babe." She shook her head. "I've never had a choice. It's time I did."

As brave as she tried to act, Chance saw the fear in her eyes, but she didn't look as if she would budge.

She planted her hands on her hips and faced the angel. "I refuse to be born again."

Chance's father turned his full attention upon Destiny, glaring at her. "You would question me? An angel?"

She drew in a deep breath and stood tall. "Yes, I would."

The angel looked at his son. "And you want her? Still? In all her stubbornness?"

"I beg your pardon?"

"And so you should," the angel told her.

Chance stepped to her side once more. He felt her body trembling, but she held her ground.

"She deserves some happiness," Chance told Jacob.

"And can you give her what she desires?"

"I think so."

"For all eternity?"

"And then some," Destiny told him, raising her chin.

The angel shook his head. "The nephilim have always been unconventional."

Jacob exhaled a deep breath, then narrowed his eyes as his gaze moved from one nephilim to the next. Dillon, Hunter, and Ryder began to fidget as they came under his scrutiny.

"But the fathers have all loved their offspring. We did not forget, as

Vetis claimed. We have watched over all of you, even though you worry us at times. You are our sons and our daughters. We could do no less."

"Then I can stay?" Destiny asked.

"Yes, you may stay." He suddenly frowned. "But be warned: you are not to meddle in the lives of mortals. Our children do enough of that already."

Chance bowed his head toward the angel. "Thank you, Father."

As Jacob began to ascend, he spoke one last time. "Remember, you are all part angel, immortals. Try to at least be somewhat circumspect in your dealings with mortals. The occasional miracle, yes, barroom fights, no."

Hunter fidgeted.

"And womanizing," his attention turned to Ryder, whose gaze dropped to his feet, "will not be tolerated." Jacob sighed. "Please try for a *little* decorum." The clouds closed as he blended in and disappeared.

"Is he gone?" Destiny asked.

"Yes, he's gone."

"That was your father?"

Chance grinned. "Yeah, it was."

Hunter frowned, not looking at all happy with the events that had transpired.

Ryder lightly punched Hunter on the arm. "What's wrong with you? Everything has turned out pretty good, but you're frowning. What's up?"

Hunter looked at everyone. "Didn't you hear him? He said all our fathers have been watching us."

Ryder shrugged. "So?"

"Oh yeah. I see what you mean," Dillon said, looking as though a light bulb was suddenly turned on.

"What?" Ryder demanded.

"Think about it, Romeo," Dillon said as he stared at Ryder. "They've been watching us—watching *us*. We haven't exactly been saints."

Ryder's mouth dropped open. "Oh fuck," he breathed, then quickly looked upward. "I mean crap... Oh hell, I don't know what I mean."

Chance laughed. "If they were going to do anything, don't you think they would've done it before now?"

Hunter slowly nodded. "Yeah, you're right."

Chance sensed how nervous Destiny had suddenly become. Being around four men would take a little getting used to, but he had no doubts she would soon fit in. When she eased out of Chance's arms, he knew he wasn't about to let her run away.

"Don't even think about it." Chance grabbed her arm and pulled her back into his embrace.

"Think about what?" she asked, evading his gaze.

"That you're not a part of me now. You're a part of me forever."

"You could at least introduce us to our new sister," Ryder said.

"Just don't get any ideas." Chance glared at the other man. "This one is taken."

"Are they really your brothers?" Destiny asked.

"Not by blood, but by the bond that flows through each of us. And now through you."

"It's going to feel strange having a family. I've never really had one," she admitted.

"Can you at least cook?" Hunter asked.

She smiled when she looked at him.

He blushed.

"I can't even boil water."

"Anybody up for Mama Paula's?" Dillon asked.

Hunter was thoughtful for a moment until his stomach began to rumble. "Okay, but don't embarrass me this time." He glared at Ryder.

"Me? Embarrass you? You're the one who ate four platters of pancakes."

"They were good," he defended himself. "But, you on the other hand, were practically having sex—" He quickly glanced toward Destiny, then cleared his throat. "You were flirting a heck of a lot with the new waitress. Made her all giggly until she almost dropped the platter of food."

"You mean your *third* platter of food," Dillon casually mentioned.

Hunter frowned. "I told you I was hungry. And even though Mama Paula keeps her restaurant nice and clean, I sure didn't want to be eating off the damn—I mean dang—floor!"

Dillon and Ryder laughed, then looked toward Chance and Destiny. "You two coming?"

She looked at Chance. Silent communication passed between them.

"We'll catch you later," Chance told them.

The other three grasped hands, then closed their eyes. In an instant, they disappeared.

"Are they always like that?" she asked.

Chance sighed. "No, sometimes they're worse."

"I like them."

"For all eternity?"

Could she love him for all eternity? He had his answer when she melted against him, then raised her face. He lowered his lips to hers. She felt so perfect, so right in his arms. He stroked her tongue as his hands caressed her back. The kiss ended, but he still held her close.

"I can and will love you for all eternity," she said.

Chapter 28

"Now what do you want to do?" Destiny asked. "I mean, here we are in your penthouse apartment. All alone. Just the two of us."

It was about time, too. They hadn't had a moment alone in the last two weeks. Hunter, Dillon, and Ryder monopolized Destiny's time. If he didn't know better, he'd think they had never been around a female.

But she was his now. "I can think of a few things we can do," he said as he slid the zipper down on the back of her dress.

Her light laugh floated around him as she stepped out of his arms, mischievously shaking her head.

Chance crossed his arms. "And just what do you have in mind?"

She put a finger to her lips. "Shh. Just follow me." She turned on her heel and made her way toward the bedroom. Chance followed at a slower pace, wondering exactly what she was up to.

She stopped, then shimmied out of her dress. She wore a skimpy pink-and-black bra and thong, except she still had on her heels, and he was already hard just looking at her.

He drew in a sharp breath right before he jerked his T-shirt over his head and tossed it away. Damn, he already liked what she had planned.

For a moment, Destiny seemed to forget what she was doing as she stared at his bare chest. "You've really got some serious muscles." She shook her head, then reached back and unfastened her bra, letting it drop to the floor.

Chance tried to swallow and couldn't. He could only stare as she blew him a kiss and sauntered down the hall. He drew in a deep breath and caught the scent of the heady perfume she wore. The alluring aroma wrapped around him, hinting at a night of untold pleasure.

And there was a reason he was standing in the middle of his living room with his tongue hanging out?

He toed off his boots, kicking them out of his way. Next went his socks. His jeans and briefs came off at the same time.

"Here I come, baby," he said under his breath as he hurried to the bedroom.

The door was closed. He grinned, but the door wouldn't be closed for long. He pictured Destiny on the other side, lying on the bed, completely naked with her legs spread in invitation. One he planned to take her up on.

He opened the door and immediately heard the sound of a waterfall. He frowned. Had she left the water running in the bathroom? His frown deepened. She wasn't in the bed waiting for him. In fact, he could barely see the bed. The whole room was cast in dark shadows.

"Dillon told me you loved the water. Especially swimming, no matter how cold it gets." Her voice came from the shadows. Even though he searched with his eyes, he couldn't make out her form.

"Dillon's an asshole," he grumbled.

She chuckled. "Rather than cold water, I thought I'd substitute the sound."

"It's nice. Now can we make love?"

"You do look as though you're ready." She sighed. "Very ready. Did I ever tell you how much I love your very thick, very long dick?"

His dick jerked in response to her words. "You're killing me."

"Nope, it's too difficult to kill a nephilim."

"You're getting pretty close."

Destiny chuckled as she snapped her fingers and half a dozen candles came to life. Then she stepped from the shadows. His torture had only begun. She wasn't naked. No, she wore what amounted to a thin red scarf that she'd draped over her body, and a red and black necklace that sparkled as it captured the candlelight. The scarf hid absolutely nothing from his view, but was sexy as hell, casting shadows over her tempting curves.

She was fire and ice as she ambled nearer. Chance couldn't take his eyes off her. She had her hands behind her back, which thrust her chest forward. Her nipples were taut, begging him to take them into his mouth.

When she was closer, Destiny unfastened the scarf and ran the silky material across his shoulders, over his chest, just brushing his dick. He shivered as the sensation she created rippled over him. Before he could get used to the scarf, she moved to a small, low table, so low it was practically on the floor. An assortment of colorful glass bottles were arranged neatly on top, along with a small warmer that had one bottle sitting inside.

He sniffed as another aroma tickled his nose. Chocolate? What had she plotted? He grinned. He might not be exactly sure what she was up to, but he had a feeling he'd like it. She stopped at the table, her back to him.

He'd liked watching her breasts bounce ever so slightly when she walked, and the thatch of curls between her legs was sweet to look upon. He didn't mind whatever game she played, though. If she wanted to be the seducer, he was more than fine with it. As long as she didn't take too long. His dick throbbed.

She spread her legs, then gave him a very saucy wink before bending at the waist and slowly leaning over to get the bottle out of the warmer.

Something close to a gurgle erupted from him. He had a clear view of her irresistible pussy and an incredible desire to kiss her in that very spot. She was torturing him.

"Destiny," he croaked, not sure how much longer he could stand the pain of not touching her.

She straightened and turned. "Is something the matter?"

"You know exactly what my problem is." He glanced down. "It's pretty obvious."

She chuckled as she moved back to stand in front of him. "I'll make it all better. I promise." She tilted the bottle and a drop of chocolate landed on her finger, then she raised her finger to his lips and lightly brushed the chocolate on.

He licked the chocolate, wanting to taste something entirely different and so much sweeter. He would let Destiny play her games a little longer, though.

"Some say chocolate works as an aphrodisiac," she said, then raised the bottle and dribbled it over his chest.

He sucked in a breath. The chocolate was thick and warm. It felt like fingers slowly caressing his chest, his abdomen.

Enough! He couldn't stand any more! He had to have her.

"It works for me," he said and grabbed her to him.

She laughed. "It hasn't had time."

"You're the aphrodisiac." He lowered his mouth to hers. She tasted sweet and hot, like chocolate. He ran his hands down her back, over the cheeks of her ass, drawing her closer. She moaned when her most intimate spot brushed against his dick. He nudged her and she opened her legs, rubbing against him. Chance loved the way she responded to his slightest touch.

When he ended the kiss, they were both panting. She rested her head on his chest.

"I'm trying to seduce you," she finally told him.

"It's working. Have your way with me." He couldn't keep the smile out of his voice.

She licked his chest and all his humor evaporated. "You taste good," she told him. "And I'm hungry."

Before she could get too deeply into her new game, he moved her to arm's length and studied her with a critical eye. "And you have chocolate all over you from rubbing against me." His expression turned wicked. "And I'm very hungry." He scooped her into his arms. She screamed with delight as he carried her to their bed.

Rather than setting her gently on top, he climbed into bed with her still in his arms. She wrapped her arms tightly around his neck when he purposefully swayed as though he might accidentally drop her. He liked her body pressed to his.

"You did that on purpose," she accused.

"Guilty."

"Have you no remorse?"

"None whatsoever."

"Whatever shall I do with you?"

"I bet you'll think of something," he said as he laid her gently against the pillows.

"I'm sure I will."

But talking stopped as he lowered his head to her breast and drew her tight nipple into his mouth. He rolled the sensitive nub around with his tongue, then gently tugged with his teeth. She gasped, squirming slightly beneath him, but it was enough of a movement that when she moved against his dick, he moaned.

Did she know what she did to him? He thought sometimes yes, sometimes no. But damn if he didn't love each of her moves.

"Now," she breathed. Her breath whispered over him, encircling him in love. "I can't stand another second without you inside me."

That was all the encouragement he needed. When he moved she opened her legs, and when he entered the heat of her body she wrapped her legs tightly around his waist and drew him in deeper.

He groaned as her moist heat caressed him when she tightened her inner muscles. He couldn't stand waiting any more. Chance moved slowly at first. His strokes long and easy. Still wanting to draw out the moment.

"Now," she said. "I need you now."

"As much as I need you," he told her. He moved faster. Harder. Stroking her body with each movement. The heat built inside him. He looked at her face. Her eyes were partially closed, her breathing rapid.

The most beautiful sight to him was a woman in the throes of passion, but when he loved that woman with all his heart, it was even more magnificent.

Her body tensed. She gasped. Trembles, like small earthquakes, rushed down her body.

Heat exploded around him. Blinding lights flashed before his eyes. He gritted his teeth, his orgasm shaking him to his very core.

When his world came back into focus, he rolled to his side, taking Destiny with him, holding her close.

"I never want to disappoint you," she whispered.

Chance moved back enough so he could look into her face. "You never will," he said in all sincerity. He pulled her close to him again, holding her tight.

Epilogue

"LeAnn shouldn't be there," Destiny argued, but Chance didn't seem concerned at all. He could be so infuriating sometimes! After being together for a whole year, she still hadn't figured out his way of thinking.

"The nephilim can't always change things," he told her with exasperating patience. "You know the rules. Sometimes we're blocked and we can't use our powers."

She clamped her lips together and glared at him. "It sucks!" She was going to let him have it!

But before she could rant and rave more, he pulled her into his arms and lowered his mouth to hers. Her bluster immediately drained as his kiss weakened her knees. Her arms circled his neck.

Chance was everything to her, even though he could be so blasted exasperating at times, and she couldn't seem to get enough of him. When he ended the kiss, her knees were so weak they barely held her up.

"Hmm, what was I saying?" she asked.

He lightly caressed her back. "Nothing. Nothing at all."

"Why do you always do that?" she asked, resting her head against his chest.

"Do what?"

"Make me forget what I was talking about."

He stroked her back. "Want me to stop?" She heard the smile in his voice.

"No."

"Good, because I wouldn't."

"I want to help LeAnn. I want her to be as happy as I am." And why not help LeAnn? Apparently there wasn't a hard and fast rule. Chance had helped the Dunlops. When they returned from Hawaii, she made sure Chance helped the couple find jobs. In no time they would have all their bills paid. It was the least Destiny could do since she'd used their apartment.

He even saw that Charles and Beulah were able to buy the best parcel of land for their money after they were married. It was just a small ranch, but Chance had stocked it with some of his own horses and cattle. They were as happy as two people could be.

"But LeAnn has everything she ever dreamed about," Chance told her, drawing her away from her thoughts.

"Pffttt." He wasn't paying a bit of attention to her!

His chest rumbled with suppressed laughter.

Destiny leaned back, frowning up at him. "She's not happy, you know. Even if she does have two songs in the top ten on the Billboard charts."

"She's an overnight success. A star. She's been on most of the talk shows, her concerts have all sold out—"

"But that doesn't mean she's happy," Destiny quietly interrupted him.

He didn't meet her eyes.

There was something he wasn't telling her. "What?"

"Duncan thinks he missed his opportunity with her. He's constantly playing her songs. It's pathetic to watch him. I might have given him a little push."

"What do you mean? I thought that was breaking the rules."

He shrugged. "More like bending them a little.

"I see."

"See what?"

"Breaking the rules is a no-no, but it's okay to bend them."

"Sort of."

She eyed him with more than a little trepidation. "What did you do?" she cautiously asked.

"Duncan was given a chance to go into a partnership with an old friend, so he sold his bar in Ft. Worth a few months ago. He's opening a new one in Nashville. Tonight, in fact." He waved his hand in an arc and a screen appeared in front of them.

She quirked an eyebrow.

"What? You think Vetis was the only one with powers?" He nodded toward the screen. "Watch."

Destiny turned her attention to the screen in front of her. She watched as downtown Nashville came to life. Country and Western bars lined the street that appeared, along with stores selling everything from Elvis memorabilia to Stetson hats to Justin boots. It might have been sleazy except the storefronts all looked as though a person had stepped back in time. The bars were more like saloons out of the Old West.

Then Destiny saw the woman walking down the street. She was all alone and huddled beneath a long black coat with the collar turned up and she wore a black floppy hat. It was a good disguise, but Destiny immediately recognized her friend.

"It's LeAnn," she whispered.

"Shh, just watch," Chance told her.

LeAnn walked timidly inside the bar. Destiny held her breath, then realized LeAnn didn't know she was watching. Destiny's heart swelled with pride. LeAnn was so beautiful, and so successful, that Destiny bubbled over with emotion. She felt like a proud mother.

It had hurt her to tell LeAnn she wouldn't be traveling to Nashville with her. LeAnn tearfully said she understood when Destiny explained she couldn't leave Chance. LeAnn remembered meeting him at the rodeo and admitted she would do exactly the same.

But LeAnn didn't. She left Ft. Worth and Duncan behind.

Destiny promised not to meddle. Mingling with mortals was frowned upon. As much as she would have liked to stay in touch, she resigned herself to only occasional visits. But she sensed LeAnn's sadness. Her loneliness.

"Look at her." Destiny sniffed. "We need to help."

"Just watch," Chance told her again.

"Okay, okay, I'm watching."

———

LeAnn wondered what the hell she was doing as she glanced nervously around before making her way inside one of the bars lining the street. She pulled her coat tighter to her body. The light was dim and the room more crowded than she expected for a Wednesday night. There was a sign out front that had GRAND OPENING plastered across it. Maybe she should've chosen another place. One that was quieter. She sighed. It wouldn't matter; even in a crowd she felt all alone. She wished Destiny was with her.

No, she didn't. Destiny was with Chance, and they were so in love. It wasn't right for her to be so darn selfish. It still didn't make LeAnn feel any less lonely. Her most loyal companion became the television, but if she had to flip through channels one more night, she knew she would start screaming like a crazy woman. How many reality shows could they come up with, anyway? It was ridiculous!

Her manager was like a mother hen. Oh, she trusted Barry's judgment and all, but he was a little pushy. Okay, if she was truthful, he was a whole lot pushy. Drat, she knew he was just trying to protect her, but she was tired of feeling like he wrapped her in cotton and tucked her away after each performance.

So she escaped.

As she sat on one of the barstools, a young bartender made his way over to her.

"What can I get you?" He smiled, showing pearly white teeth.

Oh gosh, she hadn't thought about what she would order. LeAnn was just proud she'd escaped the hotel room. She normally didn't drink.

"I can make anything," he told her. "I took a course. We don't just serve beer and whiskey here." He blushed. "My name is Tony, by the way. I mean, since we're carrying on a conversation, sort of." He frowned. "Except I guess it's just me talking, isn't it?"

She smiled, liking the young man. Although she suspected there wasn't much difference in their ages, somehow she felt a lot older.

"Surprise me," she said. "And I'm LeAnn."

He narrowed his eyes. "Okay, LeAnn. Do you like tropical drinks? Pineapple juice, coconut?"

She nodded.

He grinned. "I could tell. Okay, one frozen piña colada coming up."

She wondered if he meant she was fruity, then shook her head. Nope, no one could really tell much about her. She wore jeans, as did just about everyone in Nashville. A chill was in the air, so she didn't look out of place in a coat with the collar turned up á la Elvis, and she wore a floppy hat pulled down low.

Nope, she was just your average working girl who came in for a little company and a drink after work. Nothing unusual about that.

"Here you go." He put a coaster down and set a pretty glass on top of it. "I didn't have one of those little umbrellas."

"It looks good."

He waited.

Okay, LeAnn supposed she would have to taste it even though she just wanted something sitting in front of her. She dutifully took a drink. A blend of tropical fruits hit her taste buds.

"It's wonderful," she told him and was telling the truth. His grin grew wider.

"Yeah, I'm pretty good at judging people. Oh look, the band is setting up."

She turned toward the stage.

"It's a shame, though."

"What's a shame?"

"The singer got laryngitis. Called in sick, and on opening night, too."

She quickly became very interested in stirring what looked like snow around in her glass with the straw.

"They say your first night will make or break you in this town. The owners seem really nice, too. One of them sold his bar in Texas and sank all his money into this place. Sometimes it's hard to have dreams that never happen."

Guilt rushed through her. She quickly cleared her mind. It wasn't her problem. "But there seem to be a lot of people here."

He shook his head. "Won't last long, though. As soon as they figure out there's no singer, they'll leave for the next place quick enough. Hell, the owners are out lookin' for someone who can take her place."

"Maybe they'll find another singer."

"They haven't so far." He held up a cell phone. "Said they would call if they had any luck."

LeAnn knew all about dreams, and dreams not coming true. And maybe the bar owner from Texas made her think about Duncan. Yeah, right, as if she did anything else since the day she and her manager had left for Nashville.

Oh, what the hell. "I'll sing," she blurted before she could change her mind.

Tony studied her. "Can you really sing?"

Laughter bubbled out of her. "That's what they tell me." She pulled off her hat and shook out her blond curls.

Tony's eyes grew round. "You're... you're..." His face turned red and he began to choke.

Oh gosh, she didn't mean to kill the poor guy. She pushed her drink toward him. He automatically took it and gulped down a big swallow.

He grabbed his neck.

"What?" Ohmigosh, was he allergic to her drink?

"Cold throat," he gasped, eyes watering. "You'd really sing? I mean here? Tonight? Right now?" he finally managed to get out.

She nodded.

He took a deep breath. "Can I introduce you?"

She nodded again and he grinned as if he'd won the lottery. He practically ran to the stage. She took off her coat and laid it across the stool, then followed. Oh Lord, what had she gotten herself into?

"It's my pleasure," Tony said as he grabbed the microphone, "to introduce one of my favorite new singers, and she's going to sing for us here tonight. Miss LeAnn Wells."

The crowd jumped to their feet, applauding.

LeAnn smiled as she took the microphone. "Thanks, Tony."

Tony blushed and stumbled off the stage.

She turned to the band that was on the stage. "Do you know 'My Hero'?"

The guitar player grinned. "Do we?" He began to strum his guitar.

"My brother was my hero. I wrote this song for him." She began to hum softly.

LeAnn lost herself in the song that became her first number one hit and, when she ended on the last note, she looked around the crowd and smiled tenderly. What would her brother think if he could see her now? She had a feeling he would be proud of her. Except nothing happened. The people stared at her. Everyone was so quiet that for a moment, LeAnn wondered if maybe she should've stayed in her room channel surfing. Just her and the remote.

But then the crowd erupted and they began to clap. She breathed a sigh of relief then glanced up and smiled. *Well, what do you know, they liked us, Brother.*

"Sing 'Lost Love,'" someone yelled.

"Lost Love" was her newest number one hit. She looked at the band and they nodded, grinning from ear to ear. As they began to play softly in the background, LeAnn began to talk again.

"Sometimes we meet someone just in passing, but they leave a mark on our lives forever. I've been lucky to have known a few people like that in my life. My brother, of course. Then there was Destiny. Destiny was, well, I like to think she changed *my* destiny." She smiled before continuing. "But there was one person who swept in like a warm breeze that blows across the land, and when it's gone, we look around and wonder if we only imagined it, and wonder if we'll ever find it again."

LeAnn began to hum. She closed her eyes, and started to sing as though she sang to her lost love, and in fact she did.

Like the sound of the midnight train
As it fades into the night.

Her voice was soft at first, then grew stronger.

Like an eagle floating on the wind
Slowly drifting out of sight.
A love of long ago
Leaves a picture in my mind
One that will never fade
With the passing of the time

Visions filled her mind. That first look they'd shared. The instant when she felt the spark flowing between them. His startled expression as though he felt it, too.

Duncan encouraging her up on the stage, introducing her like she was already a star. Destiny thought she trembled because she was so scared, and she was, but Duncan had caused her to tremble too. One look and she felt such an intense connection.

She went back to that bar on skid row, only to find Duncan had sold it. A preacher on a street corner said the owner left, but he didn't know where. Then he told her how he saw demons. That he was saved from the bottle.

LeAnn was happy for the man, but she left quickly. The guy was really strange.

And Duncan became her lost love.

She finished the song, the last mournful note ending. Sadness welled inside her. It would seem she had lost everyone she ever loved or could have loved. She opened her eyes and smiled at the crowd.

Her gaze skidded to a stop on one man. She held up her hand and the band stopped playing.

"I said you would be a star one day," Duncan told her.

The audience grew quiet, waiting to see what would happen. When Duncan continued toward the stage, they parted like the Red Sea.

The crowded bar seemed to disappear until LeAnn felt as though it was only the two of them. "Everything happened so fast."

"I know."

"I went back. You were gone. The bar was sold."

"I came here looking for you," he told her as he climbed the steps to the stage. "You're famous now. I wasn't sure I'd fit into your new life, but I had to find out."

She shook her head. "I wrote that song for you."

"Am I your lost love?" He stopped in front of her.

She shook her head as her heart swelled until she thought it would burst.

His shoulders slumped.

"You're not my lost love. You're my found love." She threw her arms around his neck. As his lips met hers, the crowd of people began to clap and cheer.

"Is that better?" Chance asked as he waved his arm and the screen disappeared.

Destiny nodded, wiping the tears from her eyes. "I love happy endings." She sniffed as she went into Chance's arms and wrapped her arms around his neck.

God, he loved this woman. She was the very air he breathed, and he didn't know what he would've done if he'd lost her.

"Don't ever leave me," he told her. "If you did, I would die."

She rested her head against his chest. "As I would die if you ever left me."

"For all eternity," he said.

"For all eternity," she repeated.

Their vows slipped through the apartment and out to the balcony. The light breeze caught their words and whisked them upward, as far as the heavens above.

"PLEASE LORD, YOU HAVE to send me a miracle. A man, in case you want specifics."

Haley Tillman really needed to get laid before she incinerated. If a man looked cross-eyed at her, the only thing left would be a pile of smoking ashes.

Just one little bitty miracle. Was that too much to ask?

She was thoughtful for a moment, then decided she'd better revise her prayer. Once, she'd prayed for a stuffed bunny rabbit. The next day her dad took her to the taxidermist to pick up Fifi, the family dog that died two weeks before, or as Haley preferred to call the beast when no one was around, The Tasmanian Terror. The mongrel was more her mother's pet. Her father had the miniscule creature from *The Twilight Zone* stuffed.

There was also a sale on stuffed rabbits. She hated the glass-eyed, zombie rabbit and hid the nasty looking nightmare in the back of her closet. There was no escape from Fifi, though. Her mother placed the silent menace in the living room where everyone could see the dog.

So, a prayer revision might be in order. "Not just any man. I want a really hot, drool-worthy, sexy man." That still wasn't good enough. "No, he has to be more than a normal man. He has to stand above mere mortals. No more dweebs, losers or rejects." She figured it wouldn't hurt to ask for the best.

And no more crying jags like the one last night just because she got stood up. She threw the cover back, and grabbed her black-rimmed glasses off the nightstand before heading toward the bathroom.

A miracle would be nice. She snorted. As if a miracle was ever going to happen. She was pretty sure hot and sexy would never make it to her front door. Her *almost* date wasn't drool worthy. She supposed Ben wasn't bad looking, in a *GQ*, polished sort of way.

Haley sighed. Being stood up was nothing new. Anyone with any sense would be used to it by now, but not her. Okay, so maybe she sort of expected it because she'd cornered him. She did not wear desperation well.

"Ben could've said no," she mumbled as she walked inside the bathroom and flipped on the light. Her co-worker from the bank owed her. Haley worked all week crunching numbers for him.

She casually glanced toward the mirror and saw an apparition.

Her pulse took off and her heart pounded inside her chest. She stumbled back, her knees hitting the back of the bathtub. Before she toppled inside, she slapped a hand on the toilet seat and regained her balance.

As her pulse slowed to a more normal rate, her gaze scanned the tiny room. She was the only one there. She came to her feet, nerves stretched taut.

Please don't be the ghost of Nanny.

Haley loved Nanny, but her grandmother was gone, and though she had lots of fond memories, Haley wanted her to stay gone. Haley's eyes stopped at the mirror. Her reflection stared back. Fantastic, she'd scared herself. It had to be an all-time low.

She closed her eyes and took a deep breath, then opened them again. Mornings were not good. She should drape black silk over her mirrors until she at least had her first pot of coffee. Not that she was monstrously hideous, but she was no beauty queen, either.

She had her father's looks. Her father was tall. She was five feet, seven inches. She also had her father's dull, dishwater blond hair. Her hair turned bright orange when she attempted to color it in the eighth grade. She decided dull blond was better. Her boobs were too big, but they matched her hips.

All the magazines she read said you had to like at least one thing about yourself. Her legs were nice and long. When she wasn't tripping over her feet, she was fairly satisfied with them. Except her life was never going to change. And miracles? She stopped believing in miracles long ago.

She brushed her teeth, then dragged a comb through her tangled hair so it didn't look quite so much like a rat's nest.

There was a half gallon of ice cream in the kitchen freezer. It wouldn't be too difficult to eat herself into sugar oblivion. She could bring new meaning to the phrase, *death by chocolate*. What would her sister say? Rachael never, absolutely never, let sugar cross her lips, and she always said Haley was killing herself.

The buzz from her doorbell blasted through the tiny, two bedroom house that she inherited from Nanny, effectively drawing her away from her dreary thoughts. Bummer. She'd already begun planning her funeral. She sighed. It was way too early for doorbells.

She grabbed her faded, pink terry-cloth robe off the hook on the door and pulled it on over her green froggy flannel pajamas. Once she stood at the front door, she peered through the peephole her father installed for safety, as if anyone would ever break into her house. What would they steal? Her hand-me-down furniture?

She blinked. No one there. Were they hiding?

Hmm, serial killer lurking outside her door? Would that count as a date? Nope, they didn't have murders in Hattersville. Nothing, absolutely nothing, ever happened in the small town. She shook her head and opened the door a crack, making sure the chain was secure.

"Hello?"

A man stepped into her line of vision. Haley's mouth dropped open. *Good Lord!* This had to be the guy who invented tall, dark, and sexy! Her thighs quivered.

At least six feet one inch of pure testosterone stood on her porch. He had the dark good looks of a male stripper, only with clothes on.

The stranger removed his black Stetson, slowly dragging his fingers through thick, coal-black hair. His deep blue eyes held her gaze before sliding down her body as if he could see more than the sliver revealed from the slightly open door.

Warm tingles spread over her like a Texas wildfire in the middle of summer. She could barely draw in a breath as her gaze moved past broad shoulders and a black, western shirt that hugged his scrumptious muscles. Then her eyes slipped right down to the low-slung jeans riding his hips, past muscled thighs, all the way to his scuffed black boots.

Oh, Lord, her every fantasy stood on her front porch!

She forced herself to meet his gaze.

I want him! She felt like a kid in a candy store with lots of money to spend. *Mommy, Mommy can I have the hot sexy cowboy! Pleeeeeeeeease!*

If only it was that easy. No way would she ever have the opportunity to have sex with someone who looked like that cowboy. What was he doing at her door, anyway? Lost?

"Haley, right?" he asked with a slow drawl that made her body tremble with need.

How did he know her name? She grasped the door a little harder. He smiled as though he knew exactly what she was thinking. Her world began to tilt. She remembered that breathing might not be a bad thing so she drew in a deep breath. "What?" the word warbled out. She cleared her throat and tried again. "Do you need directions or something?"

"You're Haley."

She nodded.

He smiled wider, showing perfectly straight, white teeth. "Mind if I come in?"

Her fantasy of this cowboy's naked body pressed against *her* naked body shattered like rocks hitting a mirror. Oh, this guy was good, real good, but she wasn't born yesterday. He'd obviously seen her name on the mailbox out front. She raised her chin. "I don't need a vacuum. I have all the pots and pans I will ever use—including waterless cookware. There's a complete set of encyclopedias on my e-reader *and* I have a double-barreled shotgun for protection. Now, do you want to tell me why you're ringing my doorbell at this time of morning?"

"You prayed for a miracle. I'm the answer to your prayer." He rested his hand on her grandmother's old chair. Her rocker had always sat in that same spot on the porch for as long as she could remember. The cowboy lightly set the chair in motion. Back and forth, back and forth, his thumb lightly caressing the weathered wood.

Wow, her prayer was really answered? The man upstairs gave her more than she asked for. She reached up to smooth her hair about the same time reality set in. Had she lost her mind?

"Go away!" She slammed the door shut. Her pulse raced so fast Haley thought her heart would jump out of her chest. Who was he? Definitely the wrong house. Shoot, the wrong town. No one looked liked him and lived in Hattersville. Definitely a salesman. As if she needed another vacuum cleaner. Three were quite enough. Another magazine subscription might have been nice. One could never have enough magazines.

Her pulse slowed to a more normal rate. But wouldn't it have been nice if he was sent in answer to a prayer? How had he known she'd prayed for a miracle? Not that it mattered since she slammed the door in his face.

Oh, hell!

What was she thinking? Haley smoothed her hands down the side of her robe, took a deep breath, and started to open the door. She remembered at the last minute to remove her glasses and stick them in her pocket. Rachael had said they made her appear more professional. Haley thought the glasses made her look like Buddy Holly. She wore them more out of habit than a need to see.

The cowboy wasn't there.

Had she only imagined him? She closed the door enough so that she could slide off the chain. Her smile was firmly in place when she opened the door again. Nothing. Only Old Mrs. Monroe watering her lawn across the street. She looked up and waved as her crotchety husband came around the corner of the house, getting a face full of water. Mrs. Monroe quickly dropped the hose.

"Damn, thought we'd finally got some rain," he sputtered.

"Oh, I'm sorry." She rushed toward him, raising her flowered apron as she went.

Haley smiled, then glanced down the street. Her smile dropped. Not a soul, darn it. Her fantasy lover, possibly an answer to her prayer, showed up on her porch and what did she do? Slammed the stupid door in his face.

Maybe she only imagined the guy. Really, who could actually look that good? She took a cautious step past the doorway. Maybe Mrs. Monroe saw the cowboy. But her neighbor had already turned off the water and they were going inside.

Haley stepped off the wide, covered front porch, her eyes narrowing as she looked up and down the street. Still nothing.

Chelsea, the former cheerleader, high school football sweetheart, beauty-queen-turned-slutty-bank-teller stepped out of her house next door, then gave a surprised jump when she caught sight of Haley. Chelsea's gaze swept over her.

"You really should take a little more pride in your appearance." She shrugged. "But then, I suppose nothing would help so why try?"

Haley's lip curled. Why did her co-worker buy the house next door? To taunt her? Her ploy was working.

Chelsea closed her front door, but immediately returned her attention to Haley. Oh, no, Chelsea wore her fake pouty look. Haley braced herself.

"I'm sorry about last night. Ben and I happened to be working late at the bank, and afterward, we decided to have a drink. He totally forgot about his date with you until it was too late. I hope you weren't too disappointed."

She took a step back as Chelsea hurried down the front steps to her sporty, little, red Mustang. But Chelsea had to know about the date. Then it hit her. Of course Chelsea knew. That was exactly why she coerced Ben into taking her for a drink. Chelsea loved hurting people. It was a game to her—one she played very well.

Haley tried to think of something smart to say. "You… you…" Darn! Why couldn't she think of a good comeback? She probably would that afternoon when she wouldn't need it. "I hope you get a flat tire," she finally sputtered. Oh, that was a real winning line. Sheesh!

Chelsea was right, though. Haley's looks left a lot to be desired. But Ben was her date. Of course Ben would want to be with Chelsea rather than her. Chelsea looked hot with flaming red hair and she was cute.

Haley marched back inside and closed her door a little harder than necessary. Out of habit, she jerked the chain through the slot and turned the lock. Not that it mattered. An intruder would take one look at her frumpy froggy pj's, her thick robe, and run screaming in the other direction. Which was probably what happened to the sexy cowboy and he barely got a glimpse. What would he have done if he saw the whole picture?

No, she didn't want to think about his reaction. Her day was already depressing enough. She aimed toward the kitchen and grabbed a diet soda out of the fridge instead of the ice cream. She would get dressed, then figure out what she would do for the rest of her boring day.

She trudged into the bedroom and came to a dead stop. Her heart thumped so hard inside her chest she thought it would crack a rib. The cowboy was casually reclined on her bed with his back braced against her headboard, his booted feet crossed at the ankles.

About the Author

Karen Kelley is the award-winning author of twenty books. *I'm Your Santa* spent three weeks on the *USA Today* bestseller list. Karen lives in a small Texas town with her very supportive husband and their very spoiled Pekingese, along with many wild birds that can empty two large feeders in the course of a day. She makes jewelry as a hobby because she's a firm believer that you can never have enough bling-bling. You can visit Karen at www.authorkarenkelley.com.